KENNEL CLUB
BOOK SEVEN OF UNDERDOGS

Geonn Cannon

Supposed Crimes LLC • Matthews, North Carolina

This book is a work of fiction. Names, characters, places, and incidents are products of the author's imagination or are used fictitiously. Any resemblance to actual events or locales or persons, living or dead, is entirely coincidental.

All Rights Reserved
Copyright © 2018 Geonn Cannon

Published in the United States.

ISBN: 978-1-944591-50-2

Cover art by Natasha Alterici

www.supposedcrimes.com

This book is typeset in Goudy Old Style.

UNDERDOGS

PROLOGUE

A WOLF and her cub crouch in the dirt, surrounded by trees and shrubbery. Shoulders rising and falling with their breath. Currently in their human form, hair hanging long and dark over human faces. The cub, a girl barely eleven, shivering with her fingers splayed in the dirt underneath her. When the mother turns toward her, the cub can't see her eyes because of the shadows. There's pain... there's always pain. She's tired from all the running. Can't catch her breath. She watches her mother's arm, sees how the muscles twitch and shift under sweaty skin.

"Tired? Hurt?"

The cub nods; she can't always speak right after she changes back from the wolf.

"Good. Get ready to run again."

"Can't. Mama, can't."

The mother turns and puts a hand on the side of the cub's head. "Sometimes you have to. Even when you can't. Especially when you can't. When it hurts too much to change or you can't run another step, that's when you have to run the hardest and the fastest. That's when you need the wolf the most. When I ask you if you can change, I'm not asking if you want to. Do you understand the difference?"

The cub nods again.

"Can you change?"

"Yes, mama."

"Then let's go."

More than twenty years later, the cub was grown and remembering her mother's words. She was in Seward Park, the same old growth forest where she learned how to be a wolf. Long, painful evenings when she was sure her body wouldn't snap back into the right shape when she got home. She was older and wiser now. The pain of her transformations was greatly diminished. She grabbed a tree trunk and pivoted to the right, ducking under a low branch and vaulting over a fallen log. Her knees threatened to buckle when she landed but she couldn't afford to fall.

Her pursuers shouted. Their voices echoed so it was impossible to tell how close they were, but she knew they were too close to risk transforming. She knew these trails better than anyone. If she could just get some distance, she could rip off her clothes and transform. Even if she had to remain in wolf form all day until the search ended, she would at least be safe.

"Over here!"

No such luck, it seemed. She angled back to the west in the hopes she could reach the road. She didn't know what she planned to do at that point. Keep running? Surrender? No, surrender wasn't an option. She had to keep running. She had to disappear. There was radio chatter, there was a light shining into the woods, there was the sound of sirens, and she knew she was caught a moment before someone unfolded from the shadows to her right and grabbed her arm.

She tried to pull away and succeeded, but the move threw her off balance. She hit the ground hard and rolled. She surfed sideways on a wave of dirt, pebbles, branches, and pine needles until she reached a flat area. A body landed on top of her and she was rolled over onto her stomach. The wolf snarled in the center of her brain, seconds from breaking free, but she managed to stop the transformation before it extended beyond her eyes. A powerful hand was placed on the back of her head and pushed her cheek against the muddy ground. More footsteps as other people surrounded the area.

"Stay down," the woman on top of her demanded. She grabbed one of Ari's forearms and yanked it back. "You are under arrest for murder. You have the right to remain silent. Anything you say~"

The area was awash with red and blue lights as a squad car pulled up nearby. The radios of other officers drowned out the crickets with static and garbled voices. Ari twisted her neck and looked across Andrews Bay. Houses along the opposite shore were lit up like lanterns. She knew one of the homes belonged to her mother. Maybe she'd been getting a cup of tea and noticed the commotion across the water. Maybe her instincts would draw her to the backyard. Would she know? Would she be able to tell all this was because of her daughter?

Sorry, Mama, she thought as the handcuffs were roughly snapped onto her wrists. *I guess they finally caught up.*

The female officer who tackled her shoved her shoulder. "I asked if you understood your rights."

"Yes," she managed to say.

"Then get up."

Ari was helped upright by a firm hand on each arm. She was escorted to one of the squad cars and, with a gentleness that was surprising after the pursuit and tackle, someone guided her head down so she wouldn't bump it. She felt the bizarre urge to say thank you before the door was slammed loudly on her. Alone, Ari leaned back against the headrest and closed her eyes.

It wasn't the first time she'd been accused of murder, but last time she'd been able to get away. It didn't look like she was going to be so lucky this time. Her mother had taught her there was always a chance to escape, a route to freedom, but at the moment Ari felt well and truly caged.

CHAPTER ONE

DALE SAT on the edge of the bed and stared at her phone, which rested on a web of her interlocked fingers. The screen was blank but she could see a vague reflection of her face looking down at it. She was still in her pajamas, her hair mussed, her glasses perched precariously on the edge of her nose. Eventually she managed to squeeze the button on the side of the phone and made it light up. The brightness of the lock screen dazzled her and she closed her eyes against it.

When she opened them, she saw the photo of Ari smiling up at her. She pressed her lips together and fought back tears, her chin trembling. She swept her thumb across the image just to make it go away. Once that was done, she managed to open her contacts list and find Diana Macallan's number. It only rang twice, which was still enough time for Dale to reconsider calling.

"Dale? What's up?"

"Diana." She sniffled. "Uh, I... I don't... H-how much sleep have you gotten in the past twenty-four hours?"

In addition to her duties on the force, Diana's wife Lucy had recently been diagnosed with cancer. She seemed to be doing fine, but the Macallan household wasn't exactly a stress-free environment.

"I had a couple hours this morning. I was just about to turn in."

"I'll... I can't... I'm sorry." She hung up before Diana could argue. Less than a minute later, the phone lit up with an incoming call. Dale sighed and answered. "Go to bed, Diana."

Diana sounded as if she was wide awake now. "Not when you call me at two in the morning sounding like you're about to cry. What's wrong? Is it Ari?"

Dale felt the pressure building behind her eyes. She thought if she spoke, she would start crying.

"I'm coming over," Diana said after listening to Dale struggle to explain.

"No, don't. Diana, it's... there's nothing you can do." She took a deep breath and forced the words out. "Ari's been arrested for murder."

"What? Who... What's... Explain to me what happened?"

Dale stood up and began to pace. She hoped that moving around would help settle her emotions. "Ari got a call earlier tonight from someone she met a few months ago. Her name was Shannon Hardy. She was a receptionist at Gilles Girard and Moreau until Ari inadvertently got her fired. Shannon wanted to meet and Ari felt she owed her that much. She didn't say what it was about." She felt something on her cheek and reached up to brush it away. Her fingers came back wet. "That was around eight o'clock. Around ten-thirty, I got a call from a number I didn't recognize. I assumed it was Ari at a pay phone, that she'd been the wolf and needed me to come pick her up. But there was no one on the other end. So I went back to sleep. Then I got another call at midnight."

"Puppy?" Fumbling with her glasses and the blankets. "Where are you?"

"Dale, I need you to listen to me. I've been arrested. I need you to call Mom."

"What do you mean arrested? Ari?"

"They think I murdered~"

"Murdered?!"

"~someone. I'm being held at the East Precinct. Dale, call Mom, okay?"

"Yeah, okay. Ariadne..."

"It's going to be okay, Dale. I have to go. I love you."

"I love you, too."

Diana asked, "Have you called Gwyneth?"

"Not yet. I couldn't... I don't... I didn't know what to say to her. I thought calling you might be better, you might be able to... might... there could be strings or something you could pull..."

"Dale..."

"No, I know, I shouldn't have called you. I realize that now. I'm just... I'm trying... I don't know what to do, and I thought maybe you could tell me what to do..."

"Dale," Diana said, more firmly this time. "The very least I can do is get more information. I know some people in the East Precinct. Let me give them a call and see what's going on."

"Thank you."

"And Dale, I want you to tell me something: What would Ariadne want you to do right now?"

Dale said, "I don't..."

"What would she want?"

"She'd... she would want me to take care of myself and not freak out."

"Exactly," Diana said. "Get dressed. Call Gwen. Then the two of you can go down to the station. They probably won't let you see Ari, but at least you can be there for her. Is your phone charged up?"

"Yeah."

"Keep it with you. I'll call back when I know more."

"Thank you, Diana."

Diana said, "You're welcome, Dale. We'll figure this out."

Dale hung up and turned to look around the bedroom. A few hours ago, she and Ari had been cuddling in bed watching Netflix. Now Ari was downtown in a prison cell accused of murder. She had no idea what to expect next, but at least now she had someone in her corner.

She held a breath for a long moment, and then let it out as slowly as she could. When she was finished, she tossed her phone onto the bed and started to get dressed.

The interrogation room wasn't like the ones she'd seen on television or in the movies. There was no mirror, but there was a television and a security camera mounted in one corner of the ceiling. The only table was pressed against the wall next to the door, and that was where she had been left not long after her arrival at the precinct. One phone call, though... that was like the movies. They'd taken her cell, so she had to use their landline to make the call. Probably made it easier to record the conversations.

Ari had put her head down on the table as soon as she was alone. One arm, the one cuffed to the table, was serving as a pillow. The other arm was curled over the top of her head, fingers twisting in her hair. She'd once heard that guilty people fall asleep easily after being arrested. She didn't care who was watching through the camera or what they thought her head being down meant. She was just tired, and the lights were bright, and she wanted nothing more than to wake up in bed and discover this was all a nightmare.

The hand on top of her head trailed down to the back of her neck. The bare skin reminded her that they'd taken her collar, and this was real. She hadn't had the collar off for longer than it took to shower in years. She always tried to make sure Dale was the one who put it on her again, just to establish the sentiment behind wearing it in the first place. Now it was gone, and her neck felt completely naked and exposed without it.

There was no way of telling how long she'd been in the room before she heard the door open and close quietly behind her. It only felt like a few minutes, but part of her knew she'd drifted off a couple of times. It could have been a few hours.

"Array... um, Ariadne Willow?"

She sat up and looked at the man who was moving a chair to sit in front of her. He looked like an accountant. Average height, a pale lavender shirt with a matching tie, and a smile that almost looked apologetic as he settled into the folding chair across from her.

"Detective Alonzo Rojas. Can I have them get you anything? Water?"

Ari shook her head.

"And I said your name correctly? It's Ariadne?"

"Yeah."

"Good, excellent." He put the file down on the table and scribbled something down. "You wouldn't believe some of the names we get in here. Whatever happened to Paul and Joe?" He chuckled and flipped the folder closed. He rested his left foot on his right knee and looked at her as if he was a therapist. "So, Ariadne, why don't you tell me what happened tonight?"

Ari dropped her gaze to the knot of his tie. It was tight and neat, just like the rest of his clothes. This was either the beginning of his shift or he'd been called in specifically to cover this case.

"Miss Willow? Or can I call you Ariadne?" She didn't answer. "How did you know Shannon Hardy?"

"I didn't," Ari said. "We'd only met a couple of times."

He smiled, the picture of friendliness. "Well, which is it, Miss Willow?"

"She was a receptionist at Gilles Girard and Moreau. I was on retainer there for a while. We spoke a few times in passing. It was my fault she got fired."

"Do you think she held a grudge?"

"No. She thanked me when it happened. It's a long story. That's not a good place to work. That's why I didn't stay on retainer there."

Rojas said, "Okay, let's circle back to that. I really want to know what happened tonight, if you're up to going over everything."

"Shannon called me. I was at home, watching a movie with Dale."

"That's your boyfriend?"

"Girlfriend."

"Okay."

Ari said, "Shannon called..."

"When was this?"

"Uh. Eight? Eight o'clock, a little bit after. I don't know." He nodded. He opened the file and made another note. Ari watched his pen move like it was the pocket watch of a hypnotist. "She sounded strange. Like she was high or something. She told me there were things about the law firm I needed to know. Her boss, Cecily Parrish, is a bad person."

"I know Miss Parrish," Rojas said. "I think every cop in this place knows Parrish. And I don't think any of them would question your judgement of her." He smiled again. *Just a friendly conversation,* the smile said, *it's just some silly thing we need to work out and then we'll give you a ride home.* "Go on."

Ari wet her lips. She wished she'd taken him up on the offer of water. "She asked me to meet at her apartment. She gave me the address and I went."

"Go on."

Ari closed her eyes. *I could smell the blood from the hallway.* "I felt like something was wrong as soon as I arrived at her building. I don't know what tipped me off." *Death has a smell. The wolf almost broke out of my skin the second the elevator doors opened.* "Maybe it was my years of being a private investigator. I don't know. But I knocked on the door and I wasn't very surprised when no one answered. The lights were on. I thought I could hear music inside." She swallowed hard and furrowed her brow. "I was worried about her."

"What happened next?"

I made a stupid mistake. "I picked the lock. She sounded distressed on the phone. I thought there was a very real possibility she might have taken some pills and chased them with wine. I was worried she might be unconscious and in need of help."

She could still see the room. Blood was dripping down the back of the couch, which had been stripped of their cushions. The stuffing had been ripped out of the furniture. Books were torn apart, the table was flipped over, and picture frames were lying where they had fallen off the walls. It looked like a war had been fought in the tight space. She'd followed a trail of spilled blood into the kitchen and...

"I found her there. She was... she was lying on top of the open dishwasher. She was bleeding into the clean dishes." Ari stared at a spot just beyond Rojas, the image seemingly painted on the wall behind him. "She'd... she was..."

Rojas said, "The crime scene guys are still there. They said she'd been ripped apart. One of them said he'd seen a wild animal attack like this once, but he'd never seen one person do this to another."

Ari flinched.

"Walk me through it, Miss Willow. Were you and Miss Hardy having an affair?"

"What?"

"Maybe it started after you got her fired. The doorman said he's seen you at the building multiple times over the past few months."

"What?" Ari was snapping out of her haze. "I've never been to that building before tonight."

Rojas examined the file. "According to his statement, you were a regular visitor. He assumed you and the lady were sleeping together. This girlfriend of yours. Dale? Will she back up your alibi once she knows how you were spending your nights?"

Ari started to speak, then closed her mouth. She could almost hear Rojas interviewing their landlady, Neka. "*Well, she did seem to go out at all hours of the night. Dale was home alone an awful lot. I just assumed it was private eye stuff. But come to think of it, a lot of times she would come home wearing weird clothes. Kind of... you know, walk of shame chic.*" She spread the fingers of her uncuffed hand on her thigh.

"I'm not having an affair. I've only been with Dale since we started dating."

"Well, we're going to look into that, of course. Now... what happened after you 'discovered' the body?"

Ari could hear the air quotes around 'discovered.' On an ordinary night, she would have made him eat his snide tone. This wasn't an ordinary night. She didn't feel like her skin was fitting right, or her brain was twisted in on itself. She shouldn't be in this room answering these questions, and until that situation corrected itself, she was going to feel anchorless.

"I checked to see if she was still alive. It was..." She remembered the blood, both how it looked and how it smelled. The wolf was going ballistic in her mind, but she forced herself to focus and feel the pulse. She knew it was useless; her throat was torn open, and Ari could see more vicious wounds through the tears in her blouse. "That's when I heard the sirens."

"And you ran."

"Yeah," Ari whispered.

"Why?" He looked genuinely curious. "Most people who discover a dead body, they welcome the police showing up."

Ari said, "Because it felt like a trap."

"That's a little paranoid, don't you think?"

"I got a call to the apartment. I walk in, find the woman who called me lying dead on the floor, and two minutes later, the cops are showing up. Sounds like a set-up to me."

Rojas said, "I agree. But that's only if your story is true."

Ari covered her face with her hand. She was still searching for a response when the door opened behind her.

"Speak of the devil," Rojas said, defeat creeping into his voice. "Hello, Cecily."

"Hello, Roaches." Cecily Parrish stepped to one side and held the door open. "Get out."

Rojas said, "She never requested counsel."

"It doesn't matter. I'm here now. Please excuse us."

Despite her friendly tone, it was clear that it wasn't a request. Rojas stood and closed his file. He paused and looked down at Ari.

"If there's anything you want to say..."

"You will hear it from me," Cecily said. "Leave."

Rojas left the room, head up but shoulders beginning to slump before he reached the hallway. Cecily pushed the door shut behind him and moved to take the seat he had just vacated. She placed her briefcase on the table and thumbed open the locks.

She looked extraordinarily put-together considering how late it was, but then again, she probably always looked runway-ready. Ari hadn't seen the lawyer in months, since turning down her job offer, and the effect of her beauty would have been overwhelming if she wasn't well-trained in ignoring its pull. Cecily was a succubus. Ari was mostly immune to her charms, but she could still feel the energy coming off of her.

"It's good to see you again, Ariadne."

"Did you do this?"

Cecily looked at her. "Be more specific."

"You fired Shannon to prove a point to me. Did you kill her, too? Did you set me up for murder because I wouldn't come to work for you?"

"I'm here because you get to decide what happens next, Ariadne. You were at the crime scene. You ran from the police with blood on your hands and your clothing. There are two paths we can take now. One, I tell them I'm your lawyer. I get these charges dismissed and you go home. To show your gratitude, you close down Bitches Investigations and come to work for GG&M. In addition, you will end your relationship with Dale Frye."

"What? That was never part of any deal you offered in the past."

"I'm negotiating from a position of power now, Miss Willow. You've made this increasingly difficult for us. Asking you to break up with her is just pettiness on our part. We can admit that. But it's part of the deal."

Ari could barely unclench her jaw enough to speak. "And the other option?"

"I volunteer my services to the prosecution. I ensure that you are convicted of Shannon Hardy's murder and spend the rest of your life in prison. You lose Bitches anyway. You probably decide to end things with Dale because it's not fair to have her living alone and without love while you're locked up. At least with the first option you have the benefit of being free and out in the world."

Rage boiled inside her to the point where she couldn't trust herself with words. She would have felt more articulate as the wolf. She bared her teeth and closed her eyes, focusing everything she had on not changing, on staying in human form.

"You might want to get better at controlling that beast of yours, Miss Willow. If you end up going to prison, you'll be part of a very open community. You won't be able to transform without at least twenty people seeing you."

Ari opened her eyes. Cecily was staring at her, maddeningly serene.

"You're trying to steal my life."

"No, Ariadne. Life as you know it ended when you walked into Shannon Hardy's apartment. I'm just giving you an option about how you continue from here. Whether you spend the rest of your life in a cage--"

"Or if I spend it in *your* cage."

Cecily smiled and tilted her head. "Call it what you want, Ariadne. But I can tell you that my cage is gilded. Take your time. Think about it. You'll be arraigned tomorrow..." She twisted her wrist to look at her watch. "Actually today, in a few hours. I will be in the courtroom. When the judge asks if you have representation, you can say my name. Or you can tell him no. Either way, I'll have my answer."

She closed her briefcase, which had apparently only been there as a prop, and stood up.

"I would have just left you alone," Ari said softly.

Cecily looked down at her.

"I wasn't even thinking about you anymore. But now, you have my word, that I'm going to make it my mission in life to fuck you up."

"With what, Miss Willow?" Cecily asked. "I've already taken everything. I look forward to hearing your answer tomorrow."

Ari heard the door click shut behind her as Cecily left.

CHAPTER TWO

GWYNETH WILLOW had been asleep when Dale called her, but she was wide awake and dressed by the time she let Dale and Diana into the house. The kitchen and dining room were awash with light and filled with the smell of freshly-brewed coffee. Diana filled them in about what she'd learned while Gwen poured them cups. Dale was transfixed by Ari's mother. She seemed composed and laser-focused. She looked like a general who just learned war had been declared.

When Diana finished explaining why Ari was in jail, Gwen thanked her and guided Dale outside to the car. They were halfway to the precinct before Dale even realized they were the only two in the car.

"Where did Diana go?"

"She said she needed to sleep. You were there. You told her to go."

Dale softly said, "Right," even though she had no recollection of the exchange. She chewed her thumbnail and looked out the window. The sun was just beginning to come up. Everything had an ethereal blue glow with a lining of gold. The windows of the highest buildings reflected the sun which hadn't yet gotten high enough to reach street level.

"Are you all right?"

Dale considered her answer carefully. "Ari always comes home," she finally said. "She goes out at night. She disappears in the middle of the night and I wake up to an empty bed, but she always comes home. Or she calls me to come get her."

"I know."

"She always comes home."

Gwen reached out and put her hand on top of Dale's. She kept it there for the rest of the drive, only removing it when she had to park. When they walked into the precinct, Dale reached out and took Gwen's hand before it could be offered.

The desk sergeant was young, fresh on-duty, and actually offered them a smile when they came inside.

"How can I help you?"

"My daughter was brought in last night. Ariadne Willow."

He checked the computer. "You're her mother?"

"That's right." She nodded at Dale. "And her sister."

"I'll let someone know you're here," the sergeant said. "Have a seat."

Gwen led Dale to the waiting area. "I didn't think about it until we were here," she said, "but they probably wouldn't let a girlfriend in. They probably won't allow any contact, so it's not like you could kiss her hello anyway."

"Thank you." They took a seat under the windows. "Not just for that, but for all of this. Taking control. I don't even know what's going on."

"Ari's in trouble. You're in shock, and you've barely gotten any sleep. You'll bounce back. You just need some time." She patted Dale's hand. "It's okay. I'm here."

Dale put her head down on Gwen's shoulder. She had just reached the cusp of sleep when Gwen woke her by quietly saying her name. She opened her eyes and saw a Hispanic man coming toward them.

"Miss Willow?" he said. "I'm Detective Rojas. You're Ariadne Willow's mother?"

"That's right."

"I wish we were meeting under better circumstances. If you'll come with me, I'll take you to a room where you can speak with your daughter."

Gwen held up a bag. Dale had seen her carrying it, but hadn't even wondered what it was for. "I brought Ari something to wear for her arraignment. I know I can't give it to her, but can you... I don't know, check it out to confirm it's safe and then let her have it?"

Rojas looked at the bag, reaching up to scratch his ear as he considered the request. Dale could almost see the pros and cons being written in the air above his head. Finally, he nodded and took the bag from her.

"I'll make sure she gets it."

"Thank you."

He led them past the desk and deeper into the building. Gwen was directly behind the detective with Dale bringing up the rear. Part of her shock was caused by the certainty that there was an easy way out of this. The detective seemed friendly enough. And Gwen seemed to be handling things superbly. Add those facts to Ari's ability to get out of the tightest situations, and she could see this all being wrapped up by noon.

And then Rojas opened the door to a windowless office to reveal Ari, handcuffed to a table. They had taken her mud- and blood-stained clothes as evidence, leaving her in a pair of pale blue scrubs. She should have looked like a doctor, but she didn't. She looked like a prisoner.

Dale's breath caught in her throat and she took one step back. Gwen looped an arm around Dale's elbow and urged her forward into the room.

"Thank you, Detective," Gwen said.

"I'm afraid I can't give you more than a few minutes."

Gwen nodded. "I understand."

He left and closed the door behind him. Dale thought it was unusual they would be left alone in the room but, as she sat down, she saw the camera near the ceiling. No doubt there was a cop outside the door and three more watching their conversation on a monitor somewhere.

Ari looked completely exhausted. Her face lit up when Dale met her eyes, so Dale tried not to look away. She wanted to reach out and take Ari's hands but knew she wouldn't be allowed to do it. She put her hands in her lap, then on the table, and finally folded them together as if she was saying grace.

"Hi, puppy."

"Hey," Ari said.

"I brought some clothes for you to wear to the arraignment," Gwen said. "I gave them to the police so they can confirm there are no razor blades sewn into the lining or something."

That succeeded in drawing a weak smile. "Thanks, Mom." Her fingers twitched and then curled into fists. "Dale, I'm sorry."

Dale shook her head. "Don't."

Ari bit her lip and looked down at the table.

Gwen said, "Ariadne, look at me." Ari lifted her eyes. "Can you be certain you didn't do this?"

Dale knew she was really asking about the wolf. And while she believed Ari wasn't capable of murder, while she trusted her even in wolf form, she knew the question had to be asked.

"I'm positive," Ari said. "There's no chance I did this. I know who did it." She glanced toward the camera. "Cecily Parrish."

"The lawyer?"

Ari nodded. "This is apparently her last-ditch effort to get me working for her. I agree, she takes my case and I walk free. I don't, then she sends me to jail."

Gwen said, "So you think she..."

Ari glanced over her shoulder at the camera. "I don't think she got her own hands dirty, no. I can't just sit in a cell making wild accusations. But yeah, I think she's behind it."

"We'll do what we can to figure out what really happened," Gwen said.

"In the meantime, do you happen to know a good lawyer?"

Gwen said, "I'll look into it. There's got to be someone."

Ari looked at Dale again. "We had to pause the movie we were watching." Tears threatened to overflow. "You can go ahead and watch the end without me, babe."

Dale laughed, but it turned into a sob. She reached out and put her hand on top of Ari's. "I love you."

"I love you, too." Ari covered Dale's hand with hers. The chain of her handcuffs made a raspy hiss against the edge of the table.

Rojas came into the room. "Sorry, ladies. It's time."

Dale stood up and stepped around the table. Rojas put a hand on her shoulder before she could reach Ari.

"Can't let you touch her."

Ari said, "It's okay, Dale."

Dale let herself be guided back to the door. Gwen followed, and Rojas nodded to the officer who would take Ari back to holding.

"Let me show you ladies out." Rojas walked back toward the front of the building. He looked back at Dale. "I have to say, you and your sister don't look much alike."

"I don't have a sister," Dale said, her mind elsewhere.

Rojas smiled as he faced forward again. "My mistake."

He left them at the lobby, handing Gwen his card 'in case she needed anything' and wishing them a good day. Gwen put an arm across Dale's shoulders and took her outside. It was now fully morning, the street alive with commuters on their way to work.

"I'm so stupid," Dale said.

"It's all right. The sister lie was just to get you back there. It served its purpose." She had her phone out, scrolling with her thumb. "Damn, who do I know that's a lawyer?"

Dale hugged herself and watched the cars passing by, full of people going about ordinary days in their ordinary lives.

"What happens now?"

Gwen squeezed Dale's shoulder and walked her toward the parking lot. "Now we find someone to represent Ariadne and hopefully keep her out of prison."

"And if we can't?"

Gwen started to say something but stopped herself. She remained silent until they reached the car. "Do you know when she last transformed?"

"Yesterday afternoon," Dale said. "I was with her. We went for a run. There's no way she could have blacked out and killed Shannon."

"That's not what I'm worried about," Gwen said. "Ari has twenty-eight days before the wolf forces her to transform. If that happens when she's in prison, it will be very bad."

"God," Dale whispered.

"We'll figure something out." They got into the car. "No matter what happens."

Dale wished she had some of that confidence. But at the moment it seemed like the deck was stacked against them and their enemies still had aces up their sleeves.

When she was returned to the holding cells, she stretched out on the bench and stared at the ceiling. Seeing Dale had felt like waking up, just for a second, and catching a glimpse of real life. Now she was back in the nightmare. The cell was the size of a doctor's waiting room, and she was sharing it with three other women. She knew one of them was a prostitute - bored, pissed off, obviously accustomed to this dance - but she hadn't heard what the other two were arrested for.

The night before continued playing in her head on a loop. She left the apartment just as the officers stepped off the elevator. It was immediately obvious that she was being set up, so she ran. In retrospect it was probably a stupid idea, since she ended up getting caught anyway, but she believed there was a chance she could get away. She only had to put enough distance between her and the police to transform and she would be home free.

Unfortunately whoever had called in the tip made it sound like enough of an emergency that four different cars had shown up. Ari ran out of the building past no less than four cops. She'd hoped to get lost in the wilder areas of Seward Park, but she didn't have any luck. Cecily must have been planning this for months. The woman was smart, and devious, and used to getting her own way. Ari had turned her down repeatedly and ruined whatever plans she'd been hatching.

"Payback's a bitch," she muttered.

One of the other women said, "Preach it, sister."

She closed her eyes but didn't sleep. She didn't know what to expect and, without a map of what was going to happen, she couldn't plan. So she just put herself on autopilot and waited. The wolf part of her brain knew she was in a cage but didn't quite understand how dire things were. Not yet. It was anxious but manageable. She had no idea what was going to happen when it realized the imprisonment wasn't going to be brief.

An officer eventually delivered the bag of clothes from Ari's mother and told her to change in the bathroom. When she came out, he directed her down the hallway. For a brief moment, even still cuffed, she felt like maybe they were letting her go. Her hopes were dashed when they reached the end of the hall and she was added to a line of the women from holding.

Two more officers were waiting by the exit. The female officer directed each woman to assume the position against the wall so she could run a metal detector over them. The other, male, was using a table to mark off each woman's name before she was directed out the door into a bus. When it was Ari's turn, she placed her palms against the bare brick wall and listened to the beeping of the wand as it swept across her shoulders and down her sides.

"Name," the male officer said.

"Ariadne Willow."

He tapped the screen of his device. "Any drugs, weapons, et cetera, we need to know about on your person?"

"No, nothing."

The female officer stepped back and said, "Go on."

Ari stepped through the doors and into the alley. The van was just two steps forward. To her right, the way blocked by a linebacker in a police uniform, was the street. Ari closed her eyes and took a deep breath of fresh, clean air. The hairs on the back of her neck stood up. Suddenly her skin felt tight, every muscle tense. It was the same tug a dogwalker felt just before little Fido dashed after a squirrel. It took everything in her power not to make a break for freedom.

Not now, Ari thought.

"Keep moving, Willow," one of the many cops around her ordered.

Ari ducked her head and continued forward. She climbed onto the van, took a seat next to the prostitute, and folded her hands between her knees.

"Keep your head up," the prostitute said.

Ari managed a smile. "Are you going to tell me it's not as bad as it seems?"

"No. I'm going to tell you that you're nowhere near the hard part yet. You start hanging your head now, there's people who are going to make sure it stays down. So head up."

"Right." She sat up straighter. "Thanks."

"Mm. Gotta look out for each other. Who else is gonna?"

Ari looked out the window. "Actually, I've got people."

The other woman said, "Well, good luck to them. And to you."

"Thanks."

The linebacker got behind the wheel and, moments later, they pulled out of the alley and onto the street. Ari moved closer to the window and craned her neck to look up at the sky. She didn't know how long it would be before she had another chance to enjoy the sight, and she wasn't going to waste it.

CHAPTER THREE

A LIFETIME of courtroom dramas had trained Ari to expect something ostentatious and theatrical about the arraignment. In reality, the courtroom was about as extravagant as the DMV. She was directed to a row of chairs with uncomfortably hard cushions. As she sat down she noticed the chairs' frames had male and female hooks on either side of the seat. They were built to interlock with their neighbor so none of them could be picked up and used as a projectile. Somehow that, rather than the bars and handcuffs, was what really drove home the fact she was a prisoner.

Judge Welker was a tired-looking bald man who sat forward on his chair, elbows resting on the edge of his bench, looking like a grandfather who was perusing the menu of a restaurant he didn't particularly like. The bailiff would approach the row of chairs, say a name, and the prisoner would stand up and move to stand at a table in front of the judge.

Ari looked at the spectators and spotted her family. Dale looked like she had gotten some sleep, which was a relief, but her mother looked annoyed. Gwen caught her looking and winked, almost making it look convincing. Ari responded with a half-smile which fell as soon as he saw the cap of slicked-back blonde hair sitting a few rows farther back.

Cecily Parrish had changed into a black blazer with white

piping. She was staring, unblinking, at Ari and smiled when they made eye contact. She raised one eyebrow and Ari looked away.

"Willow," the bailiff said, "Ariadne."

Ari stood and reluctantly moved into position. Judge Welker had moved one hand to his temple, using the other hand to keep his place on the page as he read.

"Ariadne Willow." He looked up at her. "Do you have counsel?"

She could feel Cecily's eyes burning holes in the back of her head. "No."

"We could appoint someone if you like. You're entitled to have someone speaking for you at this hearing."

"I..." She resisted the urge to look at her mother. She knew if they pulled up someone from the public defender pool, she had no doubt Cecily would step up for the prosecution and bury the poor sod. "I think no, not at this time."

Welker seemed disappointed but not surprised as he lowered his gaze back to the file. "Okay, then. Miss Willow, you are charged with aggravated assault, domestic violence, resisting arrest, and murder in the second degree. How do you plead?"

"Not guilty."

Welker made a mark on his page. "On the matter of bail. Mr. Snider?"

A man Ari hadn't noticed was standing at the far end of the table answered. "Your honor, the defendant was also accused of murder six years ago..."

"I was cleared of those charges," Ari said.

Welker looked at her. "Yes, Miss Willow, but in cases like this, the charges themselves have a certain weight to them. Continue, Mr. Snider."

"In that instance, the defendant successfully eluded the police and fled. She tried to run this time as well. I believe this proves her to be a flight risk and, to that end, we recommend denying bail."

"My job is here," Ari said. "My girlfriend, my mother. I've never lived anywhere but Seattle. Where would I go?"

For a moment, he seemed to consider it. "This says you're a private investigator."

"That's right."

"You work with the police a lot?"

"Um. Occasionally."

Welker sat up straighter and then let his shoulders sag again. "I know a lot of cops. They're good people. But at the end of the day, they're human. They might look past their badge and help out a friend. Given your history with evading the law, the fact you attempted to do the same thing when you were arrested this time, and the circumstances of this crime, I have to go with the prosecution and deny bail. You will be remanded to custody until your trial."

Ari put her hand on the edge of the table. She knew it was pointless to fight or argue at this point, but she also couldn't just surrender.

"Please return to your seat, Miss Willow," Welker said.

She felt someone standing next to her and she allowed herself to be guided away. The next prisoner was brought up and the routine began all over again. Ari saw Snider, the prosecutor, return to the gallery and bend down next to Cecily. Ari wasn't the best lip-reader in the world, but she could tell Cecily told him, "Good job."

She looked to her mother for an emotional boost. It backfired when she saw Gwen was sitting alone; Dale had vanished. Ari felt herself flinch and blinked away the sudden moisture in her eyes. She tried to mouth a question but her lips were shaking too much for it to be useful.

Gwen didn't look away. She held her daughter's gaze, lips pressed tightly together and eyes steely. Ari hadn't seen that look in her eyes since wolf manoth and the war with the hunters. Gwen lowered her chin and raised her eyebrows. When she was sure Ari was paying attention, she very carefully mouthed: "I will take care of her."

Ari said, "Thank you."

Gwen winked. Ever since Ari was a child, her mother had lacked the ability to properly wink. She would close both eyes and then open one while tilting her head to the side. It was absolutely adorable and, even given the circumstances, Ari couldn't stop herself from smiling. Gwen smiled as well and blew her a kiss, then put her hand flat against her chest.

Ari faced forward. The prostitute was awarded bail and began making arrangements to pay it so she could go home. She looked at Ari as she was led away. Ari nodded to her, grateful someone was getting a happy ending, but the other woman quickly looked away. She was scared. And Ari realized she had every right to be. Ari was just a stranger who had been denied bail on her second murder charge. Who wouldn't be scared?

In the gallery, Cecily Parrish stood up and picked up her briefcase. She looked at Ari one last time before she turned and walked out of the courtroom.

Ari knew she had a good team watching her back. She knew her mother, Dale, Diana, and anyone else they could enlist would fight tooth and claw to free her.

But right now, at this moment, she couldn't help but feel like the war was over and she had lost spectacularly.

Dale hated herself for retreating. The walk out of the courtroom made her feel like a coward, like she was turning her back on the woman she loved. But she knew Ari would need her to be strong and knew she wouldn't be able to give her that. She didn't want Ari to look to her and see devastation. It would shatter whatever resolve she had. So she hurried out into the hallway, one hand over her mouth to keep any sounds of distress from breaking free, and made a beeline for the ladies room.

The floor and half the wall were faux marble, with off-white tile stretching to the ceiling. Dale went to the sink and jabbed her hands under the faucet until it finally deigned to spray water into her palms. She let a small pool gather and then splashed it onto her face. She'd always scoffed when she saw people do that in movies, but it was better than just crying. And she had to admit, it felt pretty damn good. She did it again and pressed her fingertips against her eyelids.

A toilet flushed. Someone joined her at the sink, hands were washed.

"Are you okay, sweetie?"

"No," Dale said, "but thank you."

"Do you need—"

"No. It's okay. Thank you."

The woman left. Dale went to the paper towel dispenser and pulled one free, pressing it flat against her face. Her hands were trembling but at least she didn't feel like she was about to start sobbing. She breathed in the dry, somehow scratchy odor of the towel and then lowered it. She looked in the mirror and saw that Cecily Parrish had silently entered the bathroom and was standing behind her.

"I realized," Cecily said, as casual as if they were already deep in conversation, "that I've been giving Ariadne all the power in your relationship. I've been telling her to make choices which will affect you both. So in the interest of equality, I want to make you the same offer. I will free your girlfriend if she closes Bitches, breaks up with you, and comes to work for me."

Dale kept looking at the mirror instead of the actual woman. "Oh. That makes sense."

"I knew you would see reason."

"I kept thinking, what could be worse than going to prison? Now I know. Working for you. That must suck, huh? Ari would rather go to jail than have you as a boss? I can't say I blame her."

Cecily stepped closer. "Miss Frye..."

Dale turned around. "You seem to think I'm a damsel in distress. That Ariadne is my superhero who has to swoop in and save me. You're wrong. Ari is a wolf, but I'm a fighter. Especially when someone I love is in danger. Do you know how Ari and I met? Three kids were harassing her and I jumped in and scared them off. I did that. I saved her. Just like I'm going to save her now."

"Are you going to kill me, Dale?" Cecily asked mockingly.

"You took everything away from me. Without Ari, without Bitches, I have nothing but time on my hands. You're my life now, Cecily. I don't think I could kill you. I'm just being realistic there. But I can certainly make your life hell. 'Cause you know what you've never realized about our agency?" She leaned in close enough that Cecily's perfume was almost overwhelming and lowered her voice. "Bitches is plural, you fucking cunt."

She put her wet hands on Cecily's shoulders and pushed her away. She stepped around her and left the bathroom, her sorrow and helplessness hardening into anger as she strolled back toward the courtroom where Gwen was waiting for her.

"Where did you go?" Gwen asked.

"I had to grow some ovaries. Is Ariadne still in there?"

Gwen shook her head. "They just took her."

Dale slipped her arm around Gwen's elbow. "Then let's go. We have battleplans to draw up."

Back in the van, Ari again felt the wolf struggling for control. She took slow, calming breaths and focused on maintaining control. The sun fell across her face as the driver pulled out of the garage. She mentally apologized to the wolf and hoped it understood what was about to happen. *Canidae* could usually go four weeks without transforming, although it became harder and harder to hold back the wolf closer to the deadline, but that was under normal circumstances. If it felt trapped and cornered, if it didn't understand what was happening, it could lead to something tragic.

I need you to be good, she thought. *I let you run a little bit yesterday. I wish I'd known that would be the last time for a while, but you need to be patient.*

The King County Correctional Facility was downtown, a normal-enough building on Fifth Avenue, innocuous among the other high-rises on the dangerously sloped streets leading to Elliott Bay. Despite living her entire life in Seattle, Ari's stomach still dropped a little when the van turned and seemed to roll straight down like a roller coaster. She was sitting close enough to the front that, through the windshield, she could see a little sliver of blue water directly ahead. Then the van turned off the street into a garage and the view faded along with the sunlight.

Ari allowed herself to be guided, escorted, and moved from the garage and deeper into the building. She gave her name yet again, and was taken into a little room with an older female guard. The woman reminded Ari of a TSA agent, someone who was going to do the same exact thing five hundred times over the course of a week and was eager to just get it over with.

"Strip," the woman said.

Ari began undressing.

"Huh."

"What?"

"Nothing. You're fine. Just most people are a little more squeamish about getting naked in front of a stranger."

Ari was already down to her underwear. She placed everything in a bin marked with her name, using the conversation to ignore the fact she was abandoning all her things.

"I don't have a problem with nudity. And you've probably seen so many naked women that it all just blends together for you."

"Ain't that the truth," the woman said. "Okay, cheekbones. You made it easy for me, so I'll do the same for you. Maybe we'll even end up friends."

Ari turned around and put her hands on her knees, grimacing in anticipation of what was about to happen. "Yeah, I'll put you on my Christmas ca-*haaah*-rd list..."

When the search finished, she was given a white T-shirt, underwear, an orange jumpsuit, and bedding. She also had to give up her shoes, trading them for a pair of plain white sneakers.

"Through the door."

She took her new belongings into the next room. Two men in pale blue uniform shirts were sitting at a table behind a laptop. "Name."

"Willow."

"Put down your things, hold this, stand in front of the wall."

The wall was marked for height. She stood on the line and held up the placard.

"Look here," one of them said. He tapped a key on the computer, and the other one pulled a sheet from the printer. "Step forward."

Ari did as she was told. The one who hadn't spoken pulled something from the printer, attached a clip, and held it out to her.

"Keep that on you at all times."

"Yeah, if you don't know I'm a prisoner, you might let me go home."

"Funny," the talkative one said without emotion. "Move. Next."

Ari retrieved her bedding and left the room. She found herself in a hallway with two elevators and a guard stationed in front of each one. The male guard gestured for Ari to line up with the other prisoners against the opposite wall. She rested her shoulders against the bricks and closed her eyes.

"First time?"

Ari looked at the woman next to her. She was young, black, and seemed to be genuinely curious. "Yeah," she said. "You?"

The woman smiled and rested her head against the wall, looking up toward the ceiling. "Second time for me. First time was when I was a kid. Possession. State finally changes the law so we don't have to worry about having a little weed in our cars, and they find some other nonsense to run us in for."

"What did you do?"

"Forced entry, assault, grand theft auto."

Ari raised an eyebrow. "I'm sure it was all a big misunderstanding."

The other woman grinned. "I'm Elise Gilpin."

"Ariadne Willow. Apparently I'm in for murder."

"Damn. Glad I made friendly before I found that out. I'll stay on your good side, killer."

The last prisoner came through and joined the line. The male guard sighed and stepped forward. "Listen up. I'm CO Burke, this is CO Eades. If your first name begins with A through M, you'll come with me. First name N through Z, go with Eades."

Ari and Elise lined up in front of the elevator with one other woman. The other line had four women. Burke waited for them to get into the car before he joined them.

"You will be living on the fourth floor." He consulted his computer. "Gilpin, you're in bunk 4-1C. Weiss, 4-2E. Willow, 4-1J. One means you're on the first level, two means you go up the stairs to the second level. Are we clear?"

Ari and the other women nodded.

The elevator doors opened and Burke stepped out, motioning for them to follow. The main floor was a common area with several round tables. There were ten cells on the lower level, another ten on the second level, and an elevated room shaped like a tower in the far corner. Ari could see two guards behind the most-likely bulletproof glass. The cell doors were solid, not barred, with a rectangular pane of glass that reminded Ari of high school classrooms.

A half dozen women in khaki uniforms were seated at the tables, others had been lounging in their cells, and a few more had been walking down a brightly-lit hallway that branched off from the main area. No matter what they were doing, however, everyone's attention was captured by the arrival of the elevator.

"This is Level 4, ladies," Burke said. "Make yourselves comfortable. You are all probably going to be here for a very long time." He made a grand sweeping gesture to indicate the room.

"Welcome home, inmates."

CHAPTER FOUR

FOR ALL her big talk, Dale didn't have any sort of plan to go after Cecily and save Ari. She spent the drive back to Gwen's house explaining everything they had been through with Gilles Girard and Moreau, even though she had to admit she didn't think she knew the entire story. GG&M was a law firm which, according to Ari, wasn't particularly choosy about the clients they represented. Cecily Parrish had destroyed Ari's testimony in court and then offered her a job as the firm's in-house investigator. It was during her probationary period that Ari discovered Cecily was a succubus.

"Ariadne came to me for advice about that job," Gwen said. "Maybe if I'd known the depths Cecily would sink to, I would have told her to accept the offer."

Dale said, "Not on the terms Cecily was giving. First she wanted Ari to give up Bitches. Now apparently breaking up with me is part of the bargain."

"Why?"

"To be a cruel bitch?" She winced and pinched the bridge of her nose. "Sorry."

Gwen glanced toward her. "For what?"

"Uh. Nothing."

After a moment, Gwen realized what she meant. "Ah. Because *I* once tried to force you and Ariadne to break up."

"I didn't mean anything by it," Dale said.

"Did I ever apologize for that?"

"I'm sure you did. It's in the past."

Gwen said, "Not far enough in the past. I didn't realize what the two of you had. I had no idea what you meant to one another. If I had, if I knew how lucky my daughter was to have you in her life..." She flexed her fingers on the steering wheel. "Every day I'm grateful that Ariadne forgave me for that. Because if I had someone like you, I would never forgive the person who tried to take her away. I love you like a daughter, Dale."

"I don't know how to respond to that."

"You don't have to," Gwen said. "It's just information for you to have, if it's ever needed. When you need help, I'm not just 'Ari's mom.' Not to you."

"Thank you." Dale looked out the window. "It doesn't make sense. Ari's a great detective, but why go to all this trouble just to hire her? There are other detectives in this town."

"But how many of them are wolves?" Gwen asked. "This woman is a succubus... maybe there are other creatures employed at the firm as well."

Dale considered that as Gwen pulled into the garage. "You think GG&M is making some kind of menagerie?"

Gwen shrugged. "It's possible. It would explain why she's going to such ridiculous lengths just to recruit Ariadne." They got out of the car and faced each other across the roof. "You and I know how special she is, but no employer would *kill* just because she said no to a job offer. No sane person would do it, anyway."

"Are we sure Cecily is sane, though."

"That's a good question."

Dale sighed and took the keys from her pocket. "Okay. Uh, thanks for keeping my head on straight and taking care of everything this morning. I honestly have no idea what I would have done if you hadn't been there."

"Where do you think you're going?"

"Home. I need..."

Gwen was shaking her head. "You're going inside. You're going to sleep in the guest room. You've been up most of the night, and it's been an incredibly stressful few hours. You need to sleep and you need to not be alone."

"Thank you, but~"

"Dale," Gwen said softly, "I need to not be alone, too."

"Well. When you put it that way..."

Gwen moved to the front of the car and held out one hand. Dale joined her and let Gwen drop the arm across her shoulders as they went inside.

"There's nothing we can do at this moment, so we're going to regroup and recharge. And because I don't want you to worry about anything, I'm going to take care of your bills until all this blows over. Rent for your home and the offices, whatever you need."

Dale said, "That's far too much..."

Gwen stepped in front of her. "Ariadne ran away when she was a teenager. I didn't get to take care of her during those years. This is my chance to finally make up for that lost time by taking care of the life she built for herself, and by taking care of you when she isn't able to."

Dale fought back tears. "Well, gee. You make it hard to say no."

"Good." She kissed Dale's forehead. "I'm going to let you make up the room. You remember where the linens are, right?"

Dale nodded. It had been a while since wolf manoth, when she'd camped out in Gwen's house while Ari was undercover with the hunters, but she had a fair idea of where she could find everything.

"Okay," Gwen said. "Get some rest. I have some calls to make."

Ari's cell was at the far end of the room, the last one on the lower level. The door was propped open and, as she approached, she could see someone was stretched out on one of the beds. She paused on the threshold and examined her new home. Two beds, one on either side of the door, each with a small table at the far end. On the wall opposite the door was a little window, high and narrow enough that escape wasn't an option.

"Looking for decorating tips?" The woman on the bed had been reading, but she put the book face-down on her mattress and sat up. She was wearing tan khakis and a V-neck undershirt which showed off her heavily-inked arms. A khaki button-down shirt was tossed carelessly on the foot of the bed. Her black hair was shaved at the sides and slicked back on top.

"I... no. Ah, apparently I'm your new roommate."

Her shoulders sagged. "Ah, damn. Knew it was too good to last." She motioned Ari forward. "Well, it's your home, too. Don't wait for an invitation."

"Right." Ari stepped inside and put her pillow and blanket

down. "I'm Ariadne Willow. You can call me Ari."

"No, I won't. We generally use last names in here. The guards do it, so it's just easier." She stuck out her hand. "Shae Segura. How you holding up?"

Ari shook her hand before taking a seat on her bed. There was space between her and Segura, but not a hell of a lot. The cell as just a little wider than most supply closets she'd seen.

"I don't think it's real enough for me to react yet," Ari admitted. "Twenty-four hours ago, I was at home worrying about what I'd have for dinner. Now I'm sitting in jail awaiting trial for murder."

"Murder?"

"I didn't do it, if that makes you feel better."

Segura chuckled. "I might still sleep with one eye open. No offense. I'm just in here for fraud, forgery, theft." She leaned forward and lowered her voice. "I'm what you might call a con artist."

"Is that so," Ari said.

"Yeah. I was pretty good, if I do say so myself. But I got caught by one of my marks. I'm not a murderer - again, no judgement on you - so I tried to run. I've always been better at lying than running. So I got caught. Once I was in the system, all my sins started coming back to bite me."

Ari said, "Is that what the friendliness is all about? You're trying to gain my confidence so you can screw me over at a later date?"

Segura smiled devilishly. "You're quicker than I like my marks. But no. You've seen the size of this room. You and I have to share it for the foreseeable future. I could play the alpha bitch and try to make you fall in line, or I could try to become your friend. There's plenty of time to make your life miserable later if you turn out to be an asshole."

Ari smiled at the 'alpha bitch' comment but let it go. "I'll do my best to stay on your good side."

"Good. So, Willow, you have a choice. You want to settle in, relax, settle your mind? Or do you want to find out about your new home? I'm good either way."

Ari said, "I think settling sounds good right about now."

Segura picked up her book and stretched out on top of her blankets. "Works for me. Try to do it quietly, though. House rules: don't talk to me when I'm reading."

"I'll make a note."

"See that you do. And when you've been around long enough to have rules of your own, I'll respect them. It's a partnership. That way we have harmony."

Ari nodded. She spread out her blanket, put her pillow at the far end of the mattress, and lay down. She crossed her feet at the ankles and laced her fingers over her stomach. It only took her a minute or so to quiet her mind and shut out all the extraneous noise of the prison. Segura was silent as promised, and the commotion outside the cell - voices echoing as women called to each other, the crash-clang of doors automatically locking as they were closed - was easy enough to ignore.

She liked to imagine the wolf was something deep in the center of her brain. It wasn't caged, but it was secure and restrained there until she called on it. The wolf was obedient, but only to a point. It was a part of who she was and it could only be denied for so long. Four weeks, give or take. She rarely let herself go that long. She enjoyed running as much as the wolf did, and letting herself go was a pure pleasure that no non-*canidae* could hope to understand. But now she didn't have a choice.

Listen, she said.

She felt the wildness stirring in the center of her brain.

I don't want this any more than you do. I know right now you're scared and confused. I want to tell you it'll get better, but I won't lie to you. It's going to get worse. And it's probably going to be a long time before I can let you out. Be good to us, and I'll do everything in my power to get you free. You're a part of me. I'm not locking you up, I just can't let you out.

Her focus shattered into the swirling, unhinged feeling that came right before blacking out. She felt nauseated and drunk as the wolf pressed against the edges of the barrier she had put up. Her hands curled into fists and she could feel her nails scratching through the material of her jumpsuit and shirt.

No.

She thought the word once, as firmly as she could manage. It was calm and unpanicked. She felt the bunk trembling underneath her and realized it was because she was having a very small seizure from the effort of keeping the wolf at bay.

I will let you out the moment it's safe, she thought, still calm even as the darkness closed in on her vision. *Listen to me. Trust me. I don't want you to be hurt, but I have to hold you back in order to protect you. Remember the lessons. There are right times. There are wrong times. This is the wrongest time there's ever been, baby. Trust me. Let me take whatever punishment is going to happen.*

The tremors subsided. Her muscles relaxed, and she felt the darkness retreating. She waited until it was entirely gone before she let herself sigh with relief. She blinked her eyes open and turned her head to see Segura watching her over the top of her book.

"You okay there, newbie?"

"I'm..." Her voice cracked and she coughed to clear her throat. "Yeah. I'm fine. Just a little, uh, meditation trick my mother taught me."

"I thought meditation was supposed to relax you."

Ari sat up and put her feet on the floor. Her forehead and upper lip were beaded with sweat. "Don't I look relaxed?"

Segura closed the book on her finger. "Yeah, come to think of it, you do. Are you going to be doing that a lot?"

"No, I don't think so," Ari said.

She might have calmed her wolf for the time being, but she knew it wasn't anything like a permanent solution. Sooner or later it would start to push at the edges again and she would have to fight it back. Eventually there would be no reasoning with it. She examined the cell again. Not much room to pace or prowl, certainly not enough room to run. The wolf would absolutely hate it, but if she was pushed into a corner...

"How much privacy do we get in this place? Could I close the door, put a blanket over the window, and just chill for... say an hour?"

"You got a habit?" Segura asked. "Or are you coming on to me?"

Ari shook her head. "No, I just... I'm... curious. I like my private time."

"Well, you're going to have to say goodbye to that. An hour of alone time? I would agree to make myself scarce as long as you needed, but the guards and the other ladies would get real curious about what you're up to. The guards would think you're digging a tunnel, and everyone else would think you're dealing drugs and get huffy because you aren't sharing. Secrets don't survive long in this place."

"Just making sure," Ari said. "I had to ask."

Segura nodded. "Better to get it out of the way early." She looked back at her book. "About the, uh, other thing..."

"What?"

"Coming on to me."

"Oh. No, I'm... I am gay. But I have a..." Again, that hated term. Girlfriend seemed so small and partner was just so vague. "I've found the love of my life. She's waiting for me outside."

Segura clicked her tongue against her teeth. "Damn. Well, can't have it all, I guess."

Ari stood up and went to the door. She looked out over the common space and the women who were now her neighbors. She knew her mom and Dale were working hard on getting her out, but Cecily Parrish was probably marshalling every tool at her disposal to make sure Ari stayed in jail as long as possible. She didn't want to say it sounded impossible, but she had a feeling she was going to be staying in this place a lot longer than she would like.

CHAPTER FIVE

GWEN WAITED until she was positive Dale was upstairs before she collapsed into one of her dining room chairs and covered her face with both hands. From the moment Dale showed up, almost hysterical and barely able to speak, Gwen knew she would need to be the strong one. Dale and Ariadne had both needed someone they could lean on and from whom they could draw strength. Gwen was happy to provide that for them, for both her daughters, but the entire day had been an enormous strain on her. Now that she was alone she could focus on her own emotions.

She was well-trained in worrying for her daughter. When Ariadne was a teenager and learned the truth about what Gwen had done to her as a baby, she responded by running away. Gwen still believed she had done the right thing. Ari was the daughter of a hunter and was born human. The only way to make her *canidae* was a blood transfusion which gave her the ability to transform into a wolf, but with great physical pain.

Would she still feel it was the right thing if Ari had died from the procedure? Had it still felt like the right thing when she knew that every transformation was excruciating? And now that Ari was locked up, her *canidae* nature was like a sword hanging over her head by the thinnest of threads, would she have done things differently? Risked having her daughter grow up human? The wolf helped her overcome whatever hunter DNA she might have gotten from her father. It gave her a chance to become a good person. Whatever consequences came from that decision, Gwen still believed it was the right thing to do.

Gwen wiped her hands over her face. She'd always worked out her worries and stress by Doing. For years, that had been gathering funds and recruiting wolves to help in the war against the hunters. Now her girls needed her. She took out her phone and tried to think of any lawyers she might know. She was about to begin scrolling through her contacts when she realized there was another call she needed to make first.

She checked to make sure Dale hadn't come back downstairs and then dialed. There was a time difference to consider, but her call was answered while she was still trying to figure out how late it would be on the other end.

"Hi," she said. "I need you to come to Seattle. Now."

Dale was adamant that she wouldn't sleep. Not when Ari was in such a dire situation. She went upstairs because she knew Gwen wouldn't let up, but she only planned to take a quick shower and then go back down to the kitchen to begin brainstorming. The only reason she sat on the bed was to take off her shoes, and that felt so good that she decided to put her head down. That way, if Gwen asked, she would be telling the truth if she said she'd laid down for a little bit. She was smiling at her own cleverness when she drifted off.

At some point, she was aware of Gwen bending over the bed to tuck a blanket around her shoulders. Late afternoon sunlight was streaming past her, making her look godlike.

"I'm not sleeping," Dale murmured.

"I know, sweetheart."

The light had shifted the next time Dale opened her eyes. It wasn't yet night, but her stomach was very aware of the fact she'd missed breakfast and lunch. She freed herself from the blankets, found her shoes, and went into the bathroom. She finally took her shower and dressed in the clothes Gwen had left hanging from a hook on the bedroom door. She couldn't tell if the outfit was Ari's or Gwen's, but it fit her well enough despite the fact she was curvier than either of them. She left the shirt untucked and went downstairs.

Gwen was in the kitchen, stirring something on the stove.

"Hello, Dale. Did you sleep well?"

"I didn't want to sleep at all."

"Sometimes it's not up to you. It's been an incredibly stressful day. Your brain needed time to process everything. I'm making some pesto soup, if you'd like to get the bowls."

Dale's stomach grumbled as she retrieved the bowls. The silverware was in the second drawer she checked, and she joined Gwen at the stove.

"Is she going to be okay?"

Gwen looked at her and seemed to debate between the harsh truth and a hopeful lie. In the end, she said, "I don't know. I've put in some calls and hopefully we'll have reinforcements soon. I also did some research and discovered that the prison only allows visitation on certain days. We can see Ariadne again on Monday."

"Monday?" It might as well have been a month away.

"I'm sorry, Dale, but there's no wiggle room on that."

"No, I know, it's just... I don't like being away from Ari that long. I know it's harder on her, since she can't transform, but..."

Gwen put a hand on Dale's arm. "I understand. Come on. Let's eat."

They sat together at the dinner table. Despite her stomach's protestations, Dale didn't expect to have much of an appetite. She surprised herself by emptying her bowl before Gwen, licking her lips and wondering if it was impolite to ask for seconds. Gwen saw her contemplating the question and saved her from asking by pointing out there was plenty more on the stove.

"I feel guilty," Dale said as she refilled her bowl. "We're probably eating better than Ari is."

"You'll drive yourself insane if you keep thinking like that. Ari doesn't want you to punish yourself just because she's locked up. Don't play that game."

Dale returned to her seat. "It's hard not to. But I'll try."

"That's all you can do."

Dale stirred her spoon through the pale green soup. "I don't like married couples taking each other's name. It just seems stupid and possessive, and I hate it. But there have been times when I've said 'Dale Willow' to myself, and I didn't exactly hate the way it sounds. I just wanted to let you know that I'd been thinking about stuff like that. Ari and I both have."

Gwen said, "Well, that's good to know." She tapped her finger against the handle of her spoon. "And for what it's worth, I think

Ariadne Frye has a mighty fine ring to it as well. If you decided to go that route."

Dale smiled. "Maybe if Ari was my wife, we wouldn't have to lie and say I'm her sister just so I could see her."

Gwen chuckled. "Yes, I got the feeling that's a ruse you wouldn't be able to maintain for very long."

They fell into silence, eating and looking out the window. Gwen occasionally checked her phone but obviously didn't see any news from the people she'd contacted. Dale looked out the window. She wondered if Ari's cell had a window, if she could look out at the city or over the harbor depending on which side of the building she was on. All she could picture was a medieval cell, all iron bars and exposed stone bricks, with a mattress in one corner and a bucket in the other. She saw Ari in a black-and-white striped prisoner outfit, face against the bars, begging for help.

Dale closed her eyes to prevent herself from crying, then put her head down on the table next to her bowl. Gwen reached out and put her hand on top of Dale's head, stroking her hair without saying anything.

Ari had gone to her bed, one arm across her eyes, because she had no idea what else to do. Segura kicked the bedframe. Ari looked up to see the con artist was standing up and buttoning her khaki shirt. She nodded toward the door.

"Grub time. Come on, I'll show you around."

"I'm not hungry."

Segura kicked the bed again. "When was the last time you ate? I don't care if you're not hungry, your body needs food. Or the imitation of it that gets served here. Plus this is the best time for you to get a little tour. Come on. Up."

Ari sighed and swung around to put her feet on the floor. "When do I get one of those snazzy brown outfits? Orange isn't really my color."

"A couple of days, probably." She led Ari out of the cell and gestured to the right. A few of the women Ari had seen earlier were already on their way down a hall. "Cafeteria is at the end of this hall. Infirmary is down the other way, even though it's pretty much just a nurse's station with a first-aid kit. The gym is down here, too. There's a TV in there, too, but there's a hierarchy to using the remote control. I've never bothered to figure it out. Nothing worth watching, anyway."

Ari stayed behind Segura. The other prisoners would glance her way, their attention apparently drawn by the orange jumpsuit that marked her as a new arrival. Segura used her chin to indicate an older white woman who had just picked up a tray.

"That's Leona Seymour. If you need anything, she's the one you have to go through. Just make sure you really fucking need it, though, because she's not cheap. Try not to get on her bad side."

"Noted." They joined the line. Ari looked back and saw Elise, the woman she'd met by the elevators, standing in the cafeteria entrance. She waved and Elise waved back, joining the line. "So, uh, what sort of things can Leona get?"

Segura shrugged. "What do you need? Legal stuff is easier. You need to build a relationship with her before you ask for anything illegal. That's just common sense. She's not going to stick her neck out for someone she doesn't know."

"Makes sense. I don't know what I'll need. I just know I'm probably going to need *something*, and it's not likely to be for sale in the prison commissary."

"Yo, Shae."

Segura cringed. "Oh, god. Brace yourself."

The woman seemed to have come out of nowhere, clapping her hand on Segura's shoulder but keeping her focus on Ari. She was at least six feet tall and broad in the shoulders. Her short blonde hair pulled back in a ponytail. "You have a new friend? What's your name, new friend?"

"Willow."

"Willow? *Willow?* Isn't that, like... there's a movie with, like, Val Kilmer called Willow."

Ari said, "Yeah, that's–"

"Will Smith's daughter is named Willow, too. It's not a very inspiring name, you know? What's your last name?"

"Willow is my last name," Ari said. "First name is Ariadne."

The new arrival said, "Oh, that's a lot better. Nice to make your acquaintance. Miriam Kunz."

"Seriously? And you're giving me shit for *my* name?"

There was a flash of anger in Miriam's eyes, but it passed before Ari could tell how worried she could be.

"Your friend kind of has a mouth on her, Shae."

Segura said, "Yeah, she's new. Still learning the ropes."

Miriam said, "I like when they're new. Get to them before they form any bad habits." She winked at Ari. "You come find me sometime, Willow. I'll treat you better than this hussy."

"I'm sure she's grateful for the offer," Segura said, "but how about for now we just let the poor girl have some dinner."

"Sure." She lingered a moment longer before she drifted away. "See you around, Willow."

Segura watched Miriam leave. "Watch out for her. And be lucky she's not your cellmate. That 'love of my life' stuff? I found it adorably and disgustingly sweet, but she would've taken it as a challenge. She doesn't like to hear the word 'no'."

"Boy, this is a heck of a neighborhood I've moved into."

"Yeah," Segura chuckled, "but our schools are surprisingly fantastic."

They got their food and found a seat. Segura looked around the room to see if there was anyone else worth introducing. Ari used a piece of bread to sweep up some gravy. It only took one bite for her to realize she was starving, and she ate most of the bread and half the mashed potatoes before Segura spoke again.

"I'm not going to lie, Willow, this is prison. It sucks. But for the most part, it's okay. There will be people you like, people you avoid, and you don't have much freedom. You have some, but not as much as you want. In that way it's the same as working in an office, except you don't get to go home at the end of the day. Once you find a routine, it becomes easy."

"How long have you been in here?"

"Three years. I'm at the halfway point in my sentence. Plenty of time to pass on my wisdom to you before I go."

Ari paused with the spoon in front of her mouth. The implication she would still be in jail in three years hadn't hit her until that moment. But with Cecily Parrish working against her, it was a very likely outcome. The idea of going three years without transforming was terrifying enough before she realized it was probably going to be more like fifteen, twenty, or some other life-changing number. She dropped the spoon and put her fingers against her forehead.

"It just hit you, didn't it?" Segura said. "How screwed you are."

"You have no idea," Ari said.

She'd never heard of a *canidae* suppressing the wolf for that long. She knew for a fact that other *canidae* had been imprisoned. Hell, she'd put a couple behind bars herself. But she never thought about how they managed to control their transformations. But twenty years? She could only imagine staying in one form that long would cause irreparable damage. What if, when she finally got out, she wasn't able to transform anymore? Could the wolf die?

"Just breathe, Willow." Segura chewed a bite of her bread and winked at Ariadne. "It's the first day. You're allowed to freak out a little bit. This is going to sound a little corny. But if you want to stop people like Miriam Kunz from walking all over you, you're going to have to find the animal inside yourself and let it take over for a little bit."

Ari groaned and slipped her hand over her face.

She was doomed.

CHAPTER SIX

AFTER DINNER, Dale knew she wouldn't be able to sleep. Her phone was full of messages from Diana, so she called her back before it got any later. She explained everything that had happened and where they were, and Diana promised that she and Lucy would be there for anything they needed. When she hung up, Dale told Gwen she was going home.

"We talked about this..."

"I know," Dale said, "and I'm going to take you up on it. But I need to get some things from home if I'm going to be staying here. Clothes, toothbrush, stuff like that. You can come with me if you'd like. I just... I mean, if you don't want to be alone."

"Thank you. But I think I'd like the time alone to process everything."

Dale promised she would be back soon and left. Her first stop was the Bitches office. She wanted to be sure it was properly shut down. Sometimes Ari left her computer on sleep mode overnight, and Dale didn't want that sucking up energy while Ari was... until Ari was back at work.

The lights in the antiques shop next door to the office were on, but Dale barely noticed this rare occurrence as she unlocked the office. Her desk was as she'd left it, just over a day earlier. Ari had come out and stretched, asked her opinion about Chinese versus leftovers, and then they got into a debate about how to pronounce pho. And then a few hours later, she got a call from the police station.

She walked forward so she could see Ari's desk though the open door to the inner office. It was largely unchanged from the day she'd first seen it. The giant clock still hung on one wall, the filing cabinets had gotten progressively more beaten-up, and the old couch was where it had always been. The sight of it reminded her of how many times she'd straddled Ari there, rubbing the tension out of her shoulders after a transformation. She actually smiled remembering how long she had averted her gaze when Ari took off her shirt.

Dale leaned against the door frame. The first time she'd ever come to this office, she'd been broke, unemployed, and days away from using the last of her bank account to fly home and get a job in her father's orthodontist office. Then she saved a dog from some asshole kids, took it home, and woke up with the most beautiful woman she'd ever seen in her bed. They went out to breakfast and Ari explained who (and what) she was. When she mentioned she was struggling with the business ("Not the detective part, but the boring office shit is killing me"), Dale pointed out that her unfinished degree might come in handy. She'd been hired for the day, just to get everything in order.

Dale knocked on the open office door. "Miss Willow?"

Ari grunted. "No. Absolutely not. Ariadne. Better yet, just Ari."

"Okay. Well, I think I've got you pretty much situated here. It's nothing fancy, but it should be easy enough to figure out."

"Thank you. Seriously. I was about to set fire to every piece of paper in the office."

Dale had already put on her jacket. "I did a pretty good job for one day, if I do say so myself, but there's still a bit of a mess to clean up in your case files. You didn't alphabetize any of them."

"I have a method."

"I could see that. I also saw that your method has evolved, and you didn't adjust the old files to match the new version. It's a mess. I couldn't take care of it all in one day."

Ari finally looked at her. "Oh. Do you want to come in tomorrow? Same price as today."

Dale heard coins falling into her bank account. "Uh. Sure. I could do that. It's not really a one-day job, though."

"As long as it takes. I obviously need the help."

"Yeah," Dale agreed, chuckling. "I'll see you tomorrow."

Dale was almost to the door when Ari called to her. "Would you want to grab some dinner?"

One hand on the knob, Dale had almost said no. She was tired. But she liked Ari, and she was intrigued at the possibility of getting to know her better.

"Sure," she said. "Dinner sounds great."

They didn't become lovers for another three years. She used to think of that time as wasted, but now she knew it was anything but. She spent that time learning who Ari was without sex getting in the way. Their relationship - professional and platonic - was the best Dale ever had. Ari quickly became the most important person in her life. Falling in love was an evolution of what they'd painstakingly built. She thought about their first night together as a couple, ironically in the aftermath of Ari being accused of murder the first time. She thought about being shot in the head, fighting alongside Ari and a pack of British *canidae* against the hunters. It wasn't the life she would have chosen for herself, but only because she wouldn't have known what to ask for. There was no other path she would take in exchange for the one she was currently on, no matter how it might end.

She went into the office and turned off the thermostat, then sat behind the desk and opened the laptop so she could turn it off. It came to life and revealed a lock screen image of herself and Ari at a Seattle Totems game. They were both bundled against the cold, but Ari had pulled down Dale's scarf to kiss her cheek. Lucy had snapped the picture just as Dale laughed because Ari's hand had crept under her jacket to tickle her hip.

"We've come a long way, puppy. But we've still got a lot of road left. So don't give up on me and I won't give up on you."

She pressed two fingers to the image of Ari's cheek, then shut down the computer. She would take it with her just to make sure it and the sensitive files it held were somewhere safe. The computer's bag was in the closet and Dale slung the strap over her shoulder. She put her hand on the light switch and turned to look at the office one last time.

"We'll be back." She didn't know if she was talking to the room or to the fates or god, but she knew it needed to be said. "We're not going anywhere."

The room remained silent. But Dale knew that this wasn't the end of Bitches Investigations. She turned off the light and left the office, confident she would be back before long.

Lights out was at eleven o'clock, although they were supposed to be back in their cells by nine. After dinner, Segura took Ari to the library so she'd know where it was. Ari checked out a book but didn't pay much attention to what it was until they were back in the cell: *Wuthering Heights*. She held it up so Segura could see the title.

"Is this one of the good classics?"

"I think they made a movie of it."

Ari said, "That doesn't mean it's good. They made, what, ten Transformers movies." She tossed the book to the foot of her bed and put her head down on the pillow. "I don't really feel like reading anyway."

Segura was standing by the door, watching out into the common area. "Worried about your people? What's the love of your life called?"

"Dale. And she's a woman. People always think Dale is a boy's name."

"Dale is a chipmunk's name," Segura said.

Ari smiled.

"I'm sure Dale is out there getting ready to kick some ass and get you out of here."

Ari said, "You sound pretty sure about that."

"You called her the love of your life. In my experience, people don't throw that phrase around lightly. The way you said it, I don't know, I just instantly got this picture of someone who isn't going to give up on you."

"Yeah," Ari said softly. "You pretty much nailed her."

Segura walked to her bed and sat down. "So, if you don't mind talking about why you're in here... it might be nice to know I'm not about to fall asleep next to a murderer."

Ari sighed. "I'm a private investigator. A lawyer decided she wanted to hire me for her firm, I said no. She took it personally and came after me. I thought she'd let it go, but apparently she was planning all of this. She killed someone or had her killed, and she made sure I was accused of it."

"Damn. That's pretty devious."

"This lady isn't someone you want to mess with. Then again, neither is Dale."

"I get the impression you aren't, either."

Ari looked at her. "You have a lot of impressions of people."

Segura shrugged and held her hands out. "Con artist. It's my job to read people as quickly as possible. If I met you in a bar, I wouldn't even think about trying to scam you."

"That makes me feel good."

"It should."

A guard appeared in the doorway. He clicked a device on his belt twice and started to move on, but Segura whistled to make him stop.

"Where's Vogel tonight?"

"She's taking care of a fight that happened in the gym earlier. Guess one of you ladies prefers game shows to reality crap." He moved on.

Ari said, "Who is Vogel?"

"No one." Segura pivoted and brought her feet up onto the mattress. "One of the guards. One of the good ones."

"Ah. Nice to know who those are, just in case."

"Jaekel is good. The guy who just left, Sessions, is an asshole. Burke is kind of an asshole, but it's really just because you can't negotiate with him. I'll make you a list tomorrow."

Ari said, "I appreciate it."

Segura retrieved her book. "I have this little lamp if you want to turn off the overhead light."

"You sure?"

"Yeah. You've had an enormous day. Get some sleep, Willow."

"Thank you." She reached for the switch, but stopped before she touched it. "I've had a lot of bad luck in the past twenty-four hours, but meeting you almost makes up for it. Makes up for some of it. A little bit of it."

Segura grinned. "Oh, so many people have said that right before I took 'em for everything they had. Better be careful, Willow."

"I'll keep an eye on you."

Ari turned off the light and pulled the blanket up to her waist. She put her hands under the pillow and stared at the ceiling. The narrow window was letting in some of the city light, which made her feel like she was in a hotel. But just beyond the open cell door she could hear other prisoners talking, buzzers, voices over radio. She wanted to reach out and feel Dale's hip next to her, wanted to curl up and listen to her breathing. Sleeping alone might end up being just as difficult as keeping her wolf at bay.

She closed her eyes and hoped her utter exhaustion would overwhelm her stress and racing brain. She was also stressed that the wolf might use her falling asleep as an excuse to transform. It had happened in the past under normal circumstances. If the wolf felt trapped, it would be an easy way to break through her defenses and escape.

Please behave, she pleaded. *You cannot let yourself out. Let me tell you when it's safe. The moment I can let you out, I will. You have my vow.*

There was no answer, not that she expected one, but she thought maybe a little bit of the tension faded. Hopefully that meant the wolf had agreed and there was an accord. She took a long, slow breath and let it out through her nose. She had long ago discovered that sleep was possible in any situation, it just required the proper levels of exhaustion. She had hit that level around lunchtime, so even with her whole life teetering on the edge of disaster, sleep was just a matter of letting herself go.

Ari didn't know how much time passed before she was woken up by a noise. The main lights were off but there was a dim gold-orange glow of security lights filtering in from the main room. At some point during the night she had rolled onto her side to face the wall. The sound that had awoken her was still happening as she opened her eyes: a repetitive, rhythmic squeak, the protest of springs against metal and the quiet tap of a mattress against the stone wall.

She rolled onto her back and looked across the cell. Someone was on top of Segura, one elbow on the mattress by her head while the other arm was doing something under the blankets. The woman was tall, slender, muscular. Her hair was dark and loose so that it covered her face as she continued thrusting. But the most obvious and alarming thing about the woman was the fact she was wearing the uniform shirt of a guard. It was unbuttoned, and Segura's hands were roaming eagerly across the white T-shirt. One of Segura's legs had slipped off the mattress to swing free with the motion of the guard's thrusts, and her other leg - judging from the shape the blanket made - was wrapped around the taller woman's waist.

"Hey..."

Both women looked toward her. Segura grinned and winked. She spoke in a whisper that probably didn't carry further than the cell door. "Go back to sleep, Willow. Everything's cool."

Ari furrowed her brow. "This..."

"It's fine," Segura said. "She's not doing anything I don't want her to do. Just go back to sleep."

The guard whispered, "Or watch. We're not shy."

Segura laughed and dropped her head back to the pillow.

"You're nasty."

"Damn right." The guard dropped her head and attached her lips to Segura's neck. Segura arched her back and pushed her hands under the white T-shirt, which made the guard hunch her shoulders and move faster.

Ari rolled back toward the wall and tried to ignore the gasps, sighs, and bedframe noises coming from across the cell. Apparently it was going to be a long night after all.

CHAPTER SEVEN

THE HOUSE was quiet when Dale got back, so she assumed Gwen had decided to try sleeping. She took her bag into the guest room - the room where Ari had grown up - and set up her computer. It was almost three in the morning but her nap was keeping her awake. Once she had the wifi connected, she opened a browser and ran a search for Cecily Parrish.

She skipped over the results she'd found the first time she did the search, back when GG&M first offered Ari a job. There was a slew of professional reviews, ratings, news reports covering her trials, and a dutifully-updated LinkedIn page. Originally she was trying to learn Cecily's professional reputation. Now she wanted to know absolutely everything the internet had about the bitch. A long time ago, her job had evolved to include this kind of research. All she had to do was treat Cecily like a client's cheating spouse and see what the web provided.

Working the keyboard relaxed her. The scroll of databases, columns of names and dates, unchangeable facts... it was exactly what she needed. She slowly built up a biography of the woman who was trying to rip their lives apart.

Cecily Isolde Parrish was born in L'Anse Grise, Louisiana, at some point in the early seventies, judging by her school records. Her father was a volunteer fire fighter who died when was a toddler, and her mother owned a small inn. Cecily studied law at Columbia (Dale made a note: *how? $$$*) and moved to Seattle in the mid-nineties. She was immediately hired by GG&M and quickly worked her way through the ranks to her current position as a partner.

After that, there were awards and media mentions. Cecily loved getting in front of cameras, and the local news loved getting soundbites from her. There was a whole archive on KCTV-6 tagged with Cecily's name. Dale watched a few of them but stopped after she realized the cadence of Cecily's voice was lulling her into a near-hypnotic state.

"Tricksy succubusses," she muttered. No wonder Cecily liked being on camera if she could use it as an undetectable method of tampering with public opinion. She shuddered to think of how often she had fallen prey to it without realizing.

While she was on the news site, she risked clicking over to the main page to see their most recent stories. It was right at the top, a video with the headline "Seward Park Woman Killed; Local Private Investigator Charged." Dale wrinkled her nose and clicked despite every instinct telling her she didn't want to see what was about to play. An ad played before the video, and she spent the entire thirty seconds cringing and hoping it wouldn't be too terrible.

Sofia Kennedy was seated at the Channel Six desk. A graphic over her right shoulder showed a cartoonish chalk outline of a body with the bland title chevron WOMAN MURDERED.

"An anonymous call to the police led to the discovery of a woman who had been murdered in her own apartment. This happened just off South Hawthorn Road in Seward Park." The video showed an apartment building surrounded by emergency vehicles and people in uniforms milling around. "The alleged killed led police on a foot chase which resulted in capture and arrest. Seattle Police identified the suspect as local private investigate Adrian Willow."

"God damn it," Dale muttered. It was a stupid thing to get mad about, especially under the circumstances, but she found it infuriating.

The image shifted to Ari's mugshot, and Dale had to laugh. Ari looked utterly defiant, chin up and eyes narrowed. She was clearly ready for a fight.

Sofia continued, "Police have not yet released the victim's name, but believe the crime to have been due to a domestic issue."

Dale said, "Domestic...? Oh, for crying out loud..." She closed the window and dismissed the stupid newscast and its woefully mistaken information. They couldn't even get Ari's name right, how could they be trusted with anything else?

She wanted to do research into succubi, see if she could separate myth from fact, but her eyes were tired. She decided to lie down for an hour or two in an attempt to get back on a more normal sleep cycle. She turned off the computer and changed into her pajamas. She tried not to think about if Ari got pajamas, if her bed was comfortable or not, if she had a nice cellmate or someone cruel... The last time she'd felt this detached was after Ari was cured of her painful transitions and went off with Gwen to relearn how to be a wolf. At least then she could comfort herself with the knowledge Ari was with her mother. Now, she had no one. Nothing.

"You have me," she whispered. She looked at the window and willed her words to travel across the city to Ari's cell. "You'll always have me. Sweet dreams, puppy."

She didn't know how long she was asleep before she heard voices in the house. Gwen was downstairs talking to someone, a voice Dale recognized but couldn't place while semi-conscious. She was also vaguely aware of the bedroom door opening and someone looking in on her.

"Dale?" Gwen said softly. "I just wanted to let you know I was back."

"Where'd you go?" Dale kept her eyes closed and burrowed against the pillow.

"We'll talk about it when you wake up. Get your rest, sweetheart."

Dale murmured some kind of acknowledgement and went back to sleep. When she woke up at indeterminate amount of time later, the sun had fully risen. The smell of breakfast had permeated the house enough to reach her, and she could hear people talking at the front of the house. She heard male voices, so she put on clothes before she left the bedroom. A cluster of suitcases were parked at the end of the hallway and she stared at them curiously as she passed.

The bathroom door opened behind her. "Well," a familiar and very welcome voice said, "I thought I smelled the stink of a human in here."

Dale turned and saw Milo Duncan, hair wet from the shower and wearing only a towel. The British wolf smiled at her and held her arms out for a hug, saving Dale from having to speak by substituting a hug. She was vaguely aware of how awkward it was to have her cheek against Milo's bare shoulder, which was also damp, but she didn't care.

"Where did you come from?" she finally managed.

"Gwen called me yesterday. I guess it was right after you got out of court She told me everything and suggested I hop on a plane and help out if I could." Milo stepped back and brushed Dale's hair behind her ears. "So here I am."

"But that's... what, ten hours on a plane?" The only thing *canidae* hated more than flying was water. "That must have been hell for you."

Milo shrugged. "It's for Ari. Of course we came."

"We?"

"Some of my pack decided they owed you and Ari, too. Go on downstairs and say hi. I should get dressed." She kissed Dale's forehead. "We'll get her back, right?"

Dale nodded. They still didn't have a plan or any idea how to save Ari from transforming in public, let alone how they were going to beat Cecily at a game she was so obviously amazing at, but they were making progress. Last night it had just been her and Gwen against the world.

Today they had the start of an army.

In the morning, Ari woke up before Segura. She sat on the edge of the bed and planted her feet on the floor, sitting in the silence and wondering what time it was and what the day had in store for her. The first day had been a whirlwind without a chance to truly process everything happening to her. Waking up in prison was a surefire way to drive the point home, though. She was a prisoner. She had been arrested for murder, she was denied bail, and now she was awaiting a trial in which she would be prosecuted by a woman with a vendetta against her.

Life was, from a purely objective standpoint, really shitty at the moment.

Segura stretched her arms out, flattened her palms against the wall, and grunted as she pushed her feet out from under the blanket. She flopped onto her back, smoothed her hair with one hand, and blinked her eyes open. She immediately looked toward Ari, looked at the cell door, and pushed herself up onto her elbows. She grinned and ducked her head in a gesture that was too prideful to be called shame.

"That was Vogel."

"Ah."

"It's not... I know, the visual of a guard on top of a prisoner in the middle of the night, it doesn't look good. And you actually spoke up. You were going to do something. I appreciated that, even though it wasn't necessary." She threw back the blankets and sat up. She lifted her arms and twisted one way, then the other, and Ari heard her back popping. Segura sighed and sat up straighter. "How much of the story do you want?"

Ari waved her hand. "I don't need any of the story, really. It's your business. If you say that it's all consensual, then that's all I need."

"It's completely consensual. Well... actually, last night, she had to be convinced." Segura's eyes momentarily became distant, and her lips curled into a half-smile at the memory. "She didn't expect to find you here. I was hoping she would see you when she did the count, but as you saw..."

"Right," Ari said. "And it seemed like she got real comfortable with me being here pretty quick."

Segura's eyes widened. "I know, right? The thing about letting you watch? Hell, I didn't expect that from her. But it's good information to have."

A buzzer sounded. Segura stood up and took her place next to the door. She motioned for Ari to do the same.

"So is that going to be a regular thing?" Ari asked. "No offense, but I might have to invest in some earplugs if she's going to keep dropping in."

"Alas, no." Segura sighed. "We'd been taking advantage of the fact I didn't have a cellmate, but now we're going to have to get creative about where we meet up."

"Sorry."

Segura shrugged. "It's not your fault. We were getting a little too comfortable anyway."

"This is good for me, though," Ari said. "Maybe there's a way for me to get some privacy, too."

"The fact we're talking about it means it isn't private," Segura said with a laugh. "What's going on with you that's so secret anyway?" Ari pressed her lips tightly together. "Come on. If you can't trust your cellie, who can you trust?"

Ari was saved from answering by the arrival of a guard. She was tall, athletic, and wore the uniform like it had been tailored for her. She had an amazing jaw and the high cheekbones of a model or a classical sculpture. Her strawberry blonde hair was pulled back in a severe bun that only served to accentuate her bone structure and ice blue eyes. She kept her expression neutral as she counted Ari and Segura.

"Morning, ladies."

It was the voice that did it. Ari looked at Segura, who was trying to hide a smile, and then looked at the guard again to confirm what she already knew. Her name tag said M. VOGEL, otherwise known as the woman who had visited their cell a few hours earlier.

"Everything going okay here?"

Segura said, "Yeah, everyone here is satisfied with the service they've received."

Vogel's face remained impassive, but Ari thought she could see a hint of amusement in her eyes. "Are you being snide, Segura?"

"No, boss, I know my place, boss. So does this one." She slapped Ari on the shoulder. "She's a good egg. You won't have to worry about either of us, boss."

"Uh-huh," Vogel said, already moving away from the cell door. To Ari, she said, "Don't let her be a bad influence on you, Willow."

Ari said, "Uh. I'll do my best."

Vogel walked away and Ari let her eyes drift down to see how she filled out the uniform pants. Segura slugged her on the shoulder.

"Yo. What happened to 'love of my life'?"

"Dale and I both appreciate good-looking women," Ari said. "When I tell her about this, she's going to ask if the guard had a nice ass."

Segura said, "And what are you going to say?"

"Oh, *hell* yeah."

Segura smiled proudly. "Come on. We should get in the breakfast line before all the eggs are gone." She led the way back to where they'd had dinner. "I get that you might not want to talk about your secret yet. We just met and I admitted I'm a con artist. But you've got a pretty big nuke aimed at my head if I ever betray your trust."

"I'm not going to tell anyone about you," Ari said. "And my secret isn't the sort of thing you just blurt out. But... it is something that might become an issue sooner rather than later. There's a chance I won't get a chance to spill the beans before I need your help."

Segura turned so they were facing each other. She offered her hand, and Ari took it.

"You're an interesting gal, Willow. I look forward to getting to know one another."

"Me too. If I have to be in here, at least it's with someone I like."

Segura joined the line for breakfast and Ari stood behind her. "It does make things easier. And whatever's going on, whether you tell me the whole story or not, you can count on me to help you. I'm on your side."

"That's a relief. Thank you."

The wolf had been quiet since she woke up, but she knew that wasn't an indication of how it would behave for the rest of the day. Anything might trigger it. At least now she felt like she had someone watching her back.

CHAPTER EIGHT

THE DOWNSTAIRS was full of wolves. Hannah and Mia were at the kitchen table, Tarun was in the kitchen with Paige, while Owen and Benji were lounging on Gwen's luxurious leather sectional scrolling through the options on her television. Dale recognized all of them from their last visit to Seattle during wolf manoth and smiled despite the circumstances of their visit. Hannah Milsap, the lithe tattoo artist whose life Dale had saved, was the first to spot her coming downstairs and almost knocked over her chair getting up. She ran across the kitchen and wrapped Dale in a rib-bruising hug.

"My savior," Hannah said.

Dale laughed and accepted the hug as Mia, Hannah's partner, approached and put a hand on the back of her head.

"Hello again, Dale," Mia said. There was weight in those three words that proved she still held Dale in the highest esteem for what she had done. Mia, who had never trusted a non-wolf, now owed a human a debt she could never repay. A hunter's bullet had knocked Hannah down, leaving her defenseless and surrounded. Dale rescued her without a second thought to her own safety. For that act alone, Mia would always consider Dale to be her packmate.

"Hi, Mia."

"Hannah, please. Let her breathe."

Hannah stepped back but kept her hands on Dale's hips. The

rest of the pack clustered around her. Paige O'Brien and Owen Kiernan, once married but now divorced according to Milo's emails. Tarun Conrad shyly held out his hand to squeeze Dale's fingers, while Benji Wood put a hand on her shoulder. Dale, ordinarily the kind of person who hated group hugs, couldn't help but feel comforted. It felt good to be surrounded by people who were going to help her through whatever trials were coming next.

"Where's Gwen?" she asked.

"Upstairs," Mia said. "Milo convinced her to lie down. Probably the only sleep she's gotten since Ariadne was arrested."

Dale kicked herself for not considering that. She was glad someone was there to take care of Gwen. She was still a little surprised it was Milo. "So... they're still..."

Hannah grinned. "Surprised you, huh? When Gwen came to London post-manoth, we thought she was going to hook up with Anton, our pack leader?" Dale nodded; she remembered the older wolf well, even though he hadn't played a part in their war. "But I guess the heart wants what the heart wants. Milo's actually been monogamous with her. I was more shocked by that than anything else."

"I'm not," Owen said. "Gwen's hot."

Benji held up his hands. "Okay, let's give Milo and Gwen the privacy we'd all appreciate from them if our roles were reversed, hmm? I'm sure Dale is hungry, and Tarun has made a delicious breakfast for us all. Let's eat and talk about how we can help Ariadne."

The cluster broke apart, but Hannah slipped an arm around Dale's waist to walk with her into the kitchen. Tarun had cooked enough food for a platoon. Bacon was piled on one plate, with a mountain of scrambled eggs beside it. Another plate had sausage patties and hash browns. And, "out of deference for our Yank hosts," he had brewed a pot of coffee. They each made a plate and then crowded around the table. Mia chose to stand against the wall behind Hannah's chair and steal food from her plate rather than making her own.

Owen said, "I think our top priority should be figuring out what to do about the wolf. There must be other *canidae* in prison, and none of them have ever been caught transforming."

Dale said, "A few years ago, Ari helped arrest some *canidae* thieves. They've been in jail ever since, but neither of us ever thought about how they were keeping the wolf a secret.

Unfortunately, I don't think they'll be very willing to offer us advice."

"So we know there's an answer," Mia said. "We just have to figure out what it is."

"Have you ever arrested a *canidae?*" Dale asked.

Mia nodded. "A couple of times. The subject of what happens during imprisonment never came up. You have to understand, Dale, we just don't think about stopping the transformation. It's not just that we don't want to - although we don't - but it doesn't occur to us as an option. The wolf is part of who we are. Female *canidae* only have to think about it when we become pregnant. Our bodies know it has to protect the baby, so the wolf just... goes to sleep."

Dale said, "So the wolf will protect you if necessary?"

Tarun shook his head. "You're still thinking about it wrong. My wolf doesn't protect me. It *is* me. It's protecting itself. Or rather, a female wolf is protecting itself during a pregnancy."

Paige said, "Men don't have to worry about it. Just one more way biology is anti-woman."

Owen said, "I suppose it's too late to get Ari pregnant." Paige glared at him. "What? It's not an unreasonable solution."

Paige rolled her eyes. "We'll call that Plan Z."

"The point is," Benji said, once again stepping in to get everyone back on track, "pregnancy is the only time a *canidae* naturally pauses its transitions.

"That's not true," Dale said.

Everyone looked at her. Benji looked sheepish. "To be fair, Dale, I think we know a little more about it than you do."

"You just said you don't think about it. I've been thinking about it, and there is a way to stop the transformations. You said it stops during pregnancy to protect the baby."

Hannah nodded.

"Would it also stop if the body changed in another way? I know that transforming into the wolf affects your muscles and skeletal framework. What if..." She closed her eyes and forced herself to ask the question. "What if Ari had a broken bone? An arm or a leg or some ribs. Would the wolf... I mean, would she stop transforming long enough for the bone to set?"

Paige looked at Owen. "You broke your leg when you were a kid, right? How long did it take to heal?"

"I don't remember," he said. "A couple of weeks. But she's right, I never transformed at all during that time. It was probably longer than a month and I just didn't notice."

Tarun had taken out his phone. "This says a broken leg takes about ten weeks to set, at a minimum."

Dale said, "Great. So to put off her transformations, Ari just has to get the shit beat out of her."

"Maybe there's another option." Hannah reached out to put her hand over Dale's.

"One we can come up with before it becomes an issue?" Dale asked. "One that we can implement while she's already in prison? It's making me fucking sick to think about it, but it's the only way we can be sure she won't transform in her sleep." She looked at her food, which she suddenly had no stomach for. She pushed the plate away. "I'm sorry, Tarun."

He shook his head. "It's fine. I probably couldn't eat under the same circumstances."

Dale looked at Mia, the only cop at the table. "Realistically, what are we looking at?"

Mia looked toward the stairs, obviously hoping either Gwen or Milo would come save her. "I spent the flight reading all the news I could find about the murder. So far it seems like everything they have is circumstantial, but that could change. I read somewhere that the police have a theory that Ari was having an affair with the victim."

"Bullshit," Dale said immediately. "But it's hard to deny their accusations when I can't explain where Ari goes three or four times a week when she should be in bed with me. On the outside it does look like she's hiding something because she *is*. But she wasn't having an affair."

"Are you positive about that?" Owen said, glancing toward Paige. "Cause sometimes, you can be absolutely sure about who your partner is, and realize it's total bullshit."

Paige winced.

"I'm sure," Dale said, ignoring whatever drama they had going on.

Mia shrugged. "Okay. So they basically have a bunch of toothpicks. But if you put the toothpicks in the right place, you can still build a pretty solid wall. This Cecily Parrish woman sounds like she's a pretty good architect. I read about some of her other cases. She's put people away for life with a lot flimsier cases."

"Life," Dale whispered.

"You asked for realistic."

"I did. And I appreciate you being honest with me." She stood up. "Thank you all for coming. I can't tell you what it means to me. Ari... she's going to be blown away by this. She always tells me she doesn't want a pack, she never needed a pack, but I know sometimes she wonders what it would be like to have a group of badass wolves watching her back. She's going to be so happy to know you're all here." She ducked her chin to wipe at her eyes. "I need some fresh air so, um, I'm going for a walk."

She hurried from the room and went out through Gwen's back door. Before she could get to the gate, she heard someone come out behind her.

"Dale, wait."

"I'm fine, Mia. I just need to be alone right now."

Mia said, "I get that, but there's something I want to say."

Dale turned around to face her. Mia pressed her hands together and looked across the back yard, over the fence, at the mountains in the distance. She took a moment to figure out what she wanted to say before she looked Dale in the eye again.

"The last time I was in Seattle, I saw my world shattering. I saw the woman I love more than my own life get hit by a bullet, and I saw her fall in the street surrounded by hunters. I knew there was nothing I could do to save her." Her eyes filled with tears. "And then I saw a human... a-a woman who until that point I had considered annoying at best... I saw her jump out into the line of fire to save my Hannah. I know we both thanked you before we left, but we've never stopped thinking about you. About how we could pay you back."

"There's nothing~"

"Shush," Mia said. "Listen to me. I look kind of like Ariadne. We have similar builds, our hair looks the same. If I confess..."

"No, I can't..."

"I told you to shush," Mia said. "If I confess to the crime, they'll have to let Ari go. I'll go to prison in her place."

Dale was shaking her head, lips pressed together.

"It's no different than what you did for me. For us."

"Your career as a cop would be over."

Mia nodded slowly. "Probably. I'd be willing to do that for her."

"No," Dale said. "Ari would never let you make that sacrifice. But thank you." She opened her arms and Mia stepped into the hug. "I'd do it again, you know. In a heartbeat."

"I know," Mia said. "And I meant what I said. I can never repay you."

"You'll never have to." She kissed Mia on the cheek. "I'll see you in a little bit, okay?"

Mia nodded. "We'll be here when you get back."

Dale squeezed her hand, then turned and left the backyard. She didn't know Gwen's neighborhood well enough to have a route in mind, but she already felt better being out of the house. She and Ari had a routine of running and, even though she wasn't dressed for it, she started jogging when she reached the sidewalk. She thought maybe there was a jogging path near Lake Washington. If she could get that far she could just follow the shoreline without actually setting a destination. She would keep running until Ari was able to join her.

CHAPTER NINE

AFTER BREAKFAST, Ari learned she had been assigned to work in the library. Segura was assigned to assemble office furniture so they said their goodbyes when Vogel came to escort Ari to where she needed to be. She was surprised at how reluctant she was to leave Segura's side. Her cellmate had been like a security blanket and now she felt adrift again. She glanced back and saw Segura was watching her. The other woman smiled, winked, and held her fist up to show her support. Ari grinned and winked before facing forward again.

"So, the library," Ari said.

"You have a problem with books?"

"No. It just seems like there would be a long line of people trying to get a job like that. No hard labor, just shelving books all day."

Vogel said, "It's harder than you think. It just happens to be one of the jobs where there's an opening, and you got lucky. One of the women you came in with yesterday got assigned to the cafeteria. She found out when we woke her up at three o'clock this morning so she could begin her shift. You should thank her for your breakfast when you see her again."

Ari said, "Was her three a.m. wake-up call as entertaining as mine was?"

Vogel spun to face her, apparently on the verge of violence. Ari tensed as Vogel scanned the corridor to make sure they were alone before locking eyes with her.

"Would you like to make a comment on what you *think* you saw, Inmate?"

"Not at all," Ari said. "Segura told me it was consensual, so that's all I need to know. I was just, you know, being a smartass. It's just something I do from time to time."

The tension visibly faded from Vogel's face. She swept the hallway again with her eyes, then gestured for Ari to follow her into the library. A black woman who looked to be in her sixties was behind the circulation desk. She had a pair of eyeglasses hooked on the top button of her uniform and she brought them up to her eyes when she saw Ari and Vogel approaching.

"Who you got here, Melissa?" the woman asked with a thick Haitian accent.

"Celestin, you know the rules. You can't call me by my first name."

The librarian smacked her lips and focused on Ariadne. "Everyone in here so formal. They think only using last names makes it like we're not really people."

"No," Vogel said, "it's because I'm a CO and you're a prisoner. I don't want to write you up for something so silly, so remember it next time. Okay?"

"I'm not a child. I'm Gladys Celestin. Who are you?"

"Ariadne Willow."

Gladys raised an eyebrow. "Ariadne. Good name. I like it. Ancient. Goes all the way back to the Greeks. Are you Greek?"

"Not that I know of."

"That's okay. I'm not prejudiced, just curious." She held out her hand and flapped her fingers at Vogel. "Okay, you can go now, I'll show her everything."

Vogel sighed, exasperated. "You don't get to dismiss me, Celestin."

"Oh, you're young enough to be my grandchild, and you think you give me orders? I'd like to see you try. Go. Leave me to my books."

Vogel turned to leave but paused long enough to whisper, "Every single day..." to Ari before she walked out of the library. "Keep her out of trouble, Celestin."

Gladys made a quiet cheeping noise under her breath and

shook her head. She went back to the books she'd been stacking when Ari and Vogel arrived.

"So, what have they locked you up in here for?"

Ari said, "I was framed for murder."

Gladys pursed her lips and made a bird-like sound. "Someone gets murdered, that means they're important. Someone gets *framed* for murder, that means they're important and scary. Means whoever did the killing was too afraid to hurt you directly."

"I like that philosophy," Ari said, "but in this case it's not quite accurate. The person who did it wants me alive so she can use me. Not sure how, but that's her goal. I'm not worth anything to her dead. How about you? Sorry, I don't really know the etiquette. Is it okay for me to ask why you're in prison or is that frowned upon?"

"Oh, I don't care," Gladys said. "I actually did kill someone."

Ari didn't know how to respond to that. "Oh."

Gladys smiled. "I grew up watching my mama fix people who came to her for help. Learned her tricks, started following her example when I grew up. Officially, I ran a little restaurant in Redmond. But I never felt like giving all my money to some school, so I didn't have a license. Eventually someone was too sick for me to help and he died. His family decided to take their grief out on me."

"Wow. I'm sorry."

"Don't be. I helped a lot of people. If God sees fit to punish me for not helping one of His creatures, then I'm not going to question His judgement. Besides, I've done a whole lot of good for the women locked up in here. So maybe I'm right exactly where I'm supposed to be." She patted Ari's hand. "Maybe you are, too. You'll figure it out in time."

Ari said, "I hope so."

"For now, you're exactly where I need you." She pushed the stack of books across the table. "You know the alphabet?"

"I think I've heard the song."

"Good enough. Shelve these."

Ari picked up the books and moved them to a cart. It wasn't going to help her get out of prison, but at least it would keep her mind occupied.

Gwen woke slowly with the realization there was someone in her bed. It wasn't a completely alien experience to her, although she'd never considered sex to be much of a necessity, but it still took her a second to remember who it had to be. She slid her hand across the pillow, rubbed her palm across her face, and twisted her neck to see Milo watching her sleep. She smiled, and Milo stretched to press a kiss to the corner of her mouth.

"Good morning."

"Hi."

Of all the surprises in Gwen's life, Milo was one of the biggest. It was also the one she had fought the hardest. When the war ended, Gwen realized she suddenly had the opportunity to enjoy her life for a change. So when the British pack introduced her to their leader - a man, age appropriate, handsome - she accepted his invitation to London so they could get to know each other better. They ended up not having anything in common, but Gwen didn't regret taking the chance. She booked a flight home with no hard feelings. But then, on a whim, she decided to drop by Milo's apartment to apologize for the way she had tried to use her as a pawn.

That visit ended with them in bed.

Gwen had never considered being with a woman, especially not one who was the same age as her daughter. But Milo surprised her in more ways than one. The sex was incredible enough that Gwen explored when she got back to Seattle. No one made her feel the way Milo had, but every experiment was good enough to convince her that she was bisexual. But that was just a title, because the only person she was fantasizing about was Milo. Gender suddenly didn't matter because she only had eyes for one person.

To her shock, Milo reciprocated her feelings. Long emails and online conversations evolved into phone calls, which quickly became sexual. Gwen made a few trips to London, and Milo had come back to Seattle, and their desire only seemed to grow the more time they spent together.

Gwen pushed her hand into Milo's dark hair and pulled her in for a proper kiss. Milo's bottom lip teased Gwen's, pushing her mouth open for a quick, teasing brush of her tongue. Gwen sighed and let her hand slip to Milo's shoulder.

"Thank you for coming."

"You needed me," Milo said. "I was just pissed that I had to wait so long for a flight." She traced a freckle pattern on the skin exposed by Gwen's slipping shirt collar.

Gwen said, "You came at lightning speed. And you're here now, that's what matters. Ari's going to be so grateful you came."

"I didn't come for Ari," Milo said. "I mean, I did. Ari's great.

But I came because *you* needed me. The rest of the pack came for Ari, to see what they could do to save her, and I'll lend a hand however I can. But the reason I hopped on a plane and flew across an ocean and a continent in the middle of the night was to be here, right now, where you need me. And I kind of hate saying all of that because it seems so desperate, and this... I'm not... I've never been a support system. I always run from the first sign of neediness. But I wanted to be needed by you."

Gwen smiled through the whole speech. When Milo fell silent, Gwen brushed the bangs away from where they had fallen over her eyebrows. She kissed Milo's forehead.

"I do need you more than I ever expected to, Millicent."

Milo grinned. "I hate it when people call me that."

Gwen kissed her again. "I'm not people."

"No, you're not," Milo agreed.

"Millicent," Gwen said again.

Milo kissed her, and Gwen pulled her closer. It felt good to be taken care of. When this young wolf came into the house, she abandoned her suitcase by the laundry room door, hooked her arm around Gwen's elbow, and immediately began asking when was the last time she'd slept or eaten. She marched Gwen upstairs, got her dressed for bed, and brought her a sandwich. They had sat together on the bed while Gwen ate it, Milo supervising and brushing away any crumbs that fell on the comforter, and Gwen tried to remember when she'd last been mothered like this. When she finished the sandwich, Milo helped her into some pajamas and tucked her in.

"We should go downstairs," Gwen whispered against Milo's lips.

"Why?" Milo's eyes were still closed. "This is so nice."

"It is. It's very nice." She moved her lips to Milo's cheek. "But we're at the point where I can either get up and go downstairs to help the pack, or... do something else. And while something else might be very, very fun, I don't think it would be a suitable use of our time."

Milo said, "Hm. You're probably right." She kissed both sides of Gwen's mouth and reluctantly scooted away from her. "I'll go downstairs and let you shower. I'll warm up some of the breakfast Tarun made if there's anything left."

"I just need coffee."

"You're getting eggs and bacon," Milo said.

Gwen rolled her eyes.

Milo left the bedroom and went downstairs. Paige was at the kitchen table with her laptop, Benji and Mia on either side of her. Tarun was putting away the remnants of breakfast. Milo stopped at the bottom of the stairs and looked for the missing members of the household.

Paige said, "Mia took Owen to check out GG&M. Dale went for some fresh air."

"You let her go alone?"

"She's a big girl," Hannah said. "She probably needed the time to get her head on straight."

Milo resisted the urge to run outside and see if she could spot her. Hannah was right. Dale deserve a little alone time, given everything that was happening. She went to the table and sat across from Paige.

"Okay, so what are you doing?"

"I started out reading whatever I could find about the murder. All the local stations have pretty much the same story, and it wasn't picked up by the national services." She tapped her phone and slid it across the table. Milo picked it up and skimmed the article as Paige continued. "The cops talked to the victim's doorman, who swears Ariadne was a frequent guest at the building."

Milo said, "Could she have been visiting someone else?"

"Visitors have to tell the doorman who they're coming to see. Apartment number and name. So it looks like Ari is two-timing Dale, especially if someone finds out that Ari is frequently AWOL from their apartment late at night. Thankfully that hasn't come up yet."

Benji said, "I'm sure the media will get an 'anonymous tip' about it in due time. This Cecily Parrish person spent a lot of time weaving her net. She's not going to let a potentially damning piece of evidence go unnoticed."

"So Ari is allegedly sleeping with the dead woman..."

"Shannon Hardy," Hannah supplied. "Former receptionist at GG&M. According to Dale, she got fired because of Ari, but she didn't hold a grudge. At least not that they knew about. Ari hadn't seen her since the night she lost her job. I did a little digging and found out she got eventually got a job tending bar up in Queen Anne. Her Facebook seemed fine. No depressed posts. She actually seemed pretty happy the past few months."

Milo said, "Damn, you guys have been busy."

"You were upstairs canoodling for a long time," Tarun said.

"Don't be jealous," Milo said. "What does Facebook have to say about the affair theory?"

Hannah said, "No relationship status, no pictures or oblique references to a secret girlfriend."

The back door opened and Dale came inside. "Hey."

Milo stood up. "You okay?"

"I'm as okay as possible," Dale said. "What's going on here?"

"We're trying to do Ari's job," Milo said. "Looking into the victim, the law firm, anything that might give us a foothold in defending her."

Gwen had come downstairs in time to hear the last part of what Milo said. "I'm going to call anyone I can think of who might have connections in the legal world. I know a lot of wolves who were scared shitless during the war. They'll want to help if they know Ariadne is in trouble. Our focus should be on figuring out a way to protect her from transforming."

Dale said, "Oh. We... I came up with a plan for that."

"You don't sound very relieved."

"No. It's a bad plan. A really shitty plan. But it will keep her safe." Dale looked at the ground to avoid eye contact with anyone. "Relatively speaking. I'll let her know about it the next time we talk."

It was obviously weighing on her that she didn't know when that conversation would be possible. Milo put a hand on Dale's shoulder and squeezed.

"How about we get you out of the house for a little bit? I want to check out this Shannon chick's apartment for myself."

Hannah said, "You won't get anywhere near the building, whether you go as yourself or the wolf. The cops are going to have it locked up tight."

"We should still try," Dale said. "Ariadne didn't kill this poor woman, but *someone* did. Maybe a wolf will pick up something the cops all missed. I'll get my keys and drive you."

Milo said, "Great. So we've got a shitty plan and not a lot of information, but it's a start. It's only been one day, but we're already making progress. At this rate, we'll have her out of jail by the end of the week."

As soon as the words were out of her mouth, four wolves and one human all reached out to rap their knuckles against the nearest wooden surface.

CHAPTER TEN

ARI WAS surprised by how boring her first full day in prison ended up being. Her arms burned from shelving books, and Gladys assigned her to take the cart so she could hand out books from the hold-list. The work was so monotonous and exhausting that, by the time she returned to her cell, she could almost forget where she was. Ironically, being in jail was like being forced to take an office job she didn't want. When her shift ended at three, she hesitated at the circulation desk and looked toward the door.

Gladys said, "What's wrong?"

"I'm not exactly sure what to do now. Where do I go?"

"Go back to your cell. Stay here and read." She shrugged. "No one cares too much what you do with your free time."

Ari said, "My free time in prison. Seems like that should be an oxymoron."

"Call it what you want, but your time here is done. See you tomorrow."

"Tomorrow, then."

She half-expected a guard to be waiting outside the library to escort her back to the cell, but the hall was empty. She already knew that Gladys' respect was something she definitely wanted to have, so she didn't want the older woman to see her lingering like a grade schooler waiting for permission to go to the bathroom. But what was she supposed to do? Socialize? She supposed she could take a shower. She hadn't bathed in far too long and was afraid she was beginning to stink.

Ari arrived back at the semi-circle of cells at the same time Segura approached from the opposite direction. They both altered their course to meet up next to one of the tables in the center of the space. Segura nodded for Ari to follow her.

"Hey, Segura. I thought you'd be hanging around with Vogel."

"She only works nights. I had an idea. C'mon."

"Where are we going?"

"Trust me, you're going to kick yourself for not thinking of it yourself."

Ari said, "Is it a shower? Because trust *me*, I can smell it, too."

Segura laughed. "You can do that after. Hurry up. We gotta get there before there's a crowd."

Ari, intrigued, followed her.

"I love Seattle." Milo was sitting in the passenger seat with her head against the window, looking up at the trees that formed a canopy over the street.

Dale said, "It's a beautiful place to live. I grew up in Pennsylvania. It's pretty in a different way. A lot flatter."

"Why'd you decide to come here?"

"Originally, I wanted to get some distance between me and my parents," she said. "Then my mother died and I felt guilty for thinking that. But I still wanted to get far away from anyone who knew me or my extended family. I wanted to succeed on my own. It didn't work out well. I failed pretty hard. Of course, that failure led to meeting Ariadne, so..."

Milo said, "I'd call that a solid win."

"Me too." She brushed the hair away from her face.

"So you don't regret the move?"

Dale shrugged. "I had to come here to meet Ari. What's to regret?"

Milo sat up straighter. "I'm thinking about moving here."

"Really?" They were at a stop light so Dale looked over at her. "Did Gwen...?"

"No, I haven't brought it up with her yet. To be honest, I haven't really thought it through. It was just... when I got the call from Gwen about everything that's going on, I was almost five thousand miles away. Do you have any idea how slow planes are when the woman you love is five thousand miles away? The only thing that kept me from clawing up the plane seat was knowing you were with her. So I spent the flight thinking about maybe if I'd just been across town or something, it would've been so much better."

Dale said, "It's a big step. Are things between you and Gwen... I mean, I know it's been going on for a couple of years, but I didn't think..."

"I love her, Dale. We're in love. And yeah, maybe things will go haywire, but this is the first relationship I've had where I'm not even looking for the exit." She glanced forward. "By the way, the light's been green for a while."

"Shit." Dale pulled forward and continued down the street toward Shannon Hardy's apartment. The address was right on the edge of the Bailey Peninsula, just beyond where it joined up with the mainland. "If it factors into your decision at all, I know Ari would love to have you here. Once she got used to the idea of you being her mother's girlfriend. I think she accepts it in her head, but accepting it and being forced to see it every time she goes to see her mother are two different things."

"True. I'm not going to make any decisions until this is all over, but I'm glad to know you're on board, at least."

Dale was about to pull into the parking lot of the building when her phone rang. It was plugged into the charger and resting between the seats.

"Can you get that?"

"Sure thing." Milo unplugged it. "It doesn't have a name."

"Answer it anyway." Milo swiped the screen and poked the speaker button as Dale pulled into a parking spot. "This is Dale Frye."

Ari said, "God, it's good to hear your voice, babe."

"Puppy." Dale tightened her fingers on the steering wheel, somehow managing to prevent her foot from slamming down on the gas. She parked perfectly and took the phone from Milo. "Hi. I... I don't..." She put her free hand against her forehead. "I don't even know what to say. 'How are you' seems stupid given the circumstances."

Milo gestured at the door. "Privacy."

Dale nodded and let her leave. "Are you okay, though?"

"I'm... relatively fine," Ari said.

She was sitting in a windowless room with walls made of cinderblocks. They were painted white, but they hadn't gotten a fresh coat in at least a decade. There were two wooden tables with three phones each, the stations separated by short wooden partitions. Ari had chosen the one farthest from the door where a guard was leaning. He looked bored, but she was certain that not much would get past him.

"I'm more concerned about you. And Mom. Are you eating? Sleeping?"

"Don't worry about us," Dale said. "We're okay. We have some people taking care of us." In the rearview mirror, she could see Milo leaning against the trunk of the car. "Milo is here."

"What? When did she get to town?"

"Early this morning. Your mom called her, and she came running. Most of her pack came, too. They set up camp in your mom's house. They fed us this morning and we've all been brainstorming how to help you."

Ari said, "That's fantastic. Wait... you're all... where is Milo sleeping?"

Dale rolled her eyes. "Seriously, puppy? That's what you're worried about right now?"

"No, you're right. I'm sorry."

"How are you even calling me right now? I thought there were rules and things for inmates using the phone."

Ari chuckled. "Yeah, I'm looking at the list right now. I'm not allowed to call collect to a cell phone and I don't know any landline numbers. But my cellmate is letting me use some of her prepaid account to touch base with you."

"That's so nice of her."

"She's been amazing. Her name is Shae Segura. I feel like I'm racking up a pretty sizable debt to her already, but whatever price she asks will be worth it. I've missed you so much, Dale."

Dale realized she was crying. "It's great hearing from you, too. I'm going to figure out how to get you one of those prepaid accounts so we can talk as much as possible until you get out of there."

"Sounds good to me. I feel useless just sitting here waiting for all of you to do something."

"How many times have you saved us, puppy? Let us do the saving this time."

Ari closed her eyes. "It's a deal."

"How much time do we have?"

"Not long, I'm afraid. I don't want to use up all of Segura's time."

"I understand." She worried her bottom lip with her teeth. "Puppy... w-we... we thought of a way you can stop the transformations."

Ari sat up straighter. "That's great." She tried not to look at the guard, but he didn't seem to be paying any attention to her. "I was worried that the stress would make me transform in my sleep. What do I have to do?"

The tears came in earnest now. "I'm sorry, puppy."

"Dale? Baby, what is it?"

"You have to hurt yourself."

Ari frowned. "What do you mean?"

She sniffled and wiped at her cheeks. "Milo's pack said the only way they knew to stop it was pregnancy. And I realized that it was... if a body... your body changes, the transformations would stop until you were better. If you got hurt. A broken arm or..." She smacked the heel of her hand against the steering wheel. "I fucking hate this idea!" she yelled. "I hate that it was my idea, and I hate that I'm telling you this. But you have to be safe, puppy. I want you safe, and for that to happen, you have to get hurt."

"Dale," Ari said softly.

"What?"

"I love you."

Dale whimpered and covered her eyes. "Don't say that. Not right now."

"I'll say it whenever I think you need to hear it. I love you. I love you for thinking of this, for protecting me even though it's tearing you apart. I think it will work."

"That doesn't make me feel better."

"I know. I know, baby. But as scared as I am about what's coming next, I also feel relief knowing that I'll have one less thing to worry about. This is one more thing I don't have to be afraid of in here. That's worth... that's gold to me, Dale."

"Ariadne," Dale said softly. "I barely ever just say your name anymore."

Ari said, "I know. But I love being your puppy."

"I know you do." She sniffled and blinked the moisture off her eyelashes. "I'll talk to you soon, Ariadne."

"I can't wait. I love you, Dale."

"I love you, too."

She hung up and took a moment to compose herself before she

got out of the car. Milo slowly straightened up and turned to face her.

"I wasn't sure if I should come check up on you during the little, ah, emotional moment you had in there. Decided it wasn't my business to stick my nose in."

Dale said, "You're right. But thank you for considering it." She touched Milo's arm. "I told Ari about our plan to stop the transformations." Her stomach rolled a bit. "It better fucking work."

"It's the best idea we had. I don't think Ari getting pregnant would be in anybody's best interest."

"No."

She sniffled again and looked at the building. There was no visible police presence outside, but she knew there was most likely to be at least one police officer inside watching the crime scene. It was a three-story building with a nice shield of tall evergreens blocking the ground floor from the sidewalk. It looked like a private home which had been split up into apartments. There was a lush wooded area on the lot behind the building, and Dale tried not to think about how close Ari had gotten to escaping. If she had changed just a little faster, the wolf would've been gone before the cops had any idea what happened. She pushed away those thoughts and focused on the building itself.

"What do you think?"

Milo shrugged, unimpressed. "I was expecting a much nicer building when I heard there was a doorman."

"Same," Dale said. "What do you need from me?"

"I need to know which apartment was Shannon's. If it's not listed on mailboxes in the lobby, you should be able to just walk through and see which door has a cop standing guard. I'll stay out here and wolf out. Hopefully the real killer left a trail I can pick up. You up for this?"

Dale nodded. "Yeah. I'm fine." She held out her fist. "For Ari."

Milo bumped her knuckles. "For Ari."

She crossed the lawn, which was so sloped that it was almost a climb, and entered the building. The "lobby" was technically just a small foyer leading into a spacious living room. A desk had been placed directly in front of the door, not blocking the stairs but situated so no one could pass it would being seen. Fortunately no one was stationed there as Dale walked past. The ground floor seemed to be a common area: living room with a media center, kitchen, laundry room. Beyond the kitchen she could see a second flight of stairs leading directly to the back door.

She headed upstairs and immediately saw a police officer sitting in front of the first room. He was already looking at her, obviously alerted to her arrival by the sound of the door opening. Dale froze and returned his gaze.

"Uh. Hello."

"You can't be here, ma'am."

"I'm just... my boss sent me to find one of my coworkers? She lives here and didn't show up for work today? So... uh... she lives on the third floor...?"

The officer shook his head. "Sorry, ma'am, but I can't let you go up."

"Okay. Uh." She smiled apologetically. "Sorry. Hope everything's, uh, okay. Bye."

She tried not to hurry as she went back downstairs. She took out her phone and pretended to dial. "Leese, you're not going to believe this. Well, I just got to her apartment, and there's a *cop* here..." She put the phone back in her pocket when she got outside. The back door of her car was open and Milo was sitting on the parking lot asphalt waiting for her. The Brit's wolf was gorgeous, dappled white and grey fur and golden eyes. Dale jogged over to her and passed a hand over the top of her head.

"I forgot how pretty your wolf is."

Milo chuffed proudly.

Dale shut the car door and crouched down. She nodded toward the house. "Second floor, the window to the right of the entrance." There was a bush just underneath the window, and from there was a clear path into the woods. "There was a cop, so I'm afraid I can't sneak you into the apartment itself. Whoever killed Shannon could have gone out the window, or through the front door, or out the back."

Milo stood and hurried across the parking lot. Dale stayed where she was and watched Milo sniff the grass and front walk. It didn't take long before she lifted her head and made a quiet whimpering noise. She tossed her head to the left and took off at a slow trot so she could keep her nose to the ground. Dale glanced at the house to make sure the cop wasn't watching them and hurried after her.

When Milo stopped at the edge of the property, Dale knelt beside her and waited. Eventually Milo found the thread again and was back on the move. She weaved between the trees, stepping carefully. Dale was worried about destroying evidence the killer might have left behind, but time was of the essence. They couldn't be delicate while Cecily Parrish was probably, at that very moment, working to keep Ari in prison for the rest of her life.

They quickly passed through the wooded area, passing over a weed-choked walking trail that Milo took a moment to examine before continuing on, and arrived at a one-lane road which fed into a huge parking lot shaped like a kidney. Milo stepped onto the asphalt, moved in a circle, and then looked both ways. She lifted her head and faced Dale with her ears and tail held high.

Years of working with Ari had taught Dale how to interpret a wolf's behavior. "The trail ends here?" Milo dipped her head. Dale put her hands on her hips. "So whoever the real killer is ran through the woods and most likely got into a car that was waiting here for her. But did she park and leave the car, or did someone pick her up?"

Milo moved in a wide circle.

"What would Ari do?" Dale asked herself.

The lot hugged the edge of a park. There were swing sets and picnic tables, a little cinderblock structure that housed the restrooms, and map of the peninsula posted on a squat wooden sign. Dale tapped her foot on the pavement and tried to force herself to think like Ari. She was never good at the fieldwork part. Give her a computer and an account number, and she could find out what someone had for breakfast. But looking for puzzle pieces out in the real world often just left her feeling frustrated.

"What would you see, puppy?"

They were in a park, a very secluded place with more trees than buildings. There weren't any security cameras around, no homes nearby with a helpful insomniac sitting by a window watching the street. Milo waited patiently, sitting on her haunches, alternating between staring at Dale and looking around the area.

Dale got down on her knees, placed her hands on the pavement, and lowered her head. She tried to imagine how Ari and Milo would see the park as wolves. Milo came up to stand beside her. Dale looked at Milo and was once again surprised by how she could see the person behind the wolf's eyes. This was an animal, yes, but the mind was still completely human. The light shining there was a person. She couldn't explain the difference except to say it was obvious and unmistakable once she realized what she was seeing.

"Don't make fun of me," she said to Milo. "Right now, all we know is someone left the crime scene, ran through the woods, and ended up here where a car was parked. Either it was waiting for them or the killer left it for the getaway. The car was right here." She smacked the pavement with her hand. "But there's no way to..."

She drifted off, staring past Milo at something which had just come into focus. Milo twisted to follow her gaze. The cinderblock restrooms, originally just a visual reminder of the cinderblock prison Ari was currently stuck in, had one wall completely covered with graffiti. The side of the structure facing the parking lot had a fresh coat of paint, but the spray-painted designs were still visible underneath the layer of pale tan.

"City Parks," Dale muttered.

Milo made a curious noise. Dale got up and brushed the pebbles off her palms.

"C'mon."

Milo followed Dale across the grass to the bathrooms. "Seattle Parks hate vandals," Dale explained. "When I bury Ari's stashes, I make sure I don't put any of them near these places. Mainly because I don't want her to run up against any taggers in the middle of the night, but also because the city takes vandalism seriously."

The security camera was visible as soon as they were within a few feet of the building. Dale's face spread into a wide, genuine smile as she pointed up at it.

"That's how they catch them." She turned, using her outstretched finger to trace the camera's line of sight. When she stopped, she was pointing directly at the spot where Milo lost the scent. Her smile widened as she mimed firing a gun at the spot.

"Got 'em."

CHAPTER ELEVEN

"CAN I ask you a question?"

"Yes, she's as fantastic in bed as you imagine." Segura was reclining on her bed, book open. They were biding their time until dinner.

Ari was lying on her own bed. "That's not what I was going to ask." She pushed herself up on her elbows. "Why the hell are you being so nice to me? Everything you've done since I got here, it's been a godsend. I don't want to look a gift horse in the mouth, but I'm starting to get stressed out waiting for the other shoe to drop. Am I building up a debt it's going to take murder to repay?"

Segura pressed her lips together, thought about the question, and then closed her book. "I suppose I owe you the truth. At first, yeah, being friendly was exactly what I said it was. We have to live together in this small-ass space, and I would prefer to cohabitate with someone I like than an enemy. But then you told me you were a private eye."

"So?"

"So..." Segura was looking at her hands, avoiding eye contact. "So I have a sister. She was always the good one. Smart one. She went to college while I was scamming grocery money from poker games. We argued about which of us was taking the easy road. You know, she's getting a salary at some lame office job she hates while

I'm busting my ass and risking my safety for a couple hundred bucks. But we loved each other. Anyway, uh, her final year of college, she stops showing up to classes. Quits her job, doesn't answer my emails. I finally get worried enough to come check on her, but I'm not quick enough. She jumped off a bridge three days before I got to town."

Ari said, "I'm so sorry."

"Yeah." Segura sniffed and fixed an angry expression on her face. "I, uh, I looked into it as much as I could, but I don't know the city. I didn't know her life or her friends. I didn't even know where to start looking. I had to let the trail go cold. I don't know what happened to her or why. All I know is that someone else made her jump off that bridge, and I want to know who. So if I help you in here and you eventually get out..."

"I'll look into it," Ari promised. "Pro bono."

Segura smiled. "You're a pretty good cellmate, Willow."

"You're not so bad yourself." She put her head back down on the pillow. "So... CO Vogel's pretty wild in bed, huh?"

Segura laughed and went back to her book.

Milo clambered into the backseat when they got back to the car. Dale had spotted a sign with the number for the Parks Service, but that wasn't who she was going to call. She dialed Diana's number and ignored the commotion coming from behind her.

"Tell me what you need."

Dale winced. "I'm sorry..."

"No," Diana said. "I'm sorry. That came out sounding harsh. I was being sincere. Whatever you need, I'm here. I'm ready."

"Thank you. I found a security camera in Seward Park which could possibly have caught Shannon Hardy's real killer. I was hoping maybe you would be able to get your hands on that footage."

"I know someone who knows someone in park security. I'll see what I can do. Which camera?" Dale gave her the location. "I can't promise to give you the footage, but I can watch it and tell you what I see. Is that enough?"

Dale said, "It's perfect. Thank you, Diana."

"Of course. How are you holding up?"

Milo, now bipedal and fully-dressed, crawled forward and dropped into the passenger seat.

"I'm doing well. Ari's mom and the British wolves are keeping me from going insane."

"If you need a change of scenery or dinner or whatever, our door is always open. Lucy would love to see you."

"I'd love to see her, too. How is she doing?"

"She's well. The chemo is going well and she's feeling fine. We're hopeful." Someone spoke to her on the other end. "Just a second. Dale, I'm going to have to let you go."

"Okay. I'm about to start driving anyway. Thank you for your help."

"I'll call when I've talked to park security. And I mean it, Dale. I'm here for whatever you need until Ari is a free woman again."

"Thank you." They said goodbye and Dale hung up. She looked at Milo. "Are you okay?"

Milo nodded. "Dandy. Love running through new greenery. It's invigorating." Her hair was a tangle, so she used her fingers to straighten it out. "Your cop friend gonna help out?"

"Yeah, she's going to try." She checked her phone for messages from Gwen or the rest of the pack. What she really wanted to do was call Ari, even though she doubted Ari would still be in the room even if the number accepted incoming calls. She closed her eyes and put the phone down on her thigh, struggling to return her breathing to normal so she wouldn't cry.

Milo reached over and cupped the back of her head. "You okay?"

"Yeah." She wiped at her cheeks. "If we hit a dead end, can I murder you so I get sent to prison and share a cell with Ari?"

"Sure," Milo said.

"You're a good friend."

Milo said, "Let's just be sure we exhaust all other options first, okay?"

"If you insist," Dale said. "Let's go see what else we can dig up."

Ari skipped dinner despite Segura urging her not to miss any meals. "It's not fine cuisine, but it'll get you through the day." Ari thanked her but opted to remain in their cell. Her stomach was doing something unusual. It wasn't churning or nausea, but she still didn't want to risk putting food in it. She hated being in the cell but she also didn't feel comfortable just wandering around the prison. The prisoners and guards were equal threats in her eyes. She'd watched enough *Orange is the New Black* to be wary of offending the wrong person.

She focused on what was happening outside the jail. It was a huge relief to know Milo was there for Dale. Being friends with Milo was the closest she'd ever come to having a pack, and Ari trusted her to provide a shoulder for Dale if one was needed. Of course Milo would also be providing something else for Ari's mother, something she still wasn't entirely agreeable with. Yes, Milo made her mother happy. But the age difference... and the idea her mother was slee~ was dati~ was *involved with* someone who had once kissed Dale was a big hurdle to overcome. She also conveniently let herself forget that Milo had also come onto *her* when they first met. But that was a very complicated situation, and it was best to leave it in the past.

Segura came back from dinner and stood over her bed for a long minute. "You sure you're okay, Willow? You're looking a little peaked."

"I'm fine. Just an upset stomach."

"Really? What do you have to be stressed about?"

Ari smiled weakly and moved her hands over her stomach. Segura got onto her bed and opened a book. Ari managed to get up for the count. Vogel was back and Segura sadly said, "See you tomorrow" before the CO walked away from the cell door.

"Sorry to cockblock you like that."

Segura said, "Lesbians don't say cockblock."

"What do we say?"

Segura placed her hands on her knees and considered the question. Finally she said, "Tongue-tied?"

Ari laughed, pressing one hand against her stomach. "I like it."

"Can I ask you something personal?"

"Sure," Ari grunted.

"The woman waiting for you out in the world. Dale. How did you know she was the one?"

Ari considered the question while looking at the corner where the wall met the ceiling. "Because one day I realized she was more important to me than anything else. My job or..." *The wolf*, she added silently. "I couldn't imagine being without her. I could have lost everything else but it wasn't worth imagining a life without Dale in it."

"So you asked her out, wined her and dined her..."

"No." Ari laughed again. "No, I didn't want to risk the friendship by making a move on her, so I just kept quiet. I was fine loving her without being *in* love with her. She was the one who pulled us onto the next level. She confronted me about how we both had the same feelings and we were just being stupid ignoring it. We've never looked back."

Segura said, "That's sweet."

Ari looked over at her. "Why do you ask?"

"Vogel's a cop. Well, I mean, a guard… but close enough to be uncomfortable. When I get out of here, if I want to keep seeing her, it would mean I have to stop scamming people. I've never seriously considered that before. I'm good at it. I love the thrill of it. And I don't have many other marketable skills, so quitting would mean I have to get a job making sandwiches at Arby's or something. But I don't know. Might be worth it."

"Well," Ari said, "three more years? If my agency is doing well enough to hire a consultant, I might throw some legit work your way."

"Yeah? I'll keep that in mind. What's it called, Willow Detective Agency?"

Ari smiled. "That was pretty much the name before I hired Dale. She made me change it."

"To what?"

"Bitches Investigations."

Segura laughed. "Okay, that might be worth going straight for. So to speak." She looked over and could see that Ari didn't seem to feel any better. "Get some sleep, Willow. We don't get sick days in here, so you have to be shipshape in the morning."

Ari held up her thumb and closed her eyes. Once again, the sounds of the prison seemed so loud that she would never be able to drown it all out. But, just as she had the night before and thanks to her shift in the library, she drifted off to sleep due to sheer exhaustion.

Her next memory was panic. Her entire body was rigid, immobile, but her mind was sending frantic signals for her to flee. Heart pounding, skin clammy with sweat, eyes wide and searching for the threat which had sent her into this tailspin. Someone was next to her, no, on top of her, and hands were on her shoulders. She wanted to attack but couldn't, and then was grateful because she recognized Segura.

"Willow, cut this shit out!" Segura growled.

Knowing who was holding her down didn't help. Her brain kept flashing the same signal - *Run, run, run, get out, run, flee, fight, escape, get away, RUN* - but her body refused to cooperate. She was choking on her voice. "Guh-guh-guh." Segura clapped a hand over her mouth to quiet her. Ari was aware that her cellmate had one knee on the bed, her body twisted so she could hold Ari down. Someone else was suddenly in the cell: Vogel.

"The hell did she take?"

"Nothing that I saw. She wasn't feeling well earlier..."

"Goddamn it, Shae."

"I didn't do anything to her!"

Vogel said, "If she's in withdrawal, I have to make a report."

"Mel, don't. Please, she's not on anything. She's innocent."

"You're all fucking innocent," Vogel snarled.

Ari managed to say, "Not... drugs."

"See?"

"Yeah, that was a fucking enthusiastic testimonial there."

The seizure released its grip on Ari with agonizing slowness, but she could feel it lessening with each breath. Her hands unclenched and her body sagged into the mattress. Segura was able to relax her hold, moving her hand from Ari's shoulder to her cheek.

"Willow? You calming down?"

"Think so." She was still slurring her words, but at least they were coming easier. "I... was just... it was... I've..."

Segura was still speaking in a harsh, hissed whisper. "Sh. It's okay. Don't worry about saying anything right now, okay?" She twisted to look at Vogel. "Everything is cool now. She's calm."

Vogel glared at Segura. "This could have gone south so easily."

"Yeah, but it didn't." A heavy silence hung between them. "Mel. We can discuss it in the morning, okay? She'll tell us everything and we can work out what to do then. Okay?"

"You're going to be the death of me, Segura."

"Then it'll be a murder-suicide, beautiful."

Vogel rolled her eyes and left the cell. "God, you're morbid. Keep her quiet for the rest of the night. Any further outbursts and we're going all-out on this. Say you understand."

"I understand."

Vogel looked at Ari once more, then pushed the cell door shut. Segura's shoulders sagged and she shook her head.

"I'm going to be paying for that one." She looked at Ari. "You *swear* you're okay? Because that was some harrowing shit."

"I'll be fine."

"You're clean?"

Ari nodded. "I'm not on any drugs."

"Okay." Segura got up and walked back to her bed. "We'll talk in the morning."

"Yeah. Thank you."

Segura waved her off. "You'd have done the same for me. Good night."

"Night."

Ari looked at the ceiling. They would talk in the morning, yes, but she wasn't going to tell them the truth. Because now she knew exactly why she was feeling ill, and she knew what had caused the seizure. It was the wolf. The wolf had been caged for over twenty-four hours and knew that release wasn't forthcoming. It also knew that it was forbidden from emerging. When she went to sleep, any barriers she'd put up had weakened enough for the wolf's fight or flight instincts to kick in, but her body refused to cooperate. The seizure had been her wolf brain waking up in a cage with an unresponsive body.

It couldn't happen again. She had to find a way to silence the wolf, and Dale had given her a perfectly serviceable solution. She hoped it would be a week or two before she was forced to go through with it but now it seemed clear that she had to take action as soon as possible.

In the morning, at the first opportunity, she had to find someone to break a few of her bones.

CHAPTER TWELVE

WAITING. AGAIN.

Dale was in bed, another day mostly wasted while Ari was still in jail. She didn't want to get used to that idea. She didn't want to start any routines that didn't involve the woman she planned to spend the rest of her life with. But Gwen was still trying to find a lawyer they could trust and who was willing to go up against GG&M. Apparently the firm had a reputation of burying its opposition in discovery and humiliating them in court. The two lawyers she'd contacted both refused when they saw the details of the case. Ari, with blood on her, fleeing the scene of a crime where a witness had placed her multiple times before. Ari admitted to knowing the victim. The case was circumstantial, but apparently it was enough to put fear in the hearts of Seattle's legal elite.

"We'll find someone," Gwen told Dale as they cleared dishes after dinner.

"Someone suicidal?" Owen said.

Paige glared at him.

"I'm just being honest."

Dale didn't much care for Owen, but she had to admit he was right. The internet was full of articles about GG&M, and the majority of them focused on Cecily. There didn't seem to be many other lawyers in the firm who argued in court. And why would they?

If they had a succubus on their team who could sway the judge and jurors, why not use her to their advantage?

She'd gone upstairs early because she couldn't bear the looks she kept getting from the wolves. Hannah and Mia tried to avoid her gaze, and Benji's sympathetic shoulder patting quickly began to feel condescending. She just wanted to be alone and focus on her thoughts. When she heard everyone coming up and going to bed, she again felt guilty for having a room all to herself. There was a perfectly good bed across town she wasn't using. But everyone insisted she stay, even if that meant some of the wolves had to sleep on the couch.

It did make her feel a little better to sleep in Ari's childhood bedroom again. There was a dusty stereo on top of the dresser with a stack of CDs next to it. Dale chose one at random - they were all burned off the computer and Ari seemed to have let the wolf hold the Sharpie to label them - and turned the volume down low enough so it wouldn't carry beyond the closed door. The first song was "Don't Speak," so Dale figured it had to be good enough to let it play through.

She stretched out on the bed and imagined Ari in the same position. Before meeting Dale, before becoming a private investigator, even before she first transformed into the wolf. She pictured Ariadne, all gangly limbs and hormones going crazy, singing along with Gwen Stefani. She could see the confusion on her little face as she tried to figure out why she was so attracted to Chris Cornell (it was the hair).

The CD had moved on to Nirvana when Dale drifted back to consciousness and realized she had fallen asleep. She kept her eyes closed in the hopes she could get some rest, but then another sound infringed on the music. It was a squeak followed by a thump, like someone in socks dragging their feet from one stair to the next. Her brain connected it to all the times Ari had come home exhausted from running as the wolf and her eyes snapped open.

"Puppy?" she muttered before remembering where she was and why.

But there was another sound, this time more of a slide. She looked toward the wall where it seemed to originate. Gwen's bedroom was on the other side of that wall. If something was wrong...

"Milo..."

She sounded like she was in distress. Dale sat up, kicking at the blankets and swinging her feet onto the floor.

"Oh, god, Milo."

Dale froze. The squeaking noise came again, followed by a sharp gasp that was quickly cut off. Probably by a hand, either Gwen's or Milo's. And then another, quieter, stifled cry.

"Sh, baby," Milo responded.

Dale choked in an effort to hold back her reaction, covering her own mouth. She regretted taking the time she'd taken to undress for bed. Fortunately there was a robe hanging on the closet door. She put it on and retreated before she could overhear anything else. She was wavering between horrified and amused. Gwen and Milo were both adults, and she was glad they were able to enjoy each other's company even with everything that was going on. But oh, god, it was *Milo* and *Ari's mother*. Knowing they were having sex was much easier to accept when she didn't have to overhear it.

There were two wolves curled up on the floor next to Gwen's couch. Dale didn't know how she recognized them, but she knew it was Owen and Benji. Neither stirred as she went past them into the kitchen. She turned on the light over the stove and rested her hands on the edge of the counter. She laughed, shook her head, and tried not to think about what was happening upstairs. Eventually she turned off the light and walked to the sliding door that led out onto Gwen's small back porch. She crossed her arms over her chest and looked out at the moon.

Working for Ari, being her friend and lover, led to so many more late nights than Dale had anticipated when she took the job. Sometimes she would get a call at three-thirty that the wolf had run up to Lake City and Ari needed a ride home. By the time Dale got dressed, drove north, found whatever all-night diner Ari was waiting in, and got back to her apartment, it was already past four. So she would stay up reading or drinking tea or watching a movie until it was time to go into the office.

She didn't want to do anything to disturb the wolves in the living room, so she just stared at the sky. There was a movie when she was a kid, some cartoon about a family of immigrant mice. A boy mouse was separated from the rest of his family and spent the rest of the movie trying to reunite with them. At one point, the mouse and his sister sang a song about being under the same sky, looking at the same moon. The song always made Dale cry, and she hummed a few bars.

In a way, she was luckier than the mice. She knew exactly where

Ari was. Only about two miles west of where she was standing. She could've walked that far in less than an hour. She didn't know when Ari would go through with the bone-breaking plan. She imagined how it would happen and felt every blow, all the pain, knowing it was because of her. She'd come up with the plan that would cause Ari to be hurt worse than she'd ever been hurt before, and it was sickening.

Time passed slowly. There was a possibility she had briefly fallen asleep with her head against the glass door. She heard footsteps on the stairs and turned to see Milo descending on the balls of her feet, shoulders hunched like a cartoon thief creeping through a house. She was wearing black boxer briefs and a white sleeveless top, and her hair was twisted and tangled and all pushed to one side of her head.

Milo glanced into the living room to see the boys were still asleep, then pivoted into the kitchen and spotted Dale.

"Oh. Hi. *Oh.*" She looked up at the ceiling and winced. "I thought we were being quiet, but... you were next door, weren't you?"

Dale said, "It's okay. I wasn't sleeping very well anyway."

"Sorry." She went to the fridge. "I just need some ice."

"Oh god, I don't need details."

Milo said, "Not for *that*. I'm thirsty."

"And overheated?"

Milo grinned as she found a cup and opened the freezer. The cubes rattled against the bin as she scooped them out.

"Sh, sh," Dale warned. She nodded toward the boys in the living room.

"Eh, they'll sleep through anything." She filled the glass from the tap and took a long drink. When she was finished she pressed her wrist against her mouth and looked at Dale. "Are you sure you're okay? Is it just the sleeplessness?"

Dale turned to rest her shoulders against the wall. "It's a thousand things. Nothing technically wrong, nothing that can be fixed. Actually, that's not true. It could be fixed by having Ari walk in and hug me right now. That would fix it all." She hugged herself. "Did you know Mia offered to confess to the crime just to get Ari out of jail for me?"

Milo smiled. "No, but it doesn't surprise me. Mia and Hannah are thoroughly unreligious, but ever since the war, they've been the first converts to the Church of Dale Frye. Those two would crawl through fire if you asked them to."

"I just want them to be together. I'm finding out just how hard it is to be apart from the woman you love, so I wouldn't want to be the reason they can't be together. In fact, I hope they're having sex, too. Wait, no, they can't. They're sharing a room with Paige."

Milo smiled.

"What?"

"No, nothing. Just... Paige being in the room doesn't mean anything." Dale raised an eyebrow. "Oh, come on, you know how packs work. We let the animal take over when we run together. When we change back, we're a bunch of primal, sweaty, naked people. You think we don't have sex?"

Dale said, "So you and Mia and Hannah...?"

"Sure." Milo pointed into the living room. "And Owen and Benji, too."

"But you're..."

"And they're straight. I'm just saying, it doesn't matter to the wolf."

Dale looked at the wolves sleeping in the other room. "I keep learning all the things Ari is giving up by being with me."

Milo crossed the room and put a hand on Dale's shoulder. "You know what Ari's giving up? Nothing. Not a damn thing. 'Cause that's not how it works. You're everything Ari wants. The things she's not doing? Running with a pack, having sex with a bunch of wolves when the mood strikes, whatever, those are things she doesn't even consider because it's not part of being your girlfriend. That's all she wants. That's not a sacrifice in her mind."

"But–"

"Uh-uh," Milo said. "All Ari thinks about is what *you* are giving up to be with *her*. A human dating a wolf. That's all that's on her mind, and I doubt you've let those thoughts linger too much. So... you know, get your head out of your ass and stop worrying about what Ari's missing out on. Okay?"

Dale nodded. "Thanks, Milo. Now get your hand off me, because I know where it's been."

Milo removed her hand, winked, and went to the stairs. "Go back to bed, Dale. Try to get some sleep. Gwen and I will do our best to keep it down."

"Don't," Dale said. "I think I saw some headphones in Ari's room. I'll put them on and you two can go as crazy as you want. Hell, go across the hall to see what Mia and the girls are up to."

"You sure?"

"Ari wouldn't want it any other way."

Milo raised her glass in a toast. "Goodnight, Dale. Try to get a little sleep, huh? Ari would want that, too."

"I'll try. Goodnight."

Milo retreated back upstairs. Dale turned back to the door and, without pausing to give it thought, slipped the lock and went outside. She was barefoot and in her underwear beneath the robe, but she didn't want to take the time to go back upstairs. She did, however, have to go back and get her keys from the bowl on the kitchen counter. She worried about leaving a note just in case Milo heard the car leaving and was worried, but she didn't want to overthink what she was doing. She would apologize in the morning.

She drove south, out of the neighborhood with the lake to her left. A few boats were out on the black water, their lights reflecting on gentle waves. When the trees rose up to block her view of the lake, the houses on the other side of the road grew far enough apart so she could see the lower part of Seattle shining like Christmas lights.

Dale tried to imagine these beautiful sights as seen by a young girl, on foot, angry and crying as she fled the only home she'd ever known.

"My mother was my whole world," Ari whispered against the side of Dale's head. Strands of red hair were caught on her lips, but she didn't care enough to sweep them away. "And she confessed this godawful thing to me. She admitted she was the reason I was always in so much pain. I felt like a freak, like every teenager does, and then I found out she did it on purpose. So I ran."

Dale stroked Ari's hip. It was the first time they'd made love in Ari's bed. Doing it in a familiar place helped make it real. "Where did you go?"

"At first I just sort of wandered through the neighborhoods. I guess I was moving in a generally westward direction..."

Dale took a more direct route, driving the West Seattle Bridge across the breadth of the city. Ari ended up at Alki Point just before dawn. Dale arrived while the sky was still black and parked where she could face the water. She stayed in the car with the doors locked but even so she felt utterly exposed and vulnerable. There were people on the beach, homeless men and women in tents. Ari had been one of those people after she ran away. She'd survived this. She'd survived worse than this, and she would survive prison.

"I didn't know I wouldn't be going back," Ari said. "I just couldn't

picture myself walking back into that house and hearing her excuses. So I spent a while on the beach, and eventually I looked for something more permanent."

She pictured a teenaged Ariadne sitting on the sand, crying into the crook of her elbow, feeling as if she had lost everything. Her heart broke for that little girl. She wished she could go back in time and tell her it would all work out for the better. She had an amazing life waiting for her once she got through this rough patch. In fact, this rough patch would teach her so much, make her tough and savvy. Ari was in the same place now, really. She was all by herself without a safety net and unsure of how things could possibly work out well.

"I couldn't protect you back then, Ariadne," Dale said, "but I'm here now. You just keep yourself safe in the lion's den, and I'll come save you."

She could almost feel the words lifting through the air to settle on her shoulders. It was a promise no one else had heard, but one she would force herself to keep. No matter what it took or how hard it was, she would never lose faith. She wouldn't stop fighting until Ari was free.

Dale looked at the clock and groaned when she saw the time. Milo was right, Ari would want her in bed even if she never got any restful sleep. So she would drive back to Gwen's house, take herself upstairs, and stretch out on top of the covers. She would listen to the soundtrack of Ari's teen years. She would turn off her brain and hope for the best.

In a few minutes or so.

CHAPTER THIRTEEN

SEGURA WAS already up and sitting on the edge of her bed when Ari woke the next morning. She was staring at the floor but looked up when Ari began to stir and didn't give her time to form a lie.

"I don't know what that was," Segura said, "but you need to disclose right fucking now if you're addicted to something or have some disease."

Ari said, "I'm not addicted to anything. I'm not sick."

Segura said, "Then you were possessed by Selma Blair or something, because that was some frightening shit."

"Linda Blair." Ari rubbed her face and sat up. Her muscles ached, and moving was difficult, but she managed to get upright. "If I was possessed by Selma Blair, I would've been quirky and cute."

"Don't try to be cute now," Segura said. "Do you have any idea what Melissa and I risked by not calling the doctor? If you had died~"

Ari said, "That wasn't a risk."

"I'm glad you can guarantee that, because I sure as shit couldn't last night. Is it going to happen again? Am I going to have to tie you down to the bed before we go to sleep?"

Ari shook her head. "It's not going to happen again."

Segura stared hard at her. "Willow, I swear, next time, I'm not going to risk my neck to protect you. It's not up to me to keep you safe."

"Next time, you do what you have to. Protect Meli~ CO Vogel. Protect yourself."

Segura didn't look pleased, but some of her anger had faded. She stood up and looked down at Ari. "Do you need help?"

Ari said, "No. Thank you, though." She put her hands on her knees and pushed herself up. She'd just gotten used to transforming without pain, thanks to a solution Dale came up with. Now holding back the wolf hurt just as badly. She knew the cure would be easy, knew that spending an hour or so as the wolf would loosen her up, but there was no chance she would get that. Not without revealing her secret to everyone in the block.

She got to her feet. She had worked through pain before and she could do it again. It would definitely have helped if she could get one of Dale's magnificent massages, though. She put a hand in the small of her back and tried to improve her flexibility by twisting one way, then the other. Segura was still in the doorway watching everything with a curious tilt to her head.

"I had you pegged as, like, thirty-five when you came in. Now I'm thinking it's closer to double that."

"Hey, watch it."

"I'm not being rude. My ninety-year-old grandma had more range of motion than that."

Ari stumbled to the door for morning count. "I'll loosen up in time. My girlfriend usually gives me massages when I'm this stiff."

Segura leaned against the door. "I hope you aren't expecting conjugal visits."

"Do they really have those?" She let her hope rise. If she could get into a private space with Dale or her mother, she could let the wolf out. It would be the solution to her problems.

"Yeah, in this state they do. Extended Family Visits. But you're not going to get one, not for at least six months." She nodded at the cell block. "See all these ladies? The majority of them all have requests in. You make the request and, if you even get approved, you get added to the bottom of the list."

Ari deflated. "Oh."

Plan B it is, then.

Vogel arrived at their cell and did the count, staring hard at Ari. "You're looking better, Willow. Eat something that didn't agree with you last night?"

"Something like that."

"Whatever it was," she said, "avoid it today." She looked at Segura and walked away.

Segura whispered, "You pissed off my girl, Willow. That is *not* the way to stay on my good side."

"Understood."

Ari had slept in her boxer shorts and a T-shirt, so she just pulled her jumpsuit on over it all. "When do I get a cool brown uniform like yours?"

"Probably today," Segura said. "They don't like any of us standing out in a crowd any longer than we have to." She gestured at herself. "They like us all to blend into one faceless lump of humanity. Easier to deal with us that way."

Ari was moving a little better on the walk to the cafeteria. Segura noticed but didn't say anything. Ari watched the guards. Vogel and Baker - no, not Baker. Burke - were stationed by the entrance to the cafeteria. Burke had his thumbs hooked in his belt, carefully eyeing every prisoner as if he expected them all to make a break for freedom. Ari had to wonder how many successful escapes there'd ever been from this place. It was a high-rise in the middle of the city. Once outside there were dozens of places to hide, but getting out of the building in the first place seemed like a herculean task.

The first person Ari noticed in the cafeteria was Miriam Kunz, the Amazonian blonde she'd had a brief run-in with. She was eating with her goons, smiling in a way that seemed cruel just from the way her lips curled. Ari realized what had to be done and her spirits dropped.

"Ah, shit."

Segura followed her gaze. "Just ignore her. She's like a cat. If you don't engage, she'll move on to a target who is more fun to... Willow... what the hell are you doing?"

Ari was crossing the cafeteria. She couldn't risk waking up paralyzed, or worse, mid-transformation. The wolf was in a full panic. There was no guarantee she would be able to keep the secret another night. What happened next was going to suck, but she believed in Dale. She believed in this plan.

"Kunz and her goons," Ari said as she approached the table, raising her voice loud enough to be heard. Kunz swiveled her head like a periscope seeking its target. Her eyes narrowed when she saw who had spoken. Ari stopped at the head of the table, smiling in a friendly way. "I can't believe scientists are wasting all their time in the woods when Bigfoot is right here in front of them."

One of the goons hissed through her teeth. "Bitch, you better walk away."

Ari was surprised that her tone really was worried, not threatening. Her eyes were sincere as well, but her body language was that of someone who had just spotted a snake and was trying not to get bitten.

"What the hell are you saying to me?" Kunz said, incredulous.

"I said you're the biggest fucking cow I've ever seen, Miriam. Oh. Wait, we go by last name in here. Cunts."

Miriam stood up.

"*Willow,*" Segura snapped.

She was keeping her distance, looking toward the door in the hopes Vogel would come in and defuse the situation. Ari looked at her and hoped she could convey a very complex message without words: *You said next time you wouldn't help me. I'm holding you to that. Keep your promise, Segura, and stay safe. Please.*

When she faced forward again, Kunz had advanced on her. Her face was red, embarrassment and rage mixing beneath the surface.

"I don't know you, bitch," Kunz said, "so maybe it wasn't clear when we met the other day. So I'm going to give you one warning before I snap you like a twig. Don't look at me. Don't talk to me. Show some fucking respect. That's all you have to do. Understood?"

Ari said, "Yeah." She spit in Kunz's face. "Spitting wasn't on the list. You should revise—"

Kunz's punch was so brutal and untelegraphed that Ari was legitimately caught off-guard despite the fact she'd been begging for it. Kunz punched her again, this time in the stomach, and Ari folded double. She couldn't breathe and her head was swimming as Kunz twisted and punched her hard in the kidneys once, twice, three times. She was only upright because Kunz had her free hand balled in the material of Ari's jumpsuit. When she let go, Ari collapsed on the ground.

Everything was pain. Kunz kicked her in the stomach hard enough that Ari was pushed six inches across the concrete. Another kick lifted and dropped her in the same place. She curled into a ball, instinctively protecting herself by lacing her fingers on the back of her head.

"Little coward pussy!" Kunz shouted, and stomped once on Ari's folded hands.

After that, everything went black.

"...hadn't stopped her, she would be dead." (Vogel) "She's lucky to be alive."

"I don't know." (Segura) "It can be a burden to live when you're this stupid."

The next time Ari regained consciousness, she managed to get her eyes open. One of them, anyway. She was lying in a bed. She could tell that her wrists and ankles were restrained before she even tried to move them. Looking down, she saw leather cuffs strapping her to rails on either side of the mattress. Another strap was pulled taut across her waist. The blood splattered across her T-shirt was more alarming than the restraints. She was dizzy and confused and not in any pain, but she assumed that was due to whatever painkillers they had pumped into her while she was unconscious.

"You're up."

Ari jumped. She'd been completely unaware that anyone else was in the room. The woman stepped into Ari's line of sight. She was young, with black hair that was just short enough to be pulled back in a stumpy ponytail. Ordinarily, Ari would have called her cute, but there was just enough hardness in her expression to prevent that word from being entirely accurate. One eyebrow was naturally arched to give her a look of constant skepticism.

"I'm going to give you the benefit of the doubt here and assume you aren't the biggest idiot in the world. That might sound like a compliment, but it's actually very bad for you. It means that you had a reason for provoking Miriam Kunz. Your cellmate says you had an episode last night. So just save me some time and tell me what you're on."

Ari said, "I'm not... addict." She was slurring her words.

The doctor's face softened ever so slightly. "I'm not the bad guy here. I can help you. I want to help you. But I need to know what I'm fighting."

"Nothing," Ari said.

"Fine." The hardness was back. The doctor turned and made a note on her chart. "Enjoy those painkillers currently running through your system, because they're the last you're getting. You're damn lucky you didn't break anything."

Ari lifted her head. "Wait. What? I didn't..." She looked down at her body, battered but without casts or splints or any signs of a broken bone. "I didn't break anything."

"Kunz is smart," the doctor said. "She focuses on the soft parts. Bruises are easier to explain away than broken bones."

"No, no, no," Ari dropped her head back onto the pillow, legitimately close to tears. "I can't believe this. All of that, for fucking nothing..."

The doctor frowned. "Hold on. Just calm down."

Ari looked at her. "I need you to do something for me. It's probably better this way, since you're a doctor and this is a controlled environment. I need you to break my arm."

"You need me to do what?"

"Please. I can't explain it. I just... I need a broken bone."

The doctor was standing at the foot of the bed. "If you're looking for some kind of psychiatric evaluation, you'll have to try a lot harder than this."

"I'm not trying anything. I just need a broken bone. I have... I need to..." She thumped her head down on the pillow, wishing there was a way to explain without sounding crazier than she already did. "I need help. I need help, I need... I need a broken bone, or it's all going to shit. I won't be able to control it. It's going to happen and I can't control it..."

"Control it...?" The doctor thought for a moment and then moved to the locked cabinet. She withdrew a small phial and a syringe and brought them to the bedside. "You have a head trauma. Things are obviously getting jumbled up for you because of it. I have a new drug I can give you. It's a diluted version of an experimental pharmaceutical that had some controversy a few years back. It was called wolfsbane."

Ari pushed to one side of the mattress, her unswollen eye wide with terror. "No! Get that shit away from me! Don't..."

The doctor slapped her free hand on the railing and very firmly said, "*Canidae.*"

Ari blinked at her. "Wh-what... what did you say?"

"Do you know that word?"

"Do... *you* know that word?"

The doctor grunted and shook her head. "I should have known." She returned the phial and syringe to the cabinet. "There are protocols for this sort of thing. Damn it, your pack should have taught you about this sort of thing. Where's your pack now?"

"I don't have a pack."

The doctor rolled her eyes. "Of course you don't. Okay. Just relax. I'll be right back."

Ari said, "Doctor... uh, doctor..."

"Dr. Byrne."

"Right. Thank you."

She said, "Don't thank me yet, Willow. We're still not out of the woods." She left the room, letting the door swing shut behind her.

Left alone, Ari tried to catalogue her injuries. The swollen eye, of course. Her arm and head felt like they were wrapped in gauze with something very softly thudding against it. The pain was probably just muted by whatever drugs Dr. Byrne had given her before she woke up. She wouldn't feel very good when they wore off, and she hoped the truth about her nature would convince the doctor to give her more. She started to drift off back into unconsciousness. Maybe she could just stay here in the infirmary until the trial or until Dale found a way to save her.

The door slammed open again, waking her. Byrne returned with Gladys Celestin in tow. The librarian was carrying a small leather bag and winced when she saw Ari.

"Goodness, they told me you were missing work because you were in the infirmary, but lordy. What the hell happened to you?"

Byrne walked around to the other side of the bed. "She picked a fight with Miriam Kunz hoping to break a bone to stop her transformations."

Gladys put her bag on the bed, glaring at Ari. "What, you were too shy to just ask me for help?"

"I didn't... I'm... I didn't know there were *canidae* in prison."

"There are *canidae* everywhere, girl," Gladys said. "We find our ways to survive. We get the word out however we can so people know who they can trust. Why didn't your pack know about this?"

Byrne said, "She doesn't have a pack."

Gladys pulled her head back in surprise. "Well, now. Little girl thinks she can do it all on her own, huh? Well. I'm here now, and I'm going to take care of you. I have a little concoction that will put the wolf to sleep."

Ari thought about Gladys' accent and looked warily at the small wooden box she had taken from the bag. "Is it... voodoo?"

Gladys glared at her. "Baby, I'm Protestant. Don't be racist." She thumped the box with one knuckle. "This didn't come from me, anyway. It's something that's been passed down for generations of *canidae* who want to stop the transformation for one reason or another. It isn't permanent, but it will keep you safe. If I give this to you, you won't be able to change into the wolf for six months."

Ari felt cold, and it had nothing to do with her injuries or the painkillers. Six months without the wolf. Realistically she would probably need to go much longer without changing, but the idea that she would be physically unable to do it was horrifying. Her eyes teared up and she managed to nod.

"Do it."

Dr. Byrne handed a syringe to Gladys, who filled it with the concoction from her bag. She turned Ari's arm so she could find a vein and positioned the needle. She looked at Ari.

"Do you need a minute?" Gladys asked.

Ari shook her head, but she was crying. She was surprised to feel Dr. Byrne gripping her free hand, but she didn't question it. She needed all the support she could get. She squeezed and looked away as Gladys injected her. Liquid warmth spread through her, briefly covering the cool numbness of the painkillers. Ari tightened her grip on Byrne's hand, her body going rigid as the drug began to take effect. She lost the ability to focus and her gaze drifted up to the acoustic ceiling tiles.

She expected losing her wolf to be an epic moment. She wanted to feel something, even if it was pain. Instead, once the initial burn wore off, she sank into the mattress and let her hand relax. Byrne moved her fingers and pressed them against the inside of Ari's wrist to check her pulse. Gladys returned the drug to her bag and then laid the cool palm of her hand against Ari's forehead. Ari closed her eyes and felt more tears building behind the lids, only a few thin drops of them slipping out to travel down her cheeks. There was no need to focus inward or take stock, because there was suddenly an absence she couldn't explain. It was like a sound she hadn't realized she was hearing had gone silent, leaving the world eerily still and quiet. She didn't need any confirmation from Gladys or Dr. Byrne. She knew the drug had worked.

Her wolf was gone.

CHAPTER FOURTEEN

SOMEONE KNOCKED on the window next to Dale's head. She opened her eyes and saw water and sand, then realized where she was. She sat up straighter, grabbed at the collar of her robe, and looked up into the mirrored sunglasses of a police officer. *Punch him in the dick,* the devil on her shoulder said. *Go to prison. You and Ari can roleplay as Piper and Alex, it'll be hot.* She ignored the destructive impulse and rolled down her window.

"Morning, miss," he said. "Everything okay?"

She smiled and tried to look bashful. "Everything's great. I just, uh, lost track of time."

He looked pointedly at her pajamas. "Uh-huh. Miss, if there's a reason you're sleeping in your car instead of a nice, comfy bed..."

Dale held up her hand. "Officer, I appreciate the concern. But this isn't... I'm not afraid of my partner. The whole reason I'm here is because my partner isn't at home and I'm finding it really hard to sleep without her. I probably should have gone home when I started to feel sleepy. But everything is fine. Thank you. Do you have to give me a ticket?"

He seemed to consider it. "Why don't we call it a warning this time?"

"Thank you."

"You're welcome. And, uh, next time you want to go park in

the middle of the night, you may want to choose a different place. We've had a few issues around here the past couple of months. Drug dealers moving in. You're lucky they didn't catch you on their turf."

Dale nodded. "I'll remember that."

He touched the brim of his hat, like an old-timey cowboy. "You have a good day, Miss."

She watched him walk away and thought about what he'd said. A plan was starting to form. A bad plan, maybe, but one she could imagine Ari going through with. She took out her phone and dialed Gwen's number, but it was Milo who answered.

"Where the hell are you?"

"Good morning to you, too," Dale said. "I'll explain where I am when I see you. How many of the pack are still at the house?"

Milo said, "All of us. We were getting a little worried when we couldn't find you."

"Get some of them to volunteer and meet me at my house. Gwen has the address."

"We'll be there, of course. But what's going on, Dale?" Milo's voice was cautious, but there was a hint of excitement under the words.

Dale said, "We've been doing this wrong. Evidence, lawyers, waiting until Ari goes to trial and hoping we can defeat Cecily Parrish in court... we're just playing into her hands. We're letting her fight on her own turf. Let's not do that anymore."

Now Milo wasn't bothering to hide her excitement. "What do you need?"

"Wolves, Milo," Dale said. "I'm going to need wolves."

The hardest part of the plan would be getting into the building. Dale had never been to the GG&M offices, but she had a feeling it was pretty much the same as countless others she'd visited in the past. The front entrance was a solid wall of glass which pretty much only reflected a mirror image of the sidewalk. But, parked across the street, Dale could see enough to determine that there was a sprawling tile floor, a reception desk, and a bank of elevators. She also watched dozens of people enter and exit, anonymous drones in suits who were deep in conversation with each other or their phones. Most people approached the desk, signed in, and waited for the go-ahead to approach the elevators.

Paige, Owen, and Benji were in the backseat. Milo was sitting next to Dale in the front. Everyone but Dale wore matching blue jumpsuits. Dale had gone home to change into a more appropriate outfit and, now that the building was busy enough to suit her purposes, she took out her phone and dialed the main number of the building.

"Patkanim Building, how may I direct your call?"

"Hi, sweetheart," she said, giving her voice a sweet lilt with an exasperated breathiness. "This is Sheila Flowers calling from Seth Wheeler's office up here at Grayson Carruthers?" She'd gotten the names from the website but hoped saying so many so quickly prevented any of them from sticking in the man's mind. "Listen, we had a little going away party for Sara Beth up here, you know like we do, but the darn thing just got so out of hand, and we don't want to put any strain on the custodial staff, so Mr. Lewis, what he did, he just called up a private cleaning company to come in and tidy the place, and he wanted me to be sure that I gave you the head's up, but here's the thing, I just plumb forgot!"

"Uh~"

"I'm really hoping they aren't milling around downstairs already!"

"Uh, no, I don't see anyone~"

"That's so fantastic! They should be there at any minute, and Mr. Lewis and Mr. Wheeler and all of us here at Grayson Carruthers would appreciate it if you would just be a dear and send them straight up, okay?"

The receptionist said, "We, uh, we'll send them up."

"Fantastic, thank you, sweetie, you're a doll."

She hung up. She looked at Milo, who was stifling a laugh behind her hand.

"Shut up, it's a character. And it works."

"No, I like it." She twisted to look into the backseat. "Ready?"

Owen said, "You kidding? You think I came to America so I could do internet searches and play detective? I want to have some fun."

"Okay, then," Dale said. "Let's go."

They got out of the car and crossed the street as they moved into position. The wolves formed a straight line with a slight curve. Milo was in the lead, followed by the boys, with Paige in the rear. Dale was right behind Owen's shoulder, using his bulk to block her from sight as much as possible. They moved quickly when they entered the lobby. It was a few minutes before noon, and it seemed like half the building was leaving for lunch.

Milo raised her hand, lifting her chin to the front desk. One of the receptionists noted their maintenance uniforms and waved them past; he had more important things to deal with than a cleaning crew. Milo gave him a finger-gun in thanks and led the group toward the elevators. Milo hit the up button. When the car arrived, they waited for it to empty before they got onboard. A woman in a business suit started to get on with them, but Paige put a hand on her shoulder.

"Hey," she said under her voice, employing the best American accent she could muster, "take my advice. Don't get in a confined space with these sweaty pigs if you can avoid it. Catch my meaning?"

The woman looked at Owen. He pretended not to notice her as he grabbed the crotch of his jumpsuit and tugged for a better fit. Benji snorted and subtly picked his nose. The woman retreated.

"I'll take the next one," she said.

Paige winked at her. "Good call, sister."

The doors closed. Dale stepped forward while the wolves moved to the back wall. She pressed the button for GG&M's floor and held it down even as the doors closed. It was a simple trick to turn any elevator into an express, and now they wouldn't be interrupted before they reached the law office. Behind her, she heard the jumpsuits being removed. *Don't look back*, she told herself. It was like a car accident, only not entirely terrible. Milo and Paige were both beautiful women and, at this moment, were standing naked behind her. The fact Owen and Benji would also be naked helped her fight the temptation to sneak a peek.

The elevator bell dinged. Dale finally glanced back and confirmed she was sharing an elevator with four wolves. She smiled at them and faced forward as the doors slid open.

Three young women were stationed behind a tall desk under the golden letters of GILLES GIRARD AND MOREAU. The one in the middle brought her head up as smoothly as a robot and grinned.

"Gilles Girard and Moreau, wh~" Her carefully constructed façade shattered. "Oh my god!"

Dale ignored her and strolled out of the elevator. Milo and Paige ran ahead of her, heads low with growls echoing through their bared teeth. Dale's pace was casual, hands in the pockets of her finest long coat. She was wearing a purple dress - one Ari had gotten her for Hanukkah - and knee-high leather boots. Her eyes were hidden behind dark glasses. She kept her chin high and her shoulders back as she followed the path cleared by Milo and Paige.

Behind her, Benji and Owen were taking part in a little destruction. The receptionists shrieked and fled as Owen leapt onto their desk. He sent pen cups and blotters flying. Benji threw his head back to howl and it echoed off all the glass until it sounded like an entire pack. Lawyers emerged from their offices only to curse and run. Milo chased a few of them. Paige had cornered one man who had climbed up onto a desk to escape.

And there, the corner office. Dale was almost to the door when it swung wide open to reveal Cecily Parrish. She looked at the destruction before zeroing in on Dale as its source. Her lips curled, a sneer that didn't quite achieve the grace of a smile, and she moved to intercept.

"Miss Fr~"

Dale said, "Shut the fuck up. What about this situation led you to believe you get to speak first?"

One golden eyebrow rose. She almost looked impressed.

"You came after my family. I never had much of a family, and neither has Ariadne. We're all each other has ever really had. And you're trying to take that away from us. That is a very dumb thing to do, Cecily. I spent some time being sad, but I'm done with that. I'm done crying and wondering how we'll ever get out of this. You know why? Because we don't give up. Not on each other. We called our business Bitches because the men of this world have tried to use that word to keep us down. We decided it's not an insult anymore. Because we don't give up. Once we get our teeth in you, we don't let go. Not for anything."

The wolves gathered behind her, all four harmonizing in a single growl that filled the office.

"Ariadne once told me to be careful around you. I'm only human, after all, and your power would work on me no matter how hard I fought it. And she was right, Cecily. I'm standing here right in front of you, and all I can think about is how badly I want to fuck you over. So get ready. Because I'm not going to let you decide the game anymore."

She let the silence linger between them.

"Now, is there something *you* would like to say to me?"

Cecily chuckled. "Well, I must~"

Dale slapped her. She slapped her so hard that the impact reverberated up her arm and made her hand tingle when she dropped it back to her side. She curled her fingers into a fist so Cecily wouldn't notice how badly it was shaking. It might have gone unnoticed anyway. Cecily's eyes widened while her pupils grew narrow, and a red flush spread across her cheeks. She looked like a cartoon character.

"I said you could talk. I didn't say I'd listen."

She turned and walked away just as casually as she had entered. Cecily took one step in pursuit, but Owen - the largest of the wolves - stepped in front of her. He lowered his head and raised his shoulders. The threat was clear in his eyes, and Cecily wisely didn't challenge him. Dale walked back to reception, where the women were still pressed hard against the far wall.

"Sorry, ladies," Dale said as she pressed the call button. "I know you're just doing your job."

The elevator arrived. Fortunately, it was the same one they had taken up so Dale could retrieve the jumpsuits. They had been willing to leave them behind if necessary. Milo let out a quick, loud yap to let Owen know the elevator had arrived, and Dale held the door until he came bounding in. Dale smiled at the receptionists again.

"Word of advice, ladies? Look for a new job."

The doors closed on their terrified faces.

CHAPTER FIFTEEN

THE NEXT time Ari woke, Dr. Byrne was standing at a nearby table with her back to the bed. Ari tried to determine how much pain she was in without moving, but it turned out moving wasn't necessary. She was in agony. The throbbing in her arm and head earlier had become a full-scale pulse. Worse than that was the sense of being hollowed out. Without Dale, without the wolf, she felt utterly alone in a way she'd never experienced. It was horrible, worse than the physical pain, and she couldn't stop herself from sobbing.

Byrne heard her and moved to her bedside. "Hey. It's all right. I know you probably feel like shit, but that's because the drug did what it was supposed to. You're safe for the time being."

"You're not going to yell at me again, are you?" Ari said.

"Now that I know what you were trying to do, I have a little more sympathy." She began checking Ari's vitals. "Picking a fight with Miriam Kunz is still one of the dumbest things I've ever seen in this place, but you wanted results. I can understand that. I wish you had come to me to find out if there was anything I could do."

Ari said, "The whole point was to keep the wolf under wraps."

"What, you haven't heard of doctor-patient confidentiality? It applies in here the same as it does out in the world. You're still my patient and I'm still your physician. I would have been oath-bound to keep your secret."

"So you can't tell me how many wolves are in here?"

"No. But there are a few. Gladys tells me what she needs to make the drug, I bring it in, and we give the shots to *canidae* inmates when they need it."

Ari said, "Where do you get the ingredients? Your pack?"

"My... oh. No, I'm not a wolf."

"You're not?"

Byrne smiled. "Shocking, right? A human helping out wolves." She shone a light in Ari's eyes. "My father was a hunter. He told me all about the big bad wolf. He told me it was our duty to eliminate them. My father was also a racist who said the same thing about black people, Muslims, Mexicans... basically anyone who wasn't white and Christian. So I kind of lumped all his anti-*canidae* rhetoric as the bullshit it was. When I was a resident, a man stumbled into my ER naked and scraped up from a fall through some blackberry bushes. My attending wanted a psych eval, but I knew what was happening. I took care of him. Got him home safely." She shrugged. "After that, I did what I could to help any wolves that needed me."

"That's honorable," Ari said. "For the record, I understand working with humans. My partner is a human, actually."

Byrne stiffened slightly and looked at Ari with a different expression. Ari started to wonder if she'd said something wrong when Byrne finally snapped out of it.

"Sorry. But. You're... you're her?"

"Who?"

"The *canidae* who stopped wolf manoth?"

Ari said, "How do you know about that?"

"Every *canidae* knows about it, and the ones who come through here talk like you're some kind of mythical Robin Hood figure. The wolf who loved a woman, who fought against the hunters and brought an end to wolf manoth without a drop of bloodshed."

Ari remembered the knife sticking out of her mother, the very real fear that she might not survive the injury.

"That's not entirely accurate," Ari said, "but yeah, that was me."

"You saved a lot of lives on both sides of that conflict."

Ari said, "I had a lot of help."

"You must have. But a lot of wolves are still appreciative of the part you played. In fact, it will go a long way in making sure Kunz doesn't try coming after you again."

"Why... oh, you're kidding me."

Byrne shrugged, smiling. "No group of people is all good. I'm sure you've met your fair share of bad *canidae*."

"Yeah." She lifted her arms to hug herself, and only then did she realize the restraints were gone. "Hey. You let me go."

"Once I realized you weren't psychotic or suicidal, I didn't see any reason for the straps. Don't prove me wrong."

"I won't." She rubbed her arms and grimaced. She felt low-key nauseated, a general discomfort that settled in the hollow of her stomach. "Does it get better? I mean, does it get less horrifying to be separated from the wolf?"

Byrne looked sympathetic. "I wouldn't know. It varies from one patient to another, but Gladys has been in here for over a decade. I don't think she remembers what it feels like to be *canidae*. It's tragic, but at least she's come to terms with it. Others, like Kunz, never seem to get over it. She waits until the very last day to come get her booster. The wolf is always clawing right at the edges to get out. It's part of the reason she's so hair-trigger. A word of advice, don't wait."

Ari said, "I'll take that under advisement. How long do I have to stay in here?"

"You can leave in an hour or so. I just want to make sure you don't have any unexpected reactions to the drugs. I can prescribe you something for the pain, but you'll have to come back to get each dose. You aren't allowed to have pills in your cell."

"That seems a little strict," Ari said. "What is this, a prison?"

Byrne said, "You know, I'm starting to get that impression myself. Mostly it's the guards and the bars and all the criminals." She tapped her fingers on the foot of the bed. "I'm going to get out of here and let you rest a little. I'll be back in about an hour to officially let you go."

"Thank you, Dr. Byrne."

"My *canidae* patients call me Dr. Val."

Ari nodded. "Ari."

Dr. Byrne - Val - dipped her chin in acknowledgement and shut the door behind her. Ari let her head sink into the pillow and closed her eyes. The weight of the air seemed unbearably heavy, and the silence... was it always this quiet? She could hear her own breathing. She trusted Gladys and Val, as much as she could trust two people she'd barely met, and she believed the wolf was still there but asleep. But she'd never felt so separated from it before.

She'd never felt so utterly and completely human.

Since she was alone and no one would hear her anyway, Ari gave in to her emotions and allowed herself to cry softly.

The wolves in the back seat spent the ride back to Gwen's place pawing at each other, but they were easy to ignore. They had transformed once they were back in the elevator, pulling on their jumpsuits while Dale held the button down again. No one in the lobby paid any attention to them as they walked out; one of the red flags on the plan had been the potential for Cecily to call security to prevent them from leaving. Apparently no one in the law firm wanted to confess they had just been attacked by a pack of wolves.

Milo called Gwen to let her know they'd gotten out of the building safely. Dale focused on the drive and was for once grateful for Seattle traffic. It kept her from thinking about the gauntlet she had thrown down. Standing in front of Cecily without flinching had taken every bit of strength she had. Now she felt like she had to vomit and pee and curl up in a ball and scream, all at the same time. Milo reached over and patted her knee at a stoplight.

"You did damn good."

"Mm-hmm," Dale said, afraid to open her mouth.

"You okay?"

Dale nodded.

When they got home, Paige hooked her arm around Benji's and practically dragged him out of the car. Owen followed them and left the door open behind him. By the time Dale got into the house, all three had disappeared upstairs. Dale looked up at the ceiling and then at Milo in the hopes for an explanation. Milo grinned and shrugged.

"Fucking."

"What?"

"They got to run wild in an office and see you being a total badass. They might be human now, but the animal doesn't let go easily. They have to burn off the excess energy. Sex is the best way to do that. And the most fun."

Dale said, "But... I thought Paige and Owen were estranged."

Milo went to the fridge to get a drink. "Yeah. And Benji is straight. I told you all this before, Dale, it doesn't matter when it's in the pack."

"So why didn't you go up with them?"

Gwen came downstairs, inadvertently answering the question.

She hooked a thumb over her shoulder. "Is whatever is happening in my guest room a good thing?"

"Very good," Milo said. "You'd have been proud of your girl here, Gwen."

"I'm always proud of her," Gwen said, pausing to touch Dale's hand. "Are you okay, sweetheart? You look a little green around the gills."

Dale said, "Adrenaline's wearing off."

"Why don't you go..." She looked at the stairs and then pivoted. "Lie down on the couch. It'll probably be less noisy down here for a little bit."

"I think I will. Thanks."

Gwen watched her go and then moved closer to Milo. "So it went well?"

Milo said, "Everything went like clockwork. It was a bit nerve-wracking when Dale was actually standing in front of the shrew, but I think she was so stunned that anyone would stand up to her that she didn't think to lash out." She grinned and lowered her voice. "Girlie also adlibbed a little. Gave Cecily a chance to talk and, as soon as she opened her mouth, slapped her across the face. I'd have applauded if I'd had hands at that moment."

Gwen looked toward the couch. Dale was already lying down, curled up with her back to the room. Gwen's expression was proud, but guarded.

"What is it?" Milo asked.

"I'm impressed as hell with her, obviously. But I'm also worried. Cecily has just proven how far she's willing to go. I'm worried that Dale gained an inch but it's going to cost her a yard."

Milo nodded but couldn't help smiling. "You just, ah, mixed up your distances there."

Gwen's expression softened. "I can't help it if you're corrupting me."

Milo put her hand on top of Gwen's. She traced the length of Gwen's middle finger. She lowered her voice even further. "You, ah, wanna go upstairs an' see what they're getting up to?"

"Tempting. But I'm not a member of your pack."

"I get a plus-one to stuff like this."

Gwen kissed the corner of Milo's mouth. "Be that as it may, I'll pass. You can go up if you want. I won't be offended."

"Nah, I'll wait until you're in the mood. You're worth all of them combined." She looked around as if just noticing they were alone in the kitchen. "Speaking of which, where's everyone else?"

"Mia thought you might need some backup, so she and Hannah headed downtown. When you sent the all-clear, she said they were taking the opportunity to grab some lunch. And Tarun is scouting for places you all can go for a run without getting spotted or captured. I gave him some leads, but I'm not hopeful. Six of you all running around at once is bound to garner some attention."

"We manage to make it work in London and its suburbs," Milo said. "But we can take turns if need be."

"I also called the prison to ensure we can visit Ariadne on Monday." She was looking at her hands, watching her thumbs move across the granite of the countertop.

Milo tensed. "Uh-oh. That's not a good look. What's wrong?"

"They..." She looked into the living room. Dale hadn't moved and her shoulders rose and fell with the slow rhythm of sleep. "They said that, ah, normally it wouldn't be a problem to arrange a visit so we could discuss her legal strategy. But there are mitigating circumstances if the inmate has a strike against her. Ari apparently got a strike today."

"Ah, shit. She went through with Dale's plan already?"

"Apparently. We can still visit her since it's unclear whether the fight was her fault. Apparently the woman she fought with has a few strikes on her record already, so people think she might have started it. So at least there's that." Gwen's voice was so low now that Milo had to lean in to hear it. "They said she was in the infirmary when I called. I was upstairs trying to compose myself before you girls got home. Did I look like I'd been crying?"

"No. You look beautiful, babe." Milo wrapped an arm around Gwen and pulled her close. "I'm sorry. Are you okay?"

"I will be," Gwen said, nuzzling Milo's neck and taking comfort in her familiar scent. "I wanted to tell Dale immediately but I just couldn't bear to see her face when she found out."

"I'll tell her," Milo promised.

"Thank you," Gwen said.

"You're welcome." Milo let it hang for a moment and then, holding Gwen tightly, whispered, "I love you, Gwen."

Gwen moved a hand to the back of Milo's head. "I love you, too."

They held each other silently for a long while, letting the words linger in the air around them.

CHAPTER SIXTEEN

SEGURA DIDN'T even look up from her book when Ari limped into the cell. Ari grunted when she sat down, and Segura casually licked her thumb to turn the page.

"It's not~"

"Don't care," Segura snapped. "Changed my mind, Willow. I don't need a friend in that bed. Your shit and my shit ain't going to get mingled together. So as far as I'm concerned, this cell is fucking haunted."

"I'm a werewolf."

Whatever retort Segura had planned died on her lips. She finally looked up, curiosity slipping past her anger.

"Say again?"

Ari looked toward the door to be sure no one was hanging out within earshot. "I'm a werewolf. Technically the term is *canidae*. I can control my transformations but, if I don't let the wolf out every four weeks or so it starts to get a little insistent. If that happened, I might have changed in the middle of the night while I was asleep. You and Vogel got a little preview of something that could have been infinitely worse for all of us."

Segura was sitting up now, feet on the floor. "Are you insane?"

"I swear this is the truth. My girlfriend realized that *canidae* can stop the transformations by breaking a bone. The wolf would hold back until it healed. That's all I was trying to do with Kunz. Turns out it wasn't necessary, because Dr. Byrne knows all about us and has a drug that can put the wolf to sleep for six months. I'm not a junkie, I'm not insane, and I'm not suicidal. I just had a problem I couldn't quite explain to you because... well, because you'd look at me the way you're looking at me right now."

"No, I know. I believe you. I'm a Chupacabra."

Ari rolled her eyes. "There's no way I can make you believe me. So I'll settle for saying I'm sorry for everything and assuring you that it won't happen again. I won't put you or Vogel in that kind of situation ever again. The wolf is under control and I'm... I'm just... I'm human." She blinked back tears. "If you want to believe the cell is haunted, I'll accept that. I just wanted to tell you the truth and apologize. I'll apologize to Vogel, too, the next time I see her."

Segura stared hard at her. She pushed out her jaw and narrowed her eyes. "You believe it."

"What?"

"This nonsense you're telling me. That you're a werewolf and the doc gave you a shot to make the wolf go away for a while. I think it's a lot more believable that you're delusional and she told you a pretty lie about what was in the needle she put in your arm. But regardless of which thing is true, I can tell that you believe the wolf story. That's good enough for me."

Ari said, "Really?"

"We all have to tell ourselves lies to get through the day. Yours is a little weirder than some, but there's nothing wrong with some variety." She got off the bed and moved to stand in front of Ari. "No more fits in the middle of the night, and no more suicidal attacks on Kunz?"

"I promise."

Segura stuck out her hand. "Apology accepted, Willow."

Ari gripped the hand tightly and pumped it once. "Thank you."

"So wolves, huh?" Segura said as she walked back to her bed. "Is that where you got the boulder-sized ovaries to piss off Kunz?"

"That was more desperation than anything else," Ari said.

"She and her pals won't be so willing to forgive and forget. She's in solitary for the next three days since she, you know, stomped your head. But she'll get out eventually."

Ari carefully stretched out on her bed, aware of all her various bruises. "I think I have a way to defuse that before anything happens," Ari said.

"You sure?"

"Oh, yeah. I've dealt with bitches worse than her in my life."

Segura shook her head and went back to reading. Ari closed her eyes and tried to find a position that didn't put her weight on something that hurt.

When Dale woke up, she returned a call from Diana and learned that the security camera from the park had been retrieved and examined. She made the call from Gwen's dinner table, crossing the fingers of both hands and holding her breath.

"It's good news and bad news," Diana said. "Good news is that there was definitely a car parked there after hours, and someone definitely comes up to it on foot. The person gets in and the car drives away. The bad news is that the video quality is total shit. We can't identify the person - we can't even really tell if it's a man or a woman - and the only time the license plate is facing the camera, there's glare from a security light."

"Damn it," Dale said.

"It's not as bad as it could have been. At the very least, it establishes something was going on in the park that night. It's not enough to open an official investigation..."

"I know. But it's still something. Thank you, Diana."

Diana said, "I talked to Lucy last night. She knows a lawyer who occasionally does pro bono work. She thinks he'll be willing to take Ari's case for free due to the fact she was wrongly accused. He's taking our word for that, but he trusts us enough that he's not worried."

"I appreciate that, but apparently there isn't a lawyer in Seattle willing to go up against Cecily Parrish in this case. Apparently the evidence is strong enough that no one wants to risk their career or reputation by fighting."

"This guy will. He doesn't get scared off. Hell, he might take it just to tell people he went up against that harpy. I'll let you know when I've spoken to him."

"Okay. Thanks."

"My pleasure. Are you holding up well? You sound blasted."

Dale smiled. "I had a big morning. Plus the whole underlying fear for Ariadne's safety. But I have a really good support system here. Ari's mom has been amazing."

"Have you been able to talk to your father at all?"

"Ugh." She pressed her fingers to her temple. "No. He still

doesn't really like the idea that I'm with a woman, or that I have such a dangerous job. I don't want him to know Ari's in prison. He'll probably book me a ticket home before he even hangs up the phone."

Diana said, "Ouch. That's never fun."

Mia had come in while Dale was on the phone and silently took a seat next to her at the table. Dale smiled at her, looking past her at Gwen and Milo in the living room. "It's hard, yeah. But we all get a family that's forced on us, and a family we get to choose. If one of those sucks, it makes it more important that the second one is awesome."

She reached out and put her hand on top of Mia's.

"Well said, Dale. And please remember, anything you need, don't hesitate."

"I won't." They said their goodbyes and Dale hung up. She smiled at Mia. "And thank you for watching my back this morning. Gwen told me you were ready just in case I needed backup."

Mia shrugged. "You dived into the lion's den with both feet. I respect that." She took out her phone and placed it on the table, turning it around before sliding it to Dale. "But I wasn't just sitting on my butt waiting for things to go sideways. I found a lead for you."

Dale leaned down to look at the phone, which displayed a Facebook profile. "Jennifer Libbey? Who is that?"

"Shannon Hardy's best friend. They went to college together." She reached out and scrolled the page down. "She posted about Shannon's murder."

Dale picked up the phone to read what it said. "RIP Shan. They'll get the bitch who did this to you, I know. You won't be forgotten." She grimaced and then tilted her head to the side. "Wait. They caught Ari fleeing the crime scene. Any news report announcing Shannon's death would also say there was a suspect in custody."

"Exactly," Mia said. "Why would she make the killer's capture hypothetical unless she thought the wrong person had been arrested. She knows something."

Dale was already standing up. "If I get my laptop, I can probably find out where Jennifer Libbey lives or works..."

"Already done," Mia said. "I may not be from here, but I am a cop. Some skills work in both countries. I found her home and work address. I would offer to drive you there, but I have no idea where anything is in this city."

"I can drive," Dale said. "But if you're willing to play backup for a second time today..."

Mia stood. "I'm here for you, babe."

Gwen had overheard the end of the conversation and held up her hand. "Good luck, Dale. Let us know if you need us."

Dale stopped by the back door. "Everyone keeps saying that to me. Of course I need you. I need all of you. And I know you're here for me. But it really means a lot to hear it out loud."

"Just say the word," Milo said. "Your pack is here and ready."

Dale blew her a kiss, then led Mia out of the house.

Jennifer Libbey's work address seemed like the best bet on a Friday afternoon. It was in Capitol Hill, not far from the Bitches office. Mia watched out the window, occasionally twisting to examine one of the regal brick buildings or a tall hedge towering over the sidewalk. Eventually she asked Dale what the neighborhood was called and Dale told her.

"Something about it reminds me of home."

"It does feel a little English," Dale said. "Just a bit more hilly. This is the city's gayborhood. It's where coffee and grunge got its start in the city, and now it's one of the most LGBT-friendly areas of the city. If we have time later, I'll show you the rainbow crosswalks."

Mia smiled. "Gayborhood. I like that a lot."

The address was a one-story brick building set back from the street. The signage was mostly concealed by the trees lining the sidewalk but Dale managed to spot it before she overshot by too much. She parked against the curb and walked back with Mia. The business was a restaurant called WoodInn Fine Cuisine. The front windows were large enough that the dining room was bathed with natural light, making the wall sconces unnecessary. A man was standing at a pony wall between the cash register and the kitchen. He was examining a binder when they walked in.

"Sorry, ladies, we're closed. Come back at five."

"We're actually not here to eat. We were wondering if we could speak with Jennifer Libbey."

He looked up, glanced over his shoulder, and stood up straighter. "Look, uh, Jen is kind of having a rough couple of days. Maybe this could wait."

"I'm sorry," Dale said. "We need to talk to her."

He seemed ready to argue, but gave up before he started. "Just go easy on her if you can, okay?" He twisted at the waist and called into the kitchen. "Jen! Couple'a ladies here want to talk with you." He gestured to a table next to a window. "You can have a seat there."

They had just sat down as a blonde woman appeared from the kitchen. She spotted Dale and Mia, hesitating before she started over. Dale assumed her caution was due to Mia, who carried herself like a cop even out of uniform. She was sitting up perfectly straight with her shoulders squared, her short brown hair slicked back into a ponytail. She had her hands folded together in front of her on the table. She had the same lean, athletic build that Dale had come to associate with *canidae*. The overall impression was intimidating.

"Relax a little," Dale said quietly.

"Hm?"

"You look like a cop."

"I *am* a cop."

"Not here, you aren't."

Mia relaxed as Jennifer neared the table. She looked like she had been crying. "I'm Jen Libbey. Can I help you?"

Dale smiled. "My name is Dale Frye. I'm... a private investigator. I was wondering if we could talk about Shannon Hardy."

Jennifer's eyes welled up again. "I don't think, uh... I'm... I came to work so I wouldn't have to think about that."

"I understand. I'm sorry. It's just that we saw your post online, and it implied you think the person who was arrested might be innocent. We think there's a lot more to the story, too. We want to make sure justice is served. If Shannon's killer is still out there, we want them to be caught. Please. Anything you can tell us would be enormously helpful."

Jennifer looked back at the man. He was pretending to focus on his binder, but it was clear he was eavesdropping just enough to leap into action if necessary. Finally, Jennifer took a seat across from them.

"Mostly what I know is from the news," Jennifer admitted. "They claimed Shannon was killed by some woman she was having an affair with. Shannon wasn't gay."

Dale said, "You're sure about that?"

"Uh, yeah. As sure as I can be. I had a crush on her when we met. She didn't just tell me she was straight, let me down easy. She actually tried. She said there was a chance she was bisexual. So we made out a few times. I was the one who stopped it. What's the point of kissing someone who isn't into it? I ended up letting *her* down easy. We stayed friends, and she never mentioned experimenting or a new interest in women. I'm not saying she would have jumped at the chance to be with me, but she would have at least said something."

"Do you know anything about her work with GG&M?" Dale asked.

"The law firm?" Jennifer twisted her lips and looked out the window. The sun was filtering in through the trees, creating a constantly-shifting chessboard on the sidewalk. "She was strange about that job. She always said she couldn't talk about it, but I could tell there was something going on. She was always going to these parties at her boss' house, and she would come home... like she'd been drugged. I thought she was being... I mean, I thought..."

"Rape," Mia said.

Jennifer blinked at her as if she'd been unaware Mia could speak. "Yeah. I finally asked her about it and she swore she never did anything she didn't want to do. But I don't know. I threw a little party to celebrate when she finally got fired."

"Did she ever talk about her boss? Cecily Parrish?"

"Not much, if she could avoid it. She was kind of in awe of her, but also intimidated." She scooted forward, leaning across the table and lowering her voice. "I heard Cecily was the one prosecuting the lady they arrested. I don't know, maybe I watch too many crime TV shows, but it immediately looked sketchy to me. Did she have something to do with it?"

Dale said, "That's what we're hoping to find out."

Jennifer took out her phone and put it down on the table. She swiped the screen, opened an app, and presented it to Dale.

"I played that for a detective. Rojas? He thought it just confirmed their theory. But..."

Dale leaned in close to hear. Shannon's voice was strong but quiet.

"Hey, hon. I guess you're still at work. Give me a call when you get off. Or, um, maybe I'll come in for dinner. I just really want to bounce something off of you. I think I'm going to let myself get talked into something stupid and I need you to talk some sense into me. So hopefully I'll see you tonight. Love you, lady. Bye."

Jennifer pulled the phone back, cheeks wet from tears that had finally fallen. "That was the night she died. I called her back, but she was already..."

Dale said, "What do you think she was being talked into?"

"I don't know. Rojas thought it had to do with that ridiculous affair. Like maybe Shannon wanted to call it off, but the other woman was pushing to stay together. And then..." She waved her hand. "I know Shannon wasn't perfect. I would never have judged her. I don't think she would have lied to me if she was having an affair. I just wanted her to be happy. She knew that."

Dale said, "Did she give you any reason to believe she was frightened of Cecily Parrish?"

Jennifer smiled and raised an eyebrow. "She never said it. She never had to. I could see it in how she lived. When she was working for GG&M, she closed herself off. She was withdrawn, she wasn't eating right or taking care of herself. She would get dressed up for work and everything, but on the weekends when she was home, she just hid in her apartment. She started getting better when she was fired. She was herself again."

She pressed her hands together and looked out the window again. Dale and Mia both gave her a moment to collect herself. Finally she looked at them again.

"I don't know if she would have admitted it, Miss Frye, but I think Cecily Parrish scared the shit out of Shannon. And I think no matter who actually committed the murder, the blood is going to be on Cecily's hands."

CHAPTER SEVENTEEN

ARI SPENT the majority of her weekend in bed. She was granted permission to skip her duty in the library until Monday, when hopefully most of her aches and pains would have abated. The only time she left was when she limped to the cafeteria - Segura or Vogel offering her a shoulder - and when she shuffled by herself to the infirmary to get painkillers from Dr. Val. She put off the pills for as long as she could, waiting until the very end of the dosage window before she even got off the bed. She wanted to wean herself off as quickly as possible.

Most of her time was spent on self-examination. The last time she existed without the wolf as a constant companion had been when she was a child, pre-puberty. Her body felt the same but somehow different. She would close her eyes and squeeze her hands into fists, feeling the nails dig into her palms, and she knew that there was no way they could became paws. She knew that no matter how hard she tried, she was stuck in this form until it was safe to stop taking the drug.

And when would that be? Six months seemed like an eternity but, if the case wasn't finished by then, she would have to take a second dose. It might be a year before she transformed. Just thinking that made her panic. She had to focus her breathing in order to stop a full-out attack. Segura was at work and she was alone in the cell, but she didn't want anyone overhearing and calling a guard.

The first night, she was shaken from sleep with a scream caught in her throat. Fortunately she calmed down before she woke Segura. The dream had been a confusing jumble of shapes and colors, creating a claustrophobic kaleidoscope which created a sensation of drowning. She didn't want to risk slipping back into it so she stayed awake and stared at the ceiling. The prison was never completely dark or totally silent. Some of the guards lowered their voices after lights-out, but most didn't bother. Ari heard Sessions' laugh echo down at least three hallways. Other prisoners cried. Some had sex and didn't bother keeping quiet.

Ari just thought about her new condition. She was human. There was a bright side to that, of course. Dale could finally have a normal girlfriend. No late-night runs, no waking up at four in the morning to come get her. It might be nice. When she thought of it that way, she hoped the drug was still in her system whenever she did go home. She could call it a vacation for Dale, a chance to see the life she'd given up when she chose to be with a *canidae*.

In the morning, while waiting for the count, Segura looked Ari up and down. "So what kind of werewolf are you? Standing on your hind legs, big claws..."

"No, I just look like a regular wolf. A little bit bigger than average, but for the most part, normal."

"You ever, ah..." She moved her first forward and raised her eyebrow. "You know. As the wolf."

Ari rolled her eyes. But then she smiled and said, "Yeah."

Segura laughed. "That's nasty."

"It's different. I'm still me even when I look like a wolf, so it's not like bestiality. I'm still sentient. Everyone is consenting. It just looks strange from the outside. And what sex doesn't look a little awful from the outside?"

"That's true."

A guard Ari didn't recognize did their count. Segura explained that Vogel had Sundays off as she helped Ari to the cafeteria again. The pain was noticeably less today, and Ari managed with just resting a steadying hand on Segura's shoulder.

"So there's one day a week when you can't see each other? That seems weird."

"It's a little vacation from each other. It's good. Every relationship ought to do it. I hang out here, she goes to church and sees her friends, gets drunk, goes to the movies. Is it a little lopsided? Sure. But every relationship has its give and take."

They arrived in the cafeteria and Segura stopped dead in her tracks. "Oh, shit. We might want to go back..."

Ari didn't have to ask why. Miriam Kunz was big and obvious enough that she drew the eye. Especially when she was rising from her seat and glaring directly at Ari.

"Segura, go."

"I'm not abandoning you again."

Ari said, "I'm not going to let you be collateral damage. Just go."

Segura hesitated, but self-preservation won out. Her shoulder dropped out from under Ari's hand. She moved closer to the wall and shuffled away as Kunz closed in.

"I'm going to make you hurt for every hour I spent in solitary," she growled.

"Miriam, the last time we saw each other, I didn't fight back. I still don't want to hurt you."

Kunz grinned, she was closing in fast, both fists ready. "That's okay. I think my knuckles can handle a little bruising."

She took a swing. Ari easily sidestepped it, bending her knee and throwing her weight forward to get in close. Kunz tried to correct her position and ended up bringing her feet together. She tumbled and swayed, but Ari threw a hand against her throat. It kept her from falling over at the cost of a bruised windpipe. Kunz coughed violently, her spittle landing warmly on Ari's exposed neck. She shuddered but didn't waste the time to wipe it away.

"I had my reasons for saying those things to you," Ari said. "I want you to know I sincerely apologize for~"

"Fuck your apology!" She shoved Ari against the wall and crowded her.

Ari let her get in close, then threw an elbow against Kunz's ear. Kunz recoiled and, before she could get away, Ari threw her elbow again and cracked it off her cheekbone. Kunz howled. Ari straightened up, put an arm around Kunz's neck for a headlock, and leaned in close.

"Wolf," she hissed.

Kunz tensed. Her hands stopped reaching for Ari's face. "What did you say?"

"*Canidae,*" Ari whispered. "I was desperate. It was howling at the doors and I needed a solution fast. I'm sorry for the things I said to you, but I thought I needed to be hurt. I thought you were my best chance to stopping it from getting free, so I had to be cruel."

Kunz wrestled free from the grip and backed up a few steps. She stared at Ari, eyes narrowed. Ari braced herself for a sneak attack, but she could see the rage vanishing from Kunz's posture the longer they stared at each other.

A guard, Jaekel, ran up and stood between the two of them. She had one hand on her taser. "How's everything going, ladies?"

"Everything's fine," Ari said, eyes locked on Kunz. "No problems."

Silence hung in the room. Finally, Kunz dipped her chin and waved Jaekel away. "Yeah. No problems. Bitch learned her lesson. Right?"

Ari held her hands up in surrender. "Lesson totally learned."

It wasn't important if Jaekel believed it; she just wanted to get out of wasting a morning on a couple of inmates batting each other around. She took the accord at face value and left them alone. Kunz returned to her table, casting a few measuring glances back at Ari before she reclaimed her seat. Ari spotted Segura waiting for her and went to join her. Segura was shaking her head and chuckling quietly.

"You lied to me, Willow."

"About what?" Ari leaned against the wall, grunting as her bruises protested the gymnastics she'd just put it through.

"You told me you're a wolf. But unless wolves get nine lives, I think you're a damn cat."

Ari laughed.

The wolves spent Saturday night patrolling Gwen's house. Paige and Tarun had the last shift, so they were both already awake when Dale came downstairs even though the sun was just barely beginning to light up the windows. They were sitting on the couch with laptops open. Dale tried to ignore the fact that Paige was only wearing a baggy tank top and Tarun was in boxers. Living with a houseful of wolves was teaching her to ignore casual nudity. She said good morning to them as she went into the kitchen.

"I couldn't sleep, so I thought I would steal Tarun's job and make everyone breakfast. Any requests?"

"Meat," both of the wolves said in stereo.

Dale checked the fridge. Gwen had plenty of sausage, bacon, and ham. "I can provide meat," she assured them. "I guess Cecily Parrish didn't send any of her minions to get payback on me?"

"All's clear," Tarun said. "Paige just got updates from the others before you came downstairs. No sign of anything suspicious."

Owen had been sent to stand watch at Ari and Dale's house, mainly to protect Neka. Benji had been sent to stake out the Bitches office.

Paige said, "Well, nothing external." She looked up at Dale, eyebrows twisted with worry. "Your landlady, Neka? Is she, um, single?"

"I think so, at the moment. Why?"

"No, if she's single, then yeah, it's totally fine." She focused on her laptop.

Tarun shook his head, smirking. "Never should have sent Owen to keep an eye on her."

Dale said, "Is she in danger?"

Paige chuckled and shook her head. "No, he's just charming as fuck when he wants to be. It's how he got me to marry him in the first place. Neka's fine. He'll back off if she's not interested, he just has a way of making women *want* to be interested in him. At least for a little while."

Dale wasn't entirely convinced, but she trusted Paige's judgement.

"In the meantime," Paige said, rising to carry her laptop into the kitchen. She placed it on the counter and angled it so Dale could see the screen. "I've been doing some homework."

"On Shannon or Cecily?"

"Neither. Well, technically on Cecily, but I went back a lot farther than you did. I kept thinking it was strange how focused she was on Ariadne. Then I thought, they're going after a *canidae* and they already have a succubus, so who knows what else they might have. I dug up anything I could find on GG&M and found some interesting shit."

Dale was preparing to begin breakfast. "Lay it on me."

"Okay. First of all, the earliest reference I can find to GG&M is an 1893 article talking about new businesses coming into the area. Apparently there was a big fire a few years earlier."

"I think I remember reading something about that," Dale said, trying not to smirk.

"Louis Gilles and Barthelemy Moreau immigrated from France and set up a little law firm. I found an article that talked about how they were only doing okay until the Klondike gold rush started bringing more people to the city, at which point they started getting a lot of business from fortune hunters either going up or coming back from Alaska. The article said they were doing well enough to hire a receptionist: Lillian Girard."

Dale said, "Well, all those names certainly sound familiar."

"Mm-hmm," Paige said. "So all those gold rushers were using GG&M to stake their claims or forge partnerships or whatever, and the firm was making money hand over fist. They used that to build their empire up until it's the monster we're dealing with today. Speaking of which, the current partners. I can't find any proof they've argued a case or even shown up in public for years. But check out the names."

The bacon was sizzling, so Dale moved closer and looked at the screen. "L Gilles, L Girard, and B Moreau. So they kept it in the family rather than just keeping the name."

"But the initials. The initials are exactly the same."

Dale said, "My cousins all have first names starting with J. George Foreman named all his kids George. If you have an empire to think about, names become part of the dynasty." She went back to the stove. "You don't honestly believe they're the same people who started the firm in the 1890s."

"It's not outside the realm of possibilities," Paige said. "Milo said Ari told her you two ran into a mermaid not long ago."

"True," Dale said. "Who knows? Maybe they're vampires. We can ask Gwen when she wakes up."

"She's up," Gwen said as she reached the bottom of the stairs. She was dressed in a robe, her hair pinned back. She swatted Paige's butt as she passed. "Pull down your shirt, your tail is wagging."

Paige adjusted her tank top.

"What did you want to ask me?" Gwen asked Dale.

"Immortals. Do they exist?"

Gwen said, "No. But people who have lifespans of a hundred, two hundred years? Oh yeah. Easily. There have been *canidae* who lived to be a hundred and forty-five."

That caught Dale by surprise. "Wait. Really?"

"Yeah. What are we talking about?"

Paige repeated what she had found while Gwen poured them all coffee. She had just reached the end when Milo came downstairs in pajama pants and a T-shirt.

"I'm not repeating it again," Paige said.

"Okay," Milo mumbled. "I smell bacon."

Dale said, "It's almost ready." She gestured at Paige's laptop.

"What else did you find?"

"A lot of back-patting, mostly. They've quietly been representing some of Seattle's elite for decades now."

"Like the hockey team," Dale said.

"Like the hockey team," Paige confirmed.

Gwen said, "So this prestigious law firm that's been around since the gold rush and represents the richest people in a very expensive city is willing to commit murder to hire a private investigator who is just making a comfortable living? Ari is a fine detective. But once she said no, they kept pursuing her. Because of the wolf. So the question is, why does this firm need a wolf?"

Tarun said, "Why would they need a succubus?"

"Well, that makes sense," Dale said. "A succubus is all about seduction. All she has to do is get close to the jury and they'll side with her no matter how strong her case might be. And I guess having a wolf on retainer would be useful for the same reason it works so well for Bitches. Maybe being cutthroat and going to these extremes is how they've survived for this long. But would they go this far just to get a wolf on their payroll?"

Milo, still looking half unconscious, said, "Well, there's an easy way to find out."

Dale looked at her. "How?"

Milo shrugged and smiled. "We offer her a different wolf."

CHAPTER EIGHTEEN

MONDAY MORNING, just before eight o'clock, Ari was led to a spacious room that reminded her of a high school gymnasium. The walls were white brick with warnings like KEEP VOLUME DOWN and NO PHONES - CASH painted in large red letters every few feet. The room wasn't as crowded as Ari had feared it would be. There were three other prisoners already present, so everyone could be spaced out for privacy. She was directed to a table against the far wall and told to wait quietly.

The clock on the wall ticked over to seven minutes past eight before the door opened. Ari tensed and sat up straighter. First, a guard entered. Followed by an older woman and a teenager. And right behind them...

Ari was surprised that her eyes filled with tears when she saw her mother leading Dale into the room. She started to stand, sat back down when she realized she didn't know if it was allowed, then decided she didn't care if she was scolded and stood up again. Dale looked like she had to fight back a sob and started to turn away, but Gwen put an arm around her to guide her forward. Dale pressed her face against the shoulder of Gwen's cardigan but lifted her head when they reached the table.

"Hi," Ari said.

Dale flung herself at Ari, who caught her without hesitation.

She finally released the sob, and Ari finally let a tear fall down her cheek. She closed her eyes and focused on how it felt to have Dale in her arms. She breathed deep but discovered Dale's scent was oddly blunted. A side effect from quieting the wolf, probably. It didn't matter. After almost a week without holding her, even a reduced hit was enough to make her lightheaded.

Dale kissed Ari's neck. "Hi, puppy."

Ari did cry then, a full sob that made her tighten her grip. She smiled and burrowed her face harder against Dale's sweater, focusing on the smell of her underneath the shampoo and laundry scent. It was easier now that the wolf in her wasn't smelling every single detail. She could focus on what was important.

"Inmate," a guard said, not angrily but with enough warning to confirm he wasn't making a request.

Ari reluctantly let go of Dale and took a step back. "I've missed you so much," Ari said.

Dale reached up but stopped short of actually touching Ari's face. "Oh, god, look at you. I did this. I'm so sorry."

"Hey, no. No." Ari kissed her lips. "No. You did this to save me. I'll never, ever forget that. Thank you, Dale."

Gwen cleared her throat. "Maybe we should sit before we rile up the guards."

"Right."

They sat, Dale and Gwen on one side of the table with Ari across from them. Ari didn't let go of Dale, transferring her hand from the small of Dale's back to her hand by skimming up her back and down her arm. They linked fingers and Ari squeezed.

"So did it work?" Dale said.

Ari desperately wanted to say yes, wanted to assuage Dale's guilt by saying that it had solved their problem, but she couldn't lie.

"Not directly," Ari said. "But it did introduce me to someone who did have a solution. It worked in the end, babe. Don't worry about how it looks. The important thing is that I'm safe and you're the one who made that happen."

Dale still didn't look entirely convinced. She covered their linked fingers with her free hand.

"How are you holding up?" Gwen asked.

"Surprisingly, it's not too bad. My cellmate is a godsend. She's been watching out for me. She found out I'm a private investigator and wants me to look into a case when I get out. I figure that's a fair trade. How are things going on the outside?"

Gwen said, "We're looking for ways to take Cecily Parrish down before this goes to trial. She and that law firm have some sketchy history. If we can figure out how to use that to our advantage, it would change everything."

"We meaning you and Milo's pack," Ari said.

"And Diana," Dale added. "She's been a huge help. I found a security camera in Seward Park that caught a car on the night of the murder. Diana's trying to figure out where it went. She also thinks she knows a lawyer who will take your case."

Ari said, "Be sure to thank her for me."

Dale nodded.

"Is there anything you haven't told us about your interactions with Cecily or GG&M?" Gwen asked. "Anything that might help us out?"

"I told Dale everything," Ari said. "I know next to nothing about her other than the fact she's a succubus and really, really wants to hire me to her firm."

"We're finding out more about the firm," Dale said. "Nothing we can weaponize yet, but we're hopeful. It'll just take some time. I wish we had better news."

Ari picked up Dale's hand to kiss her fingers. "It's great news, Dale. Really. I'm just glad you have such a great support team while I'm in here."

Dale finally smiled. "Yeah, I needed a dozen wolves to make up for you not being there."

Ari laughed.

Gwen cleared her throat and patted her pocket. "I see some vending machines back there. Why don't I get us something to snack on while we're talking?" She caught the guard's eye and pointed to the machines. He nodded, so she stood up and smiled at them before she made her way across the room to leave them alone.

"Mom's subtle," Ari said.

"What are you talking about?" Dale asked. "Was there an ulterior motive for her to leave? I mean, I am feeling a little snacky."

Ari said, "See, this is why I'm the detective. I notice the little clues."

Dale smiled, but her tears welled up again.

"Hey," Ari said. "Cut that out. Don't cry. I don't want you to remember this as a sad visit." She reached up with one hand to brush the tears away with her thumb. "We're going to sort this out, just like we always do."

"What if we don't?" Dale said. "She's powerful, Ari. And her law firm has been around for over a hundred years. They have experience with stuff like this and they're used to winning. We've spent so much time punching above our weight that maybe we finally bit off more than we can chew. I don't know if I'll be able to take only seeing you for one hour every Monday."

Ari looked down at the table. "If it comes to that, then of course... I mean, I don't want you to feel trapped by me. If I'm stuck in here, you should~"

Dale smacked Ari's hand. "That's not what I meant and you know it."

"I~"

"Shame on you, Ariadne."

Ari said, "I don't want to think of you being alone."

"I won't be alone. You might be in here while I'm out there, but I'll never be alone."

Ari pressed her lips together. "I love you."

"I love you, too. And if an hour per week is all I get, I'll cope. It doesn't matter if I get to spend one hour or twenty-four hours with you, Ari, it's never going to feel like enough."

Gwen slowly approached the table. She was carrying three bags of chips. "I think I've got enough snacks, but I could always go back."

Ari smiled and motioned for her to sit. "I think we have enough for right now, Mom."

Gwen put the bags on the table. "I hope you still like barbeque, Ariadne..."

"Mom," Ari said. "You were younger than I am when I was born. I never really thought about that, but it's true. Being in this situation and not knowing if there's a way out, it made me realize how you must have felt. You didn't have a Dale, Mom. You didn't have a... *you*. Or a British pack swooping in to lend a hand. You didn't have anything. I can't even fathom how terrified you must have been or how big of a leap of faith you had to take. And looking at who I've become, I can't imagine being in this position if I didn't have the wolf."

Gwen was shaking her head, jaw tight. "Ariadne, you've already forgiven me."

"Yeah. But I never admitted that you didn't need forgiving. You did what you thought was right, what was necessary at the time. I don't know if it was wrong. All I know is how it turned out, and I wouldn't have it any other way. You never needed my forgiveness, you needed an apology from me for running away when I found out the truth. I'm sorry, Mom."

Gwen covered her face. Dale put an arm around her and squeezed, and Gwen leaned on her. Ari let go of Dale with one hand and put it on top of her mother's.

"Thank you, Ariadne."

"It was overdue."

Gwen sniffled. "Apologies or forgiveness notwithstanding, I don't think either of us regrets where your path has led, Ari. I am so proud to call you my daughter." She looked at Dale. "To call *both* of you daughter."

Dale smiled. She glanced at the clock and reached for the chips just to be doing something with her hands. "I think we should eat some of these chips while we still have time. Are you allowed to take food back to... b-back with you?"

Ari snatched up the barbeque chips. "Let's not find out."

Gwen smiled and composed herself. "So... tell us more about this new friend of yours."

Ari spent the entire meeting with a low-key sense of dread, an awareness of the clock ticking down the time she could spend with Dale and her mother. Still, when the guard announced it was time to say goodbye, it felt like a cruel and unexpected surprise. She stood up and hugged her mother, then turned and fought back tears as she pulled Dale into another crushing hug. She took a deep breath, trying to make up for her newly-limited olfactory ability to take in as much as possible. She turned her head and kissed Dale's hair.

"Take care of each other for me, okay?" Ari whispered against her ear.

Dale squeezed Ari's bicep. "If you'll keep yourself safe for me. I need you, puppy."

Ari nodded and kissed Dale. "Love you."

"Love you," Dale echoed.

They stepped away from each other because that would be a better memory than having Ari pulled away, and Dale turned to leave so she wouldn't have to watch as Ari was escorted out of the room by the guard. Ari's good mood, which had bloomed inside of her the second she saw Dale, withered just as quickly when she stepped over the threshold into the darker and colder corridor which led to the visitation room.

She was scheduled to immediately begin work in the library, which meant she had to miss breakfast. She didn't mind that too much; seeing her family was worth powering through until lunchtime.

There was a full row of books waiting on a cart when she arrived, so she pushed it into the stacks to begin shelving them. None of the returned books were alphabetized which gave her something to do while she got her emotions under control. She heard the library doors close but didn't give it much thought; there had to be a lot of traffic here throughout the day. She only looked up when someone joined her in the narrow aisle between the shelves.

Kunz.

Ari tensed and looked over her shoulder. Another inmate, one she'd seen sitting with Kunz in the cafeteria, was standing behind her to block the exit. She stood up straighter and squared her shoulders as she faced Kunz again. She was holding three hardback books and was prepared to use them as weapons if necessary.

"I don't want to fight you," Ari said, "but I'll defend myself if I have to."

Kunz advanced on her. "What you said yesterday. When we were fighting. Say it again."

Ari looked at the other inmate. "I said I'm a wolf."

"What does that have to do with you attacking me?" Kunz said.

"I needed to prevent myself from transforming. My girlfriend thought that a broken bone was the only way to do it, and I thought you were my best option for getting something broken." She quietly added, "At the moment I'm kind of hoping I was wrong..."

"And why did you tell me all of that?"

"Dr. Val told me you would understand. She also said I should tell you that I helped end wolf manoth a while back."

Kunz looked legitimately surprised by that. She blinked and shook her head like she was a robot trying to compute new information.

"Wait. *You're* the wolf who took down the hunters?"

"I, uh... I convinced them it was stupid to keep up the tradition and they backed down. Most of them, anyway." She didn't feel the need to share her father's involvement in the whole war.

Kunz moved so quickly Ari only had time to drop the books and bring up her hands in a futile attempt to protect her face. It turned out to be unnecessary, though, as Kunz merely grabbed her wrist, pulled her arm out, and closed her hand in a vice. It took Ari a moment to realize it was meant to be a handshake and not some weird pressurized torture.

"My sister was being hunted by those assholes. One day they just disappeared. They were all over Seattle like damn bedbugs, and then they all just went home. There were rumors about one wolf who walked into their fortress and told them to leave, but we just assumed that was a myth. Her name was like something from a myth, too. Uh... something weird."

"Ariadne."

"Right." Her grin widened. "Holy shit. You're a goddamn hero."

"You can call me Ari."

Kunz laughed and pumped Ari's hand again. "And you can call me whatever the hell you want. Every wolf in here owes you a huge debt. Hell, every wolf in the city."

Ari glanced back to see what the other inmate was doing. She looked star stuck. Ari smiled nervously.

"Always nice to meet a fan."

"You can meet more of us tonight when your shift ends. You know where the gym is?"

Ari nodded and Kunz smacked her on the arm. It hurt, but Ari didn't let it show.

"There aren't a whole hell of a lot of us in here, but the ones there are stick together. I feel a little extra responsible for you after giving you that shiner."

"I think you'll have to answer to my girlfriend for that," Ari said.

Kunz said, "Is she tough?"

"Scares the hell out of me."

"I'll steer clear." She pointed over Ari's shoulder. "That's Frankie Compton. You'll get to know her tonight."

Ari nodded to the other woman. "Nice to meet you."

Frankie said, "I was stuck in here when wolf manoth was kicking off. My mom, she's not doing too well, and my grandma was even worse. I was losing my mind trying to figure out how to keep them safe. I was thinking about breaking outta here to go protect them. Then I heard from some other wolves that it was all cool. Heat died down 'cause of some wolf named Willow and her daughter."

Ari smiled. "I'm glad Mom's getting some credit. It was mostly her, anyway."

"Well, no matter which of you it was, I'll stand by you."

"I appreciate it."

Kunz craned her neck to look at the clock on the wall. "We have to get to our work assignments. The gym. As soon as you have free time."

"I'll be there."

"See you then." Kunz let Frankie leave first, taking a moment to stare at Ari with something close to awe. She shook her head.

"Welcome to the kennel, Willow."

CHAPTER NINETEEN

ON MONDAY morning, Milo put on the nicest outfit she'd brought from England. Gwen, of course, made Milo change into something out of her closet once she saw it. The suit she'd chosen was a dark purple pantsuit with a black shirt. It wasn't something she would have bought for herself, but she had to admit she looked damn good in it. She even put on makeup and pinned her hair back. When she went downstairs, Paige and Benji both did doubletakes.

"Shut up, you knobs," Milo grunted before they could comment.

While Gwen and Dale were visiting Ari, Milo had her own mission. She took an Uber to the Patkanim Building. She'd expected it to be the same as their last visit, but apparently GG&M had taken the wolf invasion seriously. Two armed guards were posted at the elevator banks, and every person who came in had to stop at the front desk to receive a badge before going upstairs. Milo joined the line and waited patiently until it was her turn.

"Good morning, ma'am," the young man behind the counter said. "Where will you be visiting this morning?"

"Millicent Duncan," she said. "Gilles Garnier and Moreau."

He looked apologetically up at her. "Sorry, ma'am, GG&M requires us to call up and approve any visitors."

"That's fine. I don't have an appointment, but tell her that I was recommended to them by Bitches."

His finger hovered over the keypad. "You...?"

"Bitches," Milo said again, as professionally as she could muster. She smiled sweetly.

"Oh... uh." He frowned and pressed the button. "Hi, Tasha. I have a Millicent Duncan here. She-she said she was, uh, recommended by..." His voice dropped at least three notches in volume. "..bitches?" Another drop in volume. "Well, that's what she said, Tasha!"

Milo had to keep her smile professional, but inside she was howling with laughter.

There was a pause while he listened. Finally he hung up and scanned a blank ID card. "Wear this while you're in the building."

"Thank you," Milo said.

She clipped it on her jacket and moved to the elevators. The guard scanned the card, let her into the elevator, and pressed the button for her.

"Very secure," she told him.

"They're not taking any chances, ma'am."

The doors closed as Milo wondered when she went from "miss" to "ma'am." A lot of it had to do with the outfit, she knew, but it was still irritating to hear it twice in a row. She looked over her shoulder where she and the others had stripped down and transformed during the last visit to the building. She chuckled to herself.

"Good times," she whispered.

The doors opened to reveal Cecily Parrish flanked by two guards. Her arms were crossed over her chest. Despite the muscle, she didn't look particularly frightened.

Milo stepped off the elevator. "Morning," she said.

"Hello, Miss Duncan. Kindly extend your arms out to the side, please."

"Are you going to frisk me, Miss Parrish?" She did as she was asked. "Didn't know this visit was going to come with perks."

Cecily nodded to one of the guards, who stepped forward and wrapped his hand around Milo's wrist. He tugged hard enough to throw her off-balance, and Milo stumbled. He rubbed something against the skin of her forearm and she snatched her hand away from him just as the spot began to tingle. She scratched at it.

"What the hell, man?"

"Wolf," he reported.

Milo bared her teeth at him. "*Canidae*, and yeah, I was going to tell you that. Full disclosure, I was one of the wolves who paid you a visit last week, too."

Cecily raised an eyebrow. "And what brings you back today in your respectable clothes?"

"Maybe we could talk in your office."

"Here is fine."

Milo pursed her lips. "Fine. I spent the weekend thinking about this whole mess. I thought maybe there was a simple solution that would make all parties happy. You want to hire a wolf?" She gestured at herself. "I'm a wolf who might be in need of a job here in Seattle. I'm considering a move to the States and I could use a cushy, high-paying job like this."

"We were offering the job to a wolf who also happened to be a trained private investigator."

"First," Milo said, raising a finger, "I don't like the way you say wolf. It's *canidae* for you. Secondly, I'm a fast learner. I'll figure things out pretty quick. Question is, which aspect is more valuable to you? There's dozens of private eyes in the world, but none of them could learn how to be a *canidae*."

Cecily said, "You're Ariadne Willow's friend. Why would you betray her like this?"

"Betray nothing," Milo said. "I'm offering you exactly what you want, so you can back off on her. Get her out of jail, stop threatening her and the agency, everybody is happy. Of course, you'd have to give up the person who actually killed Shannon Hardy. But screw whoever that is, she's a murderer. She deserves to be in jail."

"The die has already been cast in that situation, I'm afraid," Cecily said. "Ariadne made her choice and we can't muddy the waters at this point."

Milo stepped forward and let her mask of humor fall. "You're going to ruin her life, not to mention Dale's life, out of pettiness? You're honestly going to let her spend years in prison just because she had the audacity to say no to you? Is your ego really that fragile?"

Cecily didn't blink. "Ariadne Willow is not the only pawn in this game, the game this firm has been playing for over a century. There are others who were told there would be consequences to their actions, who made the correct choice and now see proof that our threats were not hollow. She's serving as an example to those souls who are now convinced we do not bluff."

Milo looked past Cecily. She could see people in the office watching the exchange. "So who are they? Vampires? Zombies? I don't want to be racist, but that freckle-faced motherfucker right there is screaming leprechaun. Ay, boy-o, she after yer lucky charms?"

"Are you finished, Miss Duncan?"

Milo took a step forward. She locked eyes with Cecily again. "*Canidae* don't bluff either, Miss Parrish. You know all that stuff about alphas is bullshit, right? We don't operate like that. We'll defer to our elders and our strongest members, sure, but we're all equal. Until one of us is threatened. Then the entire pack rallies around her. And we go after the predator who so stupidly tried to take us on, and we sink our teeth in, and we don't let go until it's lying bloody on the grass behind us. That's what wolves do. So you take real good care, now. Think about which lesson you want your prisoners to learn."

She turned and jabbed the elevator call button with two fingers.

"What we're doing to Ariadne Willow is the termination of a dance. Our lives briefly became entwined, and this is simply how we unravel the knot. What we do to *you*, Miss Duncan? *That* will be simple spite."

Milo stepped into the elevator and faced Cecily again. She smiled and pressed the lobby button.

"I withdraw my application to work for you. I'll move to America, and my job will be taking your bony ass down. Have a nice day."

The elevator doors closed as she smiled and waved at them with her raised middle finger.

When Ari arrived at the gym, she found a familiar face running on the treadmill. Elise Gilpin, one of the women escorted into jail with her. Elise smiled and waved without breaking her stride. Ari scanned the room but didn't see anyone else.

"Gilpin, right?" Ari said. "Car theft?"

"Among other things. You're Willow. Murder."

"Alleged murder," Ari corrected.

"Right." Ari had no idea if Elise was there for the *canidae* meeting or just happened to be working out. She didn't know how to ask without being obvious. Flashback to being in a bar and trying to figure out if the blonde at the other end was flirting or commiserating. "So, uh... you... uh..."

Elise said, "I've only got a few more minutes if you need the machine."

"I'm... yeah, okay. I can wait. No rush."

Kunz came in, followed by Frankie and another inmate. The new woman was older, with long white hair and the wide-eyed stare of a crone in an animated fairy tale. Kunz saw Elise and hooked a finger over her shoulder.

"Out."

Ari said, "Wait, c'mon. She only has a few minutes left."

Elise was already punching in a command, her stride slowing. "Thanks, Willow, but I think I'd rather cut it short and head out." She stepped off the treadmill and retrieved her towel. She looked at Ari's bruises. "Come with me. We'll grab a bite to eat. Somewhere that isn't here."

"Appreciated," Ari said, "but Kunz and I are pals now."

Elise didn't look convinced, but she obviously didn't want to risk getting on the hulking woman's bad side. She stepped around Ari and quickly fled the room. The inmate Ari didn't recognize shut the door but remained close by so she could keep watch though the windows. Kunz walked to the butterfly press and sat down on the bench.

"You're going to want to spend as much time in here as possible if you want to keep those cheekbones. You aren't getting your normal workout running through the woods every couple of nights, you aren't burning through calories to transform, and the drug kicks your metabolism in the butt. Add all that up and you've got a recipe for a new spare tire."

"Thanks for the warning," Ari said.

"By the way, do you know Henning?" She pointed at the woman by the door.

Ari nodded a greeting. "Willow."

"I know who you are," Henning said, keeping her eye on the hall. "And I know what you did."

"Okay..."

Frankie said, "It can be tough in here even with the drug. Losing your wolf is going to take its toll on you the first time."

"The first time is a *bitch*," Kunz said, "no pun intended. It's like going cold turkey on the hardest drug you can imagine. You can go a couple of days thinking you've got it beat and then bam. Most of us can go a week or two without transforming and we barely even notice. But the third week, there's an itch. There's that itch of something that needs to be done. Like a bill you forgot to pay or you forgot to turn off the oven when you left for work. By the fourth week, even though the drug makes sure you *can't* transform, your body is going by its normal routine. It knows something is supposed to happen but hasn't. I figure that's how most ladies realize they're pregnant even before they miss their period. Our bodies know when something fucked-up is happening.

Ari said, "Am I going to have more fits in the middle of the night?"

"Nah, probably not. You can deal with it during your waking hours to help take the edge off. That's what we're here for. To help you. Exercise helps. It tricks our brains into thinking 'well, maybe I *did* go for a run today'."

"And drugs," Henning interjected. "Drugs help."

Kunz shrugged. "Yeah, if you want drugs, you can get drugs."

"I think I'll steer clear of the drugs."

"Smart," Kunz said. "Basically we're a support group. Like AA, but without the higher power stuff. We don't *want* to be 'sober,' but since we've got no choice, we might as well help each other out. We can't get official support from the prison because we can't tell them what we're abstaining from, so we meet up in secret whenever we can."

Henning said, "It helps us remember we're not alone, even if we're not with our pack."

Frankie said, "But we're looking for something more specific from you." She leaned forward, staring hard at Ari. "We've all been locked up in here, taking that drug, for years. So you'll have to remind us." Her expression wavered, just a little, and Ari could see the desperation behind her eyes. "What's it like to transform?"

"It's been so long, man," Kunz said wistfully. "Remind us what we're missing."

"Okay..." Ari sat on the bench press. "Uh, well. A lot of times it just happens. There's not a real urge or instinct, you just feel it creeping up on you. It used to hurt me a lot because... well, it's a really long story about that. But lately it just feels like sliding off a wetsuit. It's not that being human is uncomfortable and neither form feels more right than the other, but it just feels good to let the wolf out."

"Like taking off your bra at the end of a long day," Henning offered.

Ari smiled. "Yeah. That's how I describe it to my girlfriend."

Henning said, "Wouldn't she already know?"

"She's not *canidae.*"

Henning and Frankie looked at each other. Kunz furrowed her brow. "The wolf who stopped the hunters really was banging a human? I thought that was just a rumor."

Ari said, "No. And we're not 'banging.' We've been together for... wow, five years. We're in it for the long haul."

"But with a *human?*" Henning said. "I know people have their kinks, but damn."

"How could she possibly understand anything you're going through?"

Ari said, "She doesn't have to transform to understand. The pain I was talking about? She's the one who figured out how to make it go away. When I go for a run as the wolf and get too far away from home, she's the one dragging herself out of bed at two in the morning to give me a ride home. She used to give me massages after a bad transformation when my muscles hurt so badly I could barely stand up. I don't care that she's human or has never run in the woods as a wolf."

Kunz said, "I guess I can't judge. I've never had a relationship like that. Maybe I should start hooking up with humans."

Henning said, "Over my dead body."

Kunz blew her a kiss. Henning sneered and went back to keeping watch.

Ari said, "I don't think it's really sunk in yet. I'm not going to transform for at least six months. Even if my people outside figure something out and get the charges dropped, I've taken the drug. Is there any way to flush it out of my system?"

"Sorry," Kunz said.

"Right. And if my people *can't* fix this, then I might be in the same boat all of you are. I can't imagine forgetting what it's like to be the wolf."

"I'd start trying to picture it real hard, wild woman," Kunz said. "It's about to become your reality."

CHAPTER TWENTY

MONDAY NIGHT, Benji and Owen abandoned the pack in favor of a hotel. "It's not that we mind sleeping on the floor," Benji said, "it's just that we can't spend another day sharing two bathrooms with a half-dozen women." Gwen offered to take care of the bill but they waved her off. Once they were gone, Paige glanced at Mia and something unspoken passed between them. Mia decided she was the one who would speak.

"The boys running out of patience brings up an interesting point. Something we need to discuss now rather than later." She wet her lips to give herself a moment to ponder her next sentence. "At some point we need to go home. We have jobs, lives... we have three pack members who didn't come with us who are probably clawing at the walls to see us again."

Gwen said, "Of course."

"We don't want to just abandon you. We obviously don't want to turn tail when Ari still needs our help. But we should think of a cut-off point."

"That's only fair," Gwen said. "It would be reasonable that you could return home at the end of this week if we haven't made significant progress by then."

Mia nodded, looking relieved. "We absolutely want to do everything we can to help."

"You have your own lives," Dale said, finally chipping in. She'd been sitting at the wall between the living room and kitchen. "You dropped everything with no warning to be here when we needed you the most. Ari and I aren't going to ever forget that." She stood up and went to Mia, hugging her tightly. "Thank you."

"If you change your mind about my offer, just give me a call," Mia said, kissing the top of Dale's head. "Hannah and I owe it to you."

"You don't owe me anything," Dale said. "Slate's clean."

Milo came downstairs and paused when she saw the tableau in front of her. "What's going on?"

Gwen said, "We've decided that if we haven't made significant progress toward freeing Ari by the end of the week, you should all go back home. As much as we appreciate having you here for us, you shouldn't sacrifice your lives for us."

"Oh." Milo looked at Paige, and past her at Tarun and Hannah in the living room. "I was kind of planning to wait until later for this conversation. But... uh... when everyone goes home, I was thinking that I would... not."

Paige said, "What do you mean?"

Milo sighed heavily and looked at her feet. "I mean that more and more over the past few months, I've been wishing I was here instead of at home. I don't miss my apartment at all. I don't miss my job. Hell, my manager hinted that the job wouldn't be there when I come back because I don't have nearly enough vacation days for this trip. I didn't care. I had to be here because there's nowhere else I want to be." She glanced at Gwen and quickly averted her gaze before she could read anything in her expression. "I'll find a place to stay here in Seattle."

Gwen softly said, "I think I know of a place with some vacancies."

Dale said, "Oh, god. Ari's going to be begging to stay in jail when she hears about this."

Milo laughed and reached out to grab Dale's shoulder. "Or she'll break down the walls of the prison to run me out of the country."

Gwen smiled clearly relieved at having the matter settled but also giddy at Milo's revelation. "Well. Now that we've confirmed everyone's schedule, perhaps we can focus on getting Ariadne out of prison."

"I'm going to meet with Diana at lunch," Dale said. "She's

going to introduce me to Ari's lawyer. Want to come?"

Gwen nodded. "I like Diana very much. How is her wife?"

"Healthy. Responding well to the chemo."

Gwen nodded. "I'm glad to hear it." She checked her watch. "I'm going upstairs to freshen up."

She left the kitchen and headed for the bathroom. She was almost there when she heard Milo behind her on the stairs.

"Hey. Hold on." Gwen stopped. The upstairs was quiet, the doors standing open to reveal the various detritus of everyone who was camping out in the house. Milo caught up and leaned in close, her voice low because she knew everyone downstairs would be trying very hard to overhear. "I kind of dumped that in your lap without warning, right in front of everyone. I don't want you to think I consider it a done deal just because you were backed into a corner..."

Gwen put two fingers over Milo's mouth. "No corners, Milo. You are in not trapping me in any sense of the word. In fact, when you said that, I wondered if maybe I had forced you into making the announcement somehow. Like maybe you thought I expected some kind of commitment. I'm happy with the way things are. But if I could have you here all the time? Of course I want that. I want that so much that I'm feeling guilty. Ari's going through hell right now, and I have this whole awful situation to thank for finally getting you here."

Milo smiled. "Glad I wasn't alone in that thought."

"We'll both get absolution later." She kissed Milo. "For right now, I'm just very happy at a time when I expected to be distraught."

"Happy to help," Milo said. Gwen started to pull away, but Milo grabbed her hand. "You said you were going to freshen up. That mean shower...?"

Gwen said, "Yes. The boys weren't wrong about the bathroom being in high demand. There probably isn't any hot water yet, but I can't function until I've at least taken a quick shower."

"Maybe I can warm the water up for you."

"Millicent," Gwen said warningly.

Milo growled and pressed herself against Gwen. "Mm, you know what it does to me when you call me that."

"Who else can get away with it?" Gwen asked, well aware of the answer.

"Nobody, baby," Milo confirmed.

Gwen linked their fingers and pulled Milo toward the master bathroom. "C'mere. Come warm up my water."

Milo kicked the bedroom door shut behind them.

Dale drove to the restaurant Diana had chosen, pretending she hadn't overheard Gwen and Milo having shower sex when she went upstairs to retrieve her phone. There was only a fraction of awkwardness to the situation, completely outshined by how ridiculously happy Gwen was. Dale remembered the first time she met Ari's mother. She had been a cold woman, singularly-focused on her mission to destroy the hunters who threatened *canidae*. Dale had actually been frightened of her. Now, sitting at a stoplight, she looked over and caught Gwen staring out the window at a flower shop on the corner like a teenager planning for prom.

"Violets."

Gwen looked at her. "What?"

"I think Milo would like violets."

Gwen faced forward. "Green light."

Dale rolled through the intersection. "I'm just saying that if someone were to get her flowers, I think you would be good with violets."

"Thank you," Gwen said. After a moment she sighed heavily. "Am I being completely ridiculous? This girl is Ariadne's age!"

"So? You were young when you had her. You're, what, mid-fifties now?" Gwen didn't confirm or deny. "It's not that huge of a leap. The important thing is that you're both adults. You met her when she was in her late twenties, so it's not like you're a cradle robber. You're both obviously consenting. I think it's amazing you found each other."

Gwen looked out the window again.

"Of course," Dale said, "I'm the one dating a whole different species, so maybe no one should take my advice on what constitutes normal in a relationship."

Gwen laughed and then sighed. "No one makes me feel the way she does, Dale. And when she looks at me, I can tell she feels the same. It's not just her age. I never saw myself falling in love with a woman. I have no idea how I ended up in this situation."

"You ended up in this situation because you took a chance," Dale said. "Don't think your way out of enjoying the benefits, okay? Just love each other while you can. I could have freaked out that I was falling in love with a werewolf, run home to Pennsylvania, and got a normal job at my daddy's office. That would've been the safe thing to do. But I wouldn't be anywhere near as happy. When in doubt, go for happy. You deserve it more than most."

"Thank you, Dale."

"No problem."

The meeting was set up at Oliver's Lounge, a swanky bar inside the Mayflower Park Hotel. It was only a few blocks away from the shootout where Dale saved Hannah's life a few years earlier; she hoped that was a good omen. She found a place to park and let Gwen lead the way into the lobby. Ari was better at faking her way through the rich parts of town. She was born into wealth and, even though she turned her back on that life, part of her still understood how to interact with people who had the luxury of doing whatever the hell they wanted to do.

Diana and the lawyer were already seated. He was impeccably dressed, blonde hair left just long enough to appear expensively mussed. He was a small and wiry man in a three-piece suit but held himself with the bearing of someone who was seven feet tall with a hundred pounds of muscle under his jacket. He stood when he saw them approaching and extended one fine-boned hand.

"Mrs. Willow?"

"Miss Frye," Dale corrected. "And she's Miss Willow."

"Of course, my apologies. I'm Graham Cosgrove." He waited for them to take their seats before he sat down. "I have two questions before we begin. First, are you absolutely positive that the woman currently incarcerated for the murder of Shannon Hardy is innocent?"

Dale said, "I would stake my life on it. I've known Ari as a friend, an employer, and a lover, and there is no part of me that thinks she did this. I believe she is capable of murder under the right circumstances. But there was no reason for her to do it, or to lie about it once she was caught."

Graham nodded. "Second." His professional mask slipped a little, and he leaned forward with a sly grin on his face. "Did you really slap Cecily Parrish in the face?"

Dale looked at Diana, who looked at Gwen, who shrugged. "It was the best part of the story."

"Yes," Dale said. "She had it coming."

"You're damn right, she did," Graham said. "A wrongfully accused woman and a woman who lived the dream of two dozen attorneys in Washington state. I'm definitely taking this case pro bono just so I can tell the story for the rest of my career."

Gwen said, "We appreciate that, Mr. Cosgrove."

"Graham, please. And may I call you Gwyneth?"

"Gwen," she said.

"Dale."

He nodded to them both and tapped his phone. It was sitting on the table beside his empty plate, which seemed to remind him they were at a restaurant. He sat up straighter, scanned the area for a waiter, and motioned one over.

"Feel free to order something. It's on me."

Dale looked at the menu and almost threw it on the floor in terror when she saw the first page. Did they use gold-plated spinach for their dip? She finally settled on a bowl of soup. Graham ordered fish and chips "for the table." When the waiter was gone, he referred to his phone again.

"Now to business. I've gone over everything Detective Macallan here has given me on the case. It's thin, but in this case a lot of weight will be given to who is presenting the evidence to the jury. Walter Cronkite could have told people the moon was populated by lemurs and half of America would have taken it as gospel. Cecily Parrish can work wonders with the thinnest of circumstantial evidence. We have Miss Willow as a frequent guest of Shannon Hardy. Is there any way that's true?"

"No," Dale said. "Ari never saw Shannon outside of GG&M's offices. And any implication she was doing it in secret? We live together, work together, commute together. I don't know when she would have the time."

Graham said, "I want you to really think about this, Dale. There's no time period during the day where Ariadne could have slipped away to meet this woman without you knowing about it?"

Well, sure, Dale thought. *During any one of her night-long runs as the wolf.* Out loud, she said, "Ari goes on stakeouts, she investigates. We're not chained together at the ankle. But there are times when we might as well be. And you might think that, oh every spouse says the same thing. But trust me, I work for a private investigator. Seven times out of ten, the spouse knows and we're just being hired to confirm what they already know. Ari... she can't eat my yogurt without feeling guilty. She reaches out to touch me when she's asleep. She doesn't even have a favorite chair in our apartment because she wants to sit next to wherever I happen to be sitting, and if you think a woman like that is cheating on me..."

"Dale," Gwen said softly, her hand on Dale's shoulder.

She realized she had been ranting and on the verge of tears. She lowered her head to catch her breath. "I'm sorry."

"Don't be," Graham said. "I like that kind of passion. It gives weight to your denial that she was having an affair. This is good, it helps us."

Gwen said, "What about the doorman? Why would he claim to have seen Ari if she'd never even been to the building?"

"The fact he never saw Ari in person could actually have caused the confusion," Graham said. "If there is a tall brunette with an athletic build who *was* a frequent visitor to the building, then the officers showed him a picture of Ari, it's easy for the brain to combine the two. I'm confident I can throw out his identification of Ari when we're in court."

Diana said, "And speaking of reasonable doubt, we tracked down the car from the security camera."

"Really?" Dale perked up. "How?"

"We got lucky with a security camera outside of the park. Apparently the locals have a problem with coyotes coming into their backyards. And I looked closely. They actually *are* coyotes. Not... anything else." She looked at Dale and Gwen, then looked at Graham, who remained clueless. "So, uh, a few of them have cameras set up at night. I had some officers go through the tapes people were willing to offer us and we got lucky. The same car from the park's camera was spotted on Orcas Street, turning north onto Wilson. The camera was at the right angle to give us a license plate."

Dale held up crossed fingers. "And it's registered to GG&M?"

Diana smiled. "We didn't get quite that lucky. The car was reported stolen the night before Shannon Hardy was killed. It was found Sunday morning after being stripped for parts. Whoever was using it probably left it in the bad part of town and let car thieves do the rest. Any chance of fingerprints or residual evidence is long gone."

"So it was a dead end," Dale said.

"For now," Diana said, "but we have leads. At the very least we believe the car was involved with something suspicious that happened the same night as everything else. We'll keep digging on it and see what we can find."

Graham said, "In the meantime, I'll go over everything GG&M sends me now that I'm officially working for Ariadne. They'll probably try to bury me in discovery, but I'm prepared for that." He looked at Dale. "As much as I respect it and as fun as it probably was, I have to ask you to refrain from further violence against Cecily Parrish."

Dale smiled. "I'll try."

"If you surrender to the urge, film it and put it on YouTube." He winked. "For now, let's just relax and have a feast to prepare for the battle to come. The world may not pay much attention to what's going to happen in that courtroom, but for us, it'll be the trial of the century. We'll need our strength."

That night, after her shower, Dale lay in bed and tried to figure out what was bothering her. Graham Cosgrove seemed like a competent lawyer. He was charming and confident. She noticed that he'd given the waiter a one-hundred percent tip, which meant he was either a good human or compensating for the fact they hadn't eaten very much. Or maybe making up karma for being a lawyer. Either way, the waiter got paid. So it went in the "plus" column.

But something was gnawing at her. She couldn't get comfortable. The house was quiet and still enough that she could hear traffic on the street outside. She also heard sounds coming from Gwen's bedroom, but she'd been a guest in the house long enough to ignore them. She sighed and closed her eyes. The awkwardness of overhearing Gwen and Milo having sex might have been gone, but she and Ari had been apart for almost a week now and she was lonely. They'd never gone a week without having sex.

Maybe the prison had conjugal visits. Or maybe they'd get lucky and Graham would find a magic bullet that completely destroyed Cecily's whole plan. That would—

Her thoughts stopped dead as suddenly as if a radio had shut off. Under her breath she said, "Destroying Cecily's plan. Oh, god..."

She didn't bother putting a robe on over her pajamas - shorts and a T-shirt - as she burst out of her room and hurried down the hall. She smacked the flat of her palm against the master bedroom's door. "Gwen! Wake up. You have to wake up."

She heard a door open behind her. She looked back to see Hannah and Mia peering out of their room. Mia said, "What's wrong?"

"We made a mistake," Dale said. When she faced forward, Gwen was standing in the open door of her bedroom. She was wrapped in a sheet while Milo, behind her, had just finished shrugging on a T-shirt. Dale refused to acknowledge seeing that and focused on Gwen's worried expression. "We made a mistake," Dale said again.

Gwen said, "In what regard?"

"In Cecily Parrish's plan," Dale said. "We've been trying to find ways to prove Ari's innocence in court. Meeting with Graham at lunch today, having Diana look for that car. We've been trying to find a legal way to win this fight and clear Ariadne's name."

"Of course," Gwen said.

Dale's eyes were wide, frantic. She shook her head. "No, but... no. We *might* win that way. Maybe Graham is a super-lawyer who will find a magic bullet or, or there might be some little piece of evidence Cecily overlooked that might bury her."

Mia had stepped out into the hallway. The other bedroom doors were open now, and the hall around her was full of wolves in various states of undress.

Gwen put her hands on Dale's shoulders and spoke calmly. "Those are all reasons to be hopeful, Dale. We can still win this."

"No," Dale said. "That's my point! We could win that way, and Cecily won't allow that."

Mia sucked in a breath. "Oh, shit."

"What?" Hannah said. "What's going on, why is she freaking out?"

Dale said, "Because Cecily isn't going to take a chance we'll find a way to trick her in front of a judge. She's not going to endanger her career with a public humiliation like that."

Mia said, "She has no intention of this going to court."

"Right," Dale said. "She's going to have Ari killed in prison."

Gwen tensed. "No."

Mia said, "The alternative is risking exposure in court. On her home turf. If Ari says, under oath, what happened and it gets put into the public record... this Parrish woman won't allow that. And even if she got a conviction, do you really think she would let Ari rot away in prison looking for a way to get her revenge?"

Dale said, "Cecily told Milo that this was the termination of her relationship with Ari. She meant that literally. She never intended this to end with a guilty verdict, it always ended with Ari dead."

"Then why didn't she kill Ari instead of Shannon?" Paige asked.

"Because..." Dale didn't have an answer. "Because..."

Milo said, "Because this way, her reputation gets killed first and

Dale's life is ruined as collateral damage."

Paige growled under her breath and shook her head. "I really hate this woman."

"We have to warn Ari," Dale said.

Milo said, "The die is cast..." Everyone looked at her. "In Cecily's office, when I offered to take the job, she said the die was cast. She seemed to believe the matter was done. If she arranged to have Ari killed, then she's probably already got all the pieces in place. The person who is going to kill Ari is probably another prisoner, probably someone she's already crossed paths with."

Hannah said, "Okay, well, how do we find out who that is?"

Gwen's face was hard, an emotionless mask to prevent herself from breaking down as she said, "I'm afraid we can't. We can't even warn her until next Monday unless Ari chooses to call us." She looked at Dale. "For the time being, our girl is on her own."

CHAPTER TWENTY-ONE

ARI TRIED to remind herself that no matter how friendly her new prison acquaintances might be, they were all prisoners. Some might have been falsely accused but she couldn't assume they all had been. She knew Segura was a con artist, which meant she was most likely non-violent. She hadn't seen any evidence of a temper or any violent behavior from her. She was probably safe.

Kunz, Henning, and Frankie were a different story. Kunz had been arrested for assaulting someone in a drunken haze. When Ari asked her about it, Kunz worrisomely referred to the victim as "the one who was willing to press charges." Frankie was in for theft. She said that she "went about ten bucks over the limit and turned it into a Class B felony." She'd shrugged indifferently. "I've always been lucky like that." Henning was in for selling drugs and running a group of prostitutes. "They were tricking anyway," Henning said. "I just took over as new management so they'd have a boss they could trust."

Not exactly the most ideal group of new pals, but they were fine in a pinch. The first dinner after making friends with the "kennel club," Ari noticed everyone in the cafeteria watching her.

Segura explained once they sat down. "You got your face beat in by Kunz, and a couple of days later after round two, you're best buddies. Everyone thinks you've got some kind of Midas touch."

"Hopefully no one calls my bluff," Ari said.

"Mm. Also, you're friends with me. That earns you some brownie points, too."

Ari said, "Good to know."

After dinner, she had an hour to kill before lights out. She still wasn't entirely confident how far she could wander, so she cautiously moved down the hall while bracing for a guard to stop her at every step. When she arrived at the infirmary, she saw Dr. Byrne through the glass and knocked as she opened the door. Val looked up and then went back to the file she was writing in.

"If you're here for more pain meds, I'm cutting you back."

"No, I'm... I'm more or less fine on that. I was just wondering if it was okay for me to hang out in here for a while."

Val looked up again. "What's wrong?"

"Nothing." She sat on one of the beds. "I'm just trying to deal with the fact everyone I'm interacting with in here is a criminal. I'm a private investigator. My job is to put people in here, to make sure they pay for crimes. Now I'm relying on those people for my safety. Segura, for instance. She's a con artist. A month ago, I would have gladly gathered evidence on her to make sure she ended up in here. Now she's my friend. I just thought that it might be nice to spend a little time with someone who is a civilian and gets to go home at the end of the day."

"I get that," Val said. "Sure, you can hang out. But fair warning, I'm going home in about twenty minutes, so it can't be a long visit."

"That's fine," Ari said.

Val had gone back to her work, and Ari took the opportunity to look at the doctor. She wasn't wearing her lab coat, so she looked like a normal person. It made her the first person who actually looked like a civilian that Ari had seen since getting to prison. Her red turtleneck was tight in the right places, and when she turned to check something on another table, her skirt showed off just enough of her legs to make Ari's mind wander.

She snapped herself out of it and focused on the ceiling tiles instead. She was really starting to feel the separation from Dale. She hadn't gone this long without sex since they started dating. She was starting to get an undeniable itch.

"So why do you do this?" Ari said. "I'm getting sick of only seeing convicts, but you could probably be making big bucks out in the real world."

"Oh, that's where you're wrong," Val said. "This is where the real money is. Private practice has nothing on correctional work."

Ari said, "Really?"

"Yep. The state does what it needs to ensure it gets qualified physicians to work here. And it's not much different from working in a small town."

"You don't have a partner who gets worried that your job is dangerous?"

"Not anymore," Val muttered.

"Sorry."

"No, don't be. It was an epiphany moment. I wasn't going to let someone else decide what was right for me."

Ari smiled. "Sounds like something I went through recently. I was trying to make a decision that affected my girlfriend's job without consulting her."

"Yeah? How'd that go over?"

"Poorly. Of course, it ended up with me in prison, so I'm not sure there was a good path out of that situation."

Val walked over to stand next to Ari's bed. "I get a lot of people in here claiming they were set up. You, I actually believe."

"Because I seem like such a good person?"

"Because you seem like the sort of person who could piss someone off enough that they frame you for murder."

Ari opened her mouth to defend herself but realized she didn't have an argument. "I'm going to take that as a compliment."

"Most people wouldn't, but okay."

Ari sat up and got off the bed. "I'll stop bugging you now. I'll stop by tomorrow to get some more painkillers."

"How are you doing on that?"

"Good. I've dealt with pain for a while, so it's no big deal."

She was at the door, but Val began speaking almost as if to herself.

"You found those girls."

Ari looked back at her. "Excuse me?"

"Melody Scott and Jenna Morris. I Googled you last night and saw you were the one who brought them home. I remembered the disappearances when they happened, but I didn't remember the name of the person who saved them. I decided that if the person who did that was in prison for murder, she's either innocent or she had a good reason."

"I appreciate the benefit of the doubt."

Val said, "I'll see you tomorrow, Willow."

Ari waved goodbye to her and left.

Her cell was empty when she got back. She hadn't seen Vogel in the halls and had to assume the two illicit lovebirds were out looking for a new place for their alone time. She wished them luck and stretched out on her bed. So far prison was what she imagined college would be like. There were cliques, she had a dormmate, she had responsibilities she didn't ask for. Val was right about it being a small town. Now that she had the wolf under control she could focus on staying alive until trial. The worst part about that was being away from Dale.

"Worst part of prison? Boredom."

Ari opened her eyes and saw who had spoken: Elise Gilpin. She was leaning against the door to Ari's cell, smiling nervously.

"Sorry to disturb your nap. I saw you come in here and thought maybe we could hang out. My cellmate is kind of... terrifying? I've never seen her sleep, and I think she has bullet scars on her back."

"Come on in," Ari said. "I don't know where my cellmate is, but she won't mind if you sit on her bed for a while."

Elise came into the cell and sat down. "Cool, thanks." She smoothed her hands over the knees of her uniform. "I just can't get comfortable in here. I've never been good about strange places. Hotels and stuff like that. So this is kind of like the absolute worst case scenario for me."

"I was just thinking it was like college," Ari said.

"Did you go to college?"

"No."

Elise smiled. "So you mean it reminds you of the movie version of college."

Ari said, "Yeah, I suppose so."

"Nothing wrong with that." She started to pull her feet up on the mattress, then seemed to change her mind since it was someone else's bed. "So the story is starting to get around about you. Private investigator, wrongfully accused. Some people even claim to have read about you in the news."

"Missing Melody?" Ari said.

"No, Katherine Gavin. I used to read about her daughter all the time in the tabloids. I was glad to hear she'd actually managed to stay clean. People are saying you're the one who made sure people knew she was on the straight and narrow when she died."

Ari said, "Wow. Information travels fast in here."

Elise shrugged. "You jumped the boogieman for no reason.

That got people talking. A couple of people happened to recognize your name, so gossip spread like wildfire. I participated 'cause it kept them from focusing on me. So thank you for the camouflage."

"Happy to help."

"So is it true?"

"Depends on the story, I guess," Ari said. "Katherine Gavin, that was me. Missing Melody, yes."

Elise said, "The gist is that you're some kind of do-gooder who defends the little guy. You go after bad guys everyone else thinks are too big to take down."

"The underdogs," Ari said.

"Yeah."

Ari said, "I try. I've been the little guy. Hell, I think I still am the little guy. But I'm good at what I do, and I've gained enough success that I can work for the people who need help the most."

"I respect that."

Segura arrived at that moment. Ari looked past her to see she was being "escorted" by Vogel. Segura looked at Elise and pressed her hand against her chest.

"I leave for five minutes and you've already got a new roommate? I expected a little loyalty from you after everything we've been through."

Elise was already up off the bed. "Sorry about that. Willow and I came in at the same time, so I thought we should stick together a little."

Segura said, "I'm just teasing. Feel free to stay and chat."

Ari looked at Vogel and noticed the collar of her uniform blouse was flipped. She gestured to her own collar as casually as possible. Vogel reached up, felt what was wrong, and fixed it. She nodded her thanks to Ari.

"I should probably get back to my own cell before lights out. Right, officer?"

"Probably smart," Vogel said.

Ari was already getting accustomed to the rhythms and rituals of prison life, and that meant being in bed and bored for the next little while until she was actually able to sleep. She'd gotten a book from the prison library, even though part of her imagined only getting halfway through it before she was a free woman again. It would be a hassle to find another copy at the public library or buying a copy at an actual store. Even worse would be if she managed to finish the book while she was still in prison. That would *mean* something. It would mean she really was a prisoner and there was no quick fix to the situation.

She left the book where it was and settled her mind. For once, she was in a mess that she couldn't do anything to fix. She couldn't go out and beat down doors or question people. Her life was entirely in the hands of Dale and the British pack. The Brits had saved her ass once before, so she wasn't concerned about that. And Dale…? What wouldn't she trust Dale with? She had provoked a madwoman into kicking her ass on Dale's say-so. She'd let her mother bite her because of a plan that Dale came up with. There was no limit to how far she trusted Dale.

There was no way to know when exactly Dale went from her friend and employee to something more. She knew that love had turned to being *in* love well before they went to bed together. But as for the moment when she first looked at Dale and saw something more than just her best friend…?

She remembered an afternoon when they'd been working together for about three years. It was winter, and Dale called in sick. It was the first time since hiring her that Ari had been all on her own, and she realized not only how much it sucked, but how much she didn't want to do it if Dale hadn't been there. So she'd closed down the office at noon and went to Freshy's to get some soup. She didn't know when she began to fall asleep, when her memories morphed into dreams, but sometime before lights-out she was back in the building where Dale lived when they first met.

The door opened to reveal Dale, in two layers of sweats, holding a mask of Kleenex over the lower half of her face. At some point she'd tried to tame her hair with a Scrunchie, but now it had amassed on one side of her head like a living creature clinging to her skull. She was wearing her glasses, which she very rarely did in public.

"Don't come in."

Ari smiled and held up the to-go bag. "Chicken and rice!"

"I'm serious. Both our paychecks depend on you not getting sick. I can't infect you."

Ari brushed past her into the apartment. "The wolf is very resilient," she said. "Come on, you need to eat." She took the soup to the couch and kicked away some balled-up Kleenex. The TV was showing a muted sitcom on a syndicated channel. Ari sat down and opened the bag, taking out the two containers of soup. Dale shuffled over to join her. "I didn't know if you would feel like having crackers, so I got you crackers. You can just leave them in the bag if you're not up to it."

"Thank you," Dale said meekly. She dropped onto the couch and sniffed, coughed, and groaned. "It does smell good."

"You can smell it?"

"No. It just seemed like a nice thing to say."

Ari smiled. "Well, take my word for it, it does smell good." She looked at the TV. "Oh, I remember this one. Antonio is using that dog to pick up women even though he's allergic." She chuckled and shook her head. "Man, the nineties... sometimes I miss them. Hey, if you ever want to use the wolf to pick up chicks in the park, I'd happily be your wingwoman. Wingwolf. Wing... something." She looked and saw that Dale had slumped over, chin on her shoulder and arms wrapped around herself. "Aw, poor kid..."

She gently guided Dale down so she was more horizontal, then searched for a blanket to draw over her. Dale only began struggling when Ari tucked it around her shoulders.

"No, too hot..."

"Okay... okay." Ari left the blanket at Dale's waist. "Is that good?"

"Mm."

Ari smiled. She plucked some of the used Kleenex off the couch and moved them to a trash can. The stuffiness made her breathe oddly. She looked like she was dying. Ari reached out and used two fingers to brush a stray hair away from Dale's lips and then used the back of her hand to test Dale's temperature. Warm, but not dangerously so. She was probably going to be okay soon. Sitting on the couch, seeing her in pain and unable to do anything to help, made her realize just how deep her feelings ran. She touched Dale's cheek again and Dale shifted on the cushion.

"Am I drooling on the pillow?"

"No," Ari said, smiling.

"Good." She burrowed deeper into the back of the couch. "Thank you for taking care of me. You're a good puppy."

Ari laughed out loud. "No one calls me puppy."

"I do."

Ari began to argue, then decided she didn't care. She patted Dale's hand, which was still loosely clinging to one of her Kleenex. "Okay," she said, assuming Dale wouldn't remember it when she woke up. "You can call me puppy if you want to."

It was the first and last time Dale had used the pet name until they started dating. Ari couldn't remember her using it before that day, so maybe it really had been a turning point in their relationship. Whatever it was hadn't been clear in the moment. Ari just knew she had a swelling of affection for the woman who had dropped into her life and made everything easier and more fun, and helping her feel better in a time of need was the *least she could do.*

She moved Dale's feet, laying them across her lap, and retrieved the remote so she could unmute the rest of the TV show.

CHAPTER TWENTY-TWO

DALE WAS moving so quickly that she passed Diana in the police department lobby without seeing her. Diana stopped and called out her name, and Dale skidded to a stop to go back.

"What's wrong?" Diana asked.

"Someone's going to try and kill Ari in prison."

Diana said, "Come with me."

Dale explained her reasoning as she walked with Diana out to her car. "It could be another prisoner or a guard who has been paid off." She pushed her fingers into her hair and scratched, face twisted with worry. "How likely is this, Diana? Be honest with me. Am I just driving myself crazy here?"

They had arrived at Diana's car, and unlocking the door gave her a chance to think before she answered. "Prison is dangerous, obviously. And Cecily has a lot of influence even without the whole succubus thing you mentioned. But there have to be limits to her reach. No matter how powerful she or her firm might be, she can't just call up a murder in prison. That being said, I think we should at least warn Ari or the guards that something could happen. Just in case."

"That's all I ask. Thank you."

"Hey, don't run off. I didn't think the fingerprints on the car would go anywhere, but we actually got a lead. Two perfect prints on the driver's side door matched a guy named Hector Cook. He's got a string of charges... assault, domestic violence, breaking and entering, car theft - but there's one thing in common with them all: GG&M always gets the charges dismissed."

Dale said, "Why would they bother with him? Sounds like a common punk."

"And how does he afford them? His nonsense is well below their pay grade. So I figured it was worth a visit to see what he had to say. You're welcome to come along, but you have to stay in the car."

"Absolutely."

When they were on the road, Dale said, "Thank you for everything you're doing for this case. I know you probably have your own cases to deal with."

Diana said, "My lieutenant is giving me some leeway on this one since he agrees there's something hinky going on. He trusts my instincts."

"Does he know you and Ari used to date?"

"Uh..." She shrugged. "He knows we work together a lot. There's no need to tell him the whole sordid history of how we met."

Dale said, "Probably not."

She looked out the window. Their route to Hector Cook's home took them past downtown. Even though the "correctional facility" wasn't visible from where they were, Dale imagined she could feel it when they drove past. Part of her had always been aware of its presence, but now it was like a dark and ominous hole in the middle of the city she loved. Ari was there, she was locked away and out of reach, and that made it the most horrible place in the world.

"Ari is going to be okay," Diana said softly.

"I know." She faced forward and said it again, louder. "I know. She always is, right? She always gets out of whatever jam she gets into. But it just takes once, Diana. And if this is the one time she doesn't get out of it, then she's either in prison for the rest of her life or she gets killed in the next few days. Forgive me for worrying."

Diana drove in silence for almost a mile before she spoke. "Every time Lucy goes in for a treatment, I worry there will be some horrible discovery or the medicine will stop working. I go in every time bracing myself for a doctor to come out and tell me I should start preparing for the worst. She probably thinks the same thing every time I leave for work. I wish there was some easy answer or that it goes away, but it doesn't. It can't. Worry comes with the love."

"I wouldn't have it any other way," Dale said. "Logically, I mean. Physically, I could do without the butterflies in my stomach every time Ari's out of my sight."

"Side effects of love are so harsh. We should just dump them both and drive off into the sunset, Thelma and Louise style."

"Become nuns," Dale said.

"It would be so much less stressful."

Dale said, "Yeah. Less sex, though."

"Oh, god, you're right. Never mind."

Dale laughed. "Thanks for taking my mind off of it, though."

Diana said, "No problem."

Hector Cook's address directed them to an acupuncturist shop in the International District. Diana parked at the curb and double-checked her information. "One-A." She leaned forward to look at the building through the windshield. There was an open stairwell next to the shop entrance. "I guess that means apartments on the second floor. Stay here."

"I could be back-up."

"Stay in the car," Diana said again. She unfastened her seatbelt and got out of the car. As she crossed in front, a man came down the stairs. Dale had seen his picture when Diana checked the file and knew he was the guy, and Diana recognized him as well. "Hector Cook?"

He half-turned toward her. "What do you want?"

"I need to ask you a few questions about your lawyers."

Cook turned to face her fully. Dale didn't see the gun before it exploded at waist-level; it had barely cleared his belt before he pulled the trigger. Diana must have seen something suspicious because she was reaching for her weapon when she was hit. She rocked back on her heels and hit the car. Cook aimed better the second time, and Diana's body twitched as the second bullet hit her in the chest. She dropped out of sight below the end of the hood. The whole exchange took less than two seconds.

Dale was completely frozen. Cook noticed her and adjusted his aim. Every muscle in her body tensed as if it could turn to steel to stop the bullet. When a third gunshot sounded, Dale let out a scream and pressed back into the seat. But the windshield remained intact, something she only noticed when Cook collapsed inward on himself and fell onto the pavement.

Dale's hands were shaking worse than they ever had as she figured out how to open the car door and maneuvered herself out onto the sidewalk. Cook was lying a few yards away with blood darkening the back of his shirt. Dale somehow ended up on her hands and knees crawling forward until she could see around the front of the car. She saw Diana's shoes first, her legs spread out in front of her on the pavement. Then she saw Diana propped up against the front of the car, slumped to one side like a rag doll, breathing heavily with her phone pressed against her ear.

"Diana?"

"Get back in the car, Dale."

"You were shot!"

"Vest." Diana was watching Cook, making sure he was really down. She spoke the address into her phone while her other hand held the gun as steady as possible on the suspect. "Dale, get back in the fucking car right now."

Dale didn't think she would win an argument, so she got to her feet and returned to the car. Not that it would protect her if Cook jumped back to his feet and opened fire again. It was only a matter of seconds before she heard the sirens. Seconds later the first squad car came around the corner with its lights shining. Two more followed in quick succession, followed by an ambulance. Dale decided it was safe to get out of the car and went to Diana again.

"So," Diana said, "I guess he was involved." Her voice was shaking and her face had become deathly pale. She tried a smile but it didn't last long.

"I'm so sorry," Dale said.

Diana shook her head. "Don't. Don't do that, don't take the blame. Just doing my job." She swallowed hard. "I need you to--"

"I will."

"In person. One of the officers will take you back to your car. *Do not* pull up to my house in a squad car, Dale."

Dale nodded. "I'll go right now." She kissed Diana's cheek and moved back so the EMTs could take position around her. Dale pushed her hair out of her face and looked around for someone in a uniform. She chose one man at random and ran to him. "I need a ride. I need to tell Detective Macallan's wife that she's okay."

He nodded and motioned for her to follow him. "Come with me."

Dale cast a final look back at the scene, then followed him to his car.

Lucy was a comic book artist and worked out of their home. Dale parked in front of the house, silently congratulating herself for being able to drive when she felt like she was about to throw up every thirty seconds. She kept hearing the gunshot, seeing Diana fall, and worried she'd only imagined the good outcome. Her hands were still shaking. She realized she should have called Gwen and Milo with an update, but it was too late now. She needed to tell Lucy before the news got out some other way.

She had to knock twice before Lucy answered. "Dale! Sorry, I was in my studio and had the music blasting..." Her smile fell. "What's wrong? Is it Ariadne? I can call Diana..."

Dale said, "Diana's fine. She was wearing her vest."

The color drained from Lucy's face. She reached out and put her hand on Dale's shoulder, her fingers tightening until Dale was certain she would draw blood. She didn't care.

"What happened?"

"She was shot. Twice. In the chest. But she was wearing her vest. She's fine."

"You're *positive?*"

"I was there," Dale said. "I saw it all happen. She's hurt, but she's... it's not... she was conscious and she told me to come tell you in person."

Lucy had started to silently cry. She loosened her grip on Dale's shoulder. "I'll get my keys. Come in. Tell me everything while I'm figuring out where they took her."

Dale allowed herself to be ushered into the house. As awful as it sounded, she was grateful to deal with someone else's trauma for a little while. The truly attractive thing about it was that this story, no matter how scary it might be to tell or hear, had a definitely happy ending. That gave her hope that Ari's situation would have an equally happy conclusion.

It didn't hurt to hope, anyway.

Ari's morning was filled with more routine. Wake up. Get counted. Breakfast. Go to work. She felt like an extra in a dystopian movie about conformity. It was easy to see why some of the inmates who had been incarcerated for years had such a defeated look in their eyes. She didn't mind working in the library. There were far worse assignments she could have gotten, and Gladys was a great companion. But finding things to appreciate in her situation didn't equal enjoyment or anything close to happiness. She wanted a boring day at the office. She wanted to sit in a hot car for the chance to take a picture of a cheater leaving a house they weren't supposed to be visiting. She wanted her perfect life, with all its imperfections.

At a quarter past ten, halfway between the start of work and lunch, Ari decided it was time to take a break. She headed out, passing by Gladys' office on the way.

"Bathroom."

"Why don't you go in the morning like a normal person?"

"Shy bladder."

Gladys said, "You're gonna have to get over that real quick, honey."

Ari hoped that wasn't true, but said, "I'm working on it."

She went to the bathroom that was closest to their cellblock, since it was the one furthest from most work areas and therefore likely to be less occupied. She was fortunate enough to find a stall with an actual closing door and took advantage of it. When she finished, she turned around and used her foot to press the plunger so it could flush. She wondered why prisons hadn't taken advantage of automated toilets and faucets. Less water usage would probably look good on their budgets. Then again, a lack of funds was probably the reason they couldn't~

Something dropped over her head and settled around her neck. When she looked down and was bringing her hand up to see what it was, it tightened and jerked her back until she slammed into the stall door. The loop of cloth around her neck pulled even tighter and she was lifted off her feet, her shoulders sliding up the metal until they were almost at the top of the door. She grabbed at the noose and kicked her heels against the door.

Her instinct was to surrender to the wolf. But the wolf was gone, which threw her into a panic. The door opened inward, which meant the hinges were working in her attacker's favor. She couldn't get her fingers beneath the noose. She reached back and slapped her fingers against the knot, hoping she could loosen it enough to let her weight pull her free, but it was too tight. Her lips parted in a futile gasp for air.

She could guess exactly how it was going to end. Once she stopped fighting, she would be dragged to her cell and strung up from a convenient high point. Cecily Parrish would probably push the story that she'd killed herself out of guilt. The case would be closed and that would be the end of her story. After everything she'd survived, she was going to die in a toilet stall.

The hell I am.

Whoever was hanging her had to be using her own weight as an anchor. That meant they were just as vulnerable as she was. She just needed to get better leverage, and take the pressure off her throat. She twisted so she was facing the door, the noose burning her neck as she moved. She planted her feet against the door and shoved backward as hard as she could. The pressure immediately let up, and the person on the other side was knocked off balance. She hit the door hard enough to shake the entire stall, and the sheet slithered over onto Ari's side like a long white snake.

Ari's freedom meant that she fell hard, bouncing off the edge of the toilet and fortunately falling onto the ground beside it instead of into it. The unfortunate part was that it took her a precious few seconds to extricate herself from the awkward position, coughing hard enough that her chest hurt. While she was down, she caught a glimpse of her attacker's feet in a pair of blue slip-on shoes as she fled.

Still coughing, Ari burst out of the stall and ran out of the bathroom. The corridor was empty. She saw a few prisoners at the far end of the hallway, but neither of them seemed to be paying attention to her. A quick glance down revealed they were both wearing white shoes. Ari tugged at the noose until she was able to pull it over her head. It dangled from her fingers as she coughed, her heart still racing and her breathing irregular.

"Okay, Cecily," she said, her voice rough. "You want to play, we can play."

CHAPTER TWENTY-THREE

DALE EXPLAINED to Lucy what happened on their way to the hospital. The lieutenant Lucy got on the phone assured them both that Diana was just being examined as a precaution. Both bullets hit her vest, leaving her bruised but completely intact. Lucy let that news calm her nerves but she refused to completely relax until she saw Diana with her own eyes to confirm she was in one piece. Dale also learned that Hector Cook also survived the shooting, unsurprising since Diana had taken care to ensure his wounds weren't life-threatening but still enough to eliminate him as a threat.

Dale stayed behind in the waiting room to give them privacy for their reunion. That was where Gwen found her, swooping in to gather her into a hug before Dale had even realized she was there.

"Oh. Hey."

"Are you all right?" Gwen asked as she took the seat next to her. "I can't imagine how terrified you must have been."

Dale said, "I'm... I was, at first, but then I had to tell Lucy. I had to take care of Lucy. So I haven't really had a chance to process all of it."

Gwen took Dale's hand in both of hers. "Take as much time as you need."

"I just feel like this is the end. This is already the end, and we've barely even started."

"What do you mean?"

"Well, after this, we don't have Diana working the case on the official side. And in a few days, Milo's pack is going back to their real lives. We had all these people backing us up and we didn't even make a dent, and Cecily Parrish is still going strong. Do we even really stand a chance against her?"

Gwen said, "Of course we do, Dale. We have the lawyer Diana found for us."

"He won't do us any good if Ari doesn't survive to see a courtroom. This Hector Cook guy felt like a lead, but tracking him down just cost us one of our strongest allies. We didn't even learn anything from him in return. And right now, Ari is probably in immense danger, and we aren't able to warn her or do anything at all to protect her. It just feels hopeless."

"That doesn't sound like the Dale Frye I've come to know."

Dale closed her eyes. "That Dale is very tired, Mom."

Gwen raised an eyebrow at that, but didn't say anything. Either it was a mistake or it wasn't, and at the moment it didn't matter which. She guided Dale's head to her shoulder and stroked her hair.

"We are losing some of our allies," Gwen admitted, "and I'm scared. I might be more scared than I've ever been. But one thing I'm sure of, and it's something Ariadne knows with all her heart: you and I are never going to stop fighting for her."

Dale smiled. "That does make me feel a little better."

"Good."

Dale closed her eyes and let Gwen stroke her hair. It wouldn't solve any problems, but it was doing wonders for her anxiety. She didn't like to think about what her life would be like without Ari in it, didn't want to think about how she was starting to get used to waking up in an empty bed, so instead she focused on memories. She thought about a day not long after they started working together. It was a few months into her tenure, and Ari was out on a case.

Ari announced her return by pawing at the door. She did it softly so her claws wouldn't leave permanent scratches on the wood, but Dale was already attuned to the sound. She got up, let Ari in, and shut the door behind. Ari's fur was wet with mud, so Dale followed Ari into the inner office to get a towel for her. Ari stopped in front of the couch, hunched her back, and began to transform.

"Wait, I'm still in the~"

It was too late. Dale cringed at the first sound of bones snapping. She tried so hard to be out of the room when Ari changed. Muscles pulled her shoulders back, broadening her torso, as her legs snapped and extended. Her shoulders popped and repositioned themselves, her feet and hands became flatter, and her hips shifted back to where they should have been. The dark brown fur that covered her body withdrew and exposed a pale grey pelt that faded into slightly tanned flesh.

A naked human woman now crouched on the floor in front of the couch. She was shuddering, so Dale overcame her revulsion at the process to drape the towel over her. She was close enough to see how tightly Ari's eyes were squeezed shut, and to see the tremors still running through her body. She was sweating and making an almost inaudible mewling sound.

"Are you okay?"

Ari's shoulders were hunched up by her ears. "I'll b-be f-f-fine. Hurts."

"You said it always hurts."

"Bad day," Ari said, baring her teeth and hugging herself against a new wave of pain.

"Is there anything I can do?"

Ari shook her head and slumped against the couch. "No. It passes."

Dale said, "Really? Because you look like you're in a lot of pain. Let me get you an aspirin or ice pack? I could give you a massage..."

The reaction was minor but still noticeable. "That's n-not in your job description."

"What? A massage? If you think it will help, I'm willing."

Ari closed her eyes and shook her head. "No, it's f-fine."

"Get on the couch."

"I-"

"On the couch, Ariadne!"

Ari started to straighten her back, but she cried out and fell against the cushions. Dale ignored her boss' nudity and helped her get up onto the cushions. Ari groaned as she settled onto the soft cushions, her arms by her sides. Dale stood up and took a moment to debate the best logistical position for her. Nice ass, Miss Willow, she thought, then mentally slapped herself. Your friend needs help, Dale Elizabeth. Focus.

She straddled Ari's waist. Her hands hovered briefly above Ari's shoulders before she dropped them to the clammy skin. She applied pressure with her thumbs while she gently squeezed the muscles leading to Ari's neck. The tension was unbelievable at first, almost as if Ari had been frozen solid, but after a few seconds she could feel it begin to release. Ari sighed loudly and pressed her forehead against the arm of the couch.

"God, that feels amazing."

Dale moved her thumbs in wide circles on either side of Ari's spine. As *she worked her way south, she could feel Ari becoming more relaxed.*

"Okay?" Dale asked.

"Amazing," Ari said again. She managed to bring her arms up and used them to pillow her head. "How much do I have to bump your pay to make this a regular thing?"

Dale smiled. "Well, I'm not opposed to a raise. But if it helps, I'm happy to do it. Do all canidae have someone to do this for them?"

"I'm not like other wolves," Ari said.

"Is that like the bullshit 'not like other girls' thing?"

"No," Ari said. "It means I'm wrong. Broken."

Dale's smile faded. "Oh. I'm sorry."

"Don't be. It's okay. Just keep going, please."

"Sure."

Dale opened her eyes and sat up. Gwen looked at her. "Hi there."

"Did I fall asleep?" She wiped her hand over her eyes.

"For a little bit. I figured you needed it."

Dale stretched and stood up. "Stay here."

"Where are you going?"

"I'm channeling my inner Ari. I'll be right back."

She walked toward the elevators. She moved with purpose, as if she knew exactly where she wanted to be, and hoped that confidence kept anyone from asking what she was up to. She could see the waiting area from the second floor landing and waved to Gwen, who looked concerned. Dale hoped that concern was unfounded but given that she had no real plan, it was probably was.

It didn't take her long to find Hector Cook's room. A uniformed officer was stationed by the door. He looked up when he noticed Dale was walking toward him and locked his gaze on her.

"Sorry, ma'am, you can't go in."

She looked up at him; he was a good six inches taller than her. "Officer Sheehan, I was going to trick you. Maybe steal a set of scrubs, tell a lie to make you abandon your post, maybe get you in trouble with the boss, but I don't want to do that. I just want to go in there and talk to the motherfucker who shot our friend. Do you know Diana?"

He said, "Not personally." After a moment, his steely exterior cracked and he added, "I know her reputation, though. She's a good cop."

"Yeah, she is. I watched the asshole in this room shoot her today. I didn't know she was wearing her vest. I know her *wife*, man.

I had to tell Lucy that this guy shot Diana today. All I want to do is go in the room for five minutes and ask the questions Diana was going to ask him at his apartment. I don't want her to have been shot for nothing."

He continued staring forward. Dale tried to think of a new tactic before she noticed his posture relax slightly.

"Ma'am, did you threaten to steal scrubs?"

"I... I didn't..."

"Ma'am, that's a serious security threat. I have to inform hospital security."

Sheehan half-turned and put a hand to his radio, but he didn't say anything into it. Dale brushed past him and stepped into Hector's room. He was propped up in bed, his chest looking oddly puffed-up by bandages. He was paler than he'd been in the street, but he was conscious. He opened his eyes but didn't turn his head when she came into the room.

"You're not a nurse."

"No."

He lifted his head slightly. "Hey, wait. I saw you. You're the bitch in the car."

Dale said, "I'm the bitch you were trying to kill when Detective Macallan saved you from becoming a murderer."

His smile was lopsided. "Lady, I've killed people before."

"Bully for you," Dale said. "The point is, you aimed a gun at me and it didn't work out well. You lost. So now you're going to answer my questions."

"Why?"

"Because that's the way this works, asshole!" Dale snapped. "You're a nobody hoodlum who has one of the most expensive firms in Seattle bailing him out of prison. Why? What does GG&M get out of helping save your ass?"

He glared at her without speaking. Dale pushed down her anger and tried to think rationally. She tried to look at it as a puzzle Ari had given her. *Babe, I'm having trouble with this case. Can I run the facts by you real quick?* She walked to the foot of his bed and rested her hands on the metal frame. She returned his stare. He was a car thief. A common criminal. And yet, whenever he was in trouble, GG&M and Cecily Parrish came to his rescue. What was their interest in him?

"Are you special?" she asked.

His lip curled in a sneer. "Come closer, baby, I'll show you how

I'm special."

Dale grimaced at him. He didn't have the right build to be a wolf. He might have been a different breed of shifter, but she doubted it. What could he possibly have to offer the firm that would justify the expense they'd wasted on him? It came to her in a flash.

"It was for this," she said.

"What?"

"You're their redshirt." She stood up straighter. "They kept you out of jail all these years and let you run wild because you made a deal with them that you'd take the fall later. This is just the bill coming due. Let me guess, you're going to ask for a deal with the cops. You were just the getaway driver, but you can give them the name of the killer."

He smiled. "Ariadne Willow."

Dale wanted to murder him. She was legitimately, unapologetically homicidal in that moment. She was grateful she didn't have any weapons on her.

"Just between you and me, I never met the broad," Hector said. "But my baby and his mama are going to be set for life, so I figure it's a fair trade. I was gonna end up in jail anyway eventually. At least this way, my people get something out of it. They get a chance at a better life."

"An innocent woman died, and another innocent woman is going to jail for it. How many people's lives are you willing to ruin for a lie?"

"We look out for our own," Hector said. "That's what you're doing, right? Who is this Willow chick to you? Sister? Boss? Doesn't matter, don't care. All I care about is the deal I made, and the money that's going to get my girl into a good neighborhood with a good school. That's what I'm concerned about."

"Congratulations," Dale said, her voice emotionless. "I hope it's a fucking fantastic school with great teachers, because god knows she's not going to have a father worth looking up to."

She turned and went to the door.

"Hey."

She looked back at him, and he aimed a finger-gun at her.

"I shouldn't have wasted my second bullet on that cop. Should've blown your fucking head off. That might have been worth getting shot for."

Dale left the room before he could see her shudder.

CHAPTER TWENTY-FOUR

THERE WERE at least seven women in the cellblock wearing blue shoes, and none of them seemed particularly out of breath. Her attacker also had thin legs, which helped narrow it down but not enough for her to name any suspects. She bypassed the library and went directly to the infirmary. Val was in her office, a small windowless closet next to the treatment room.

"Someone just tried to kill me."

Val looked up, her eyes immediately locking onto Ari's bruised throat. "Shit." She pushed back her chair and pointed over Ari's shoulder. "Bed. Now."

Ari led the way, rubbing her neck as she sat down. Val paused to put on gloves before she began examining the injured area. Her brow was knit together in concern as she gently probed.

"What happened?"

"Someone made a noose out of some sheets." She cleared her throat; it felt raw. "Caught me like a fish while I was in the bathroom. Strung me up. Tried to hang me using the stall door."

"Kunz?"

"I don't think so. She's my number one fan now."

Val said, "Okay, look here." She used a penlight to test Ari's pupils. "Was there any loss of consciousness?" Ari shook her head. "You said you were strung up. Did you drop?"

"No."

"How long were you hanging?"

Ari tried to remember. It felt like minutes, but she knew that couldn't be accurate. "Probably only a couple of seconds. No one else came into the bathroom during the whole thing."

"That bodes well," Val said. "Of course, if someone had come in and seen who your attacker was, it might have been helpful."

"Yeah. All I saw were her shoes. They were blue. Why does the prison allow two different colors of shoes? Isn't there... I don't know, gang affiliations to worry about?"

Val said, "Mm, there are only two colors. Blue and white. They're handed out at random, and people aren't allowed to request a specific color when they get new ones. It's not really worth it to use them as a symbol."

Ari grunted. "That's too bad. I was hoping I could narrow down the suspect pool."

"You've really pissed off enough people that you don't know who did this? Also, you've already spent more time in the infirmary than some women who have been in here for years. Kudos for that."

"What can I say, I have a punchable personality."

Val smirked. "I've known some people like that. I could have you stick around here for observation, but I don't think you would take too kindly to that."

"I don't have to stay?"

"You don't *have* to..."

Ari slipped off the bed. "I need to figure out who is trying to kill me before she takes another shot." She took a step toward the door before she stopped. "Wait, you get to leave at the end of the day."

Val held up her hands. "Whatever you're going to ask, the answer is no. I don't do errands for prisoners, Miss Willow."

"This is a special circumstance."

"They all are!"

Ari said, "I was framed by the same woman who is going to prosecute me. And I'm pretty sure she's behind the attack, to make sure I never actually see the courtroom. Some serious shit is going on here. I have good people working to unravel everything on the outside, but they can't do it alone. And I'm completely blind. I need to know what they're doing. I'm not asking you to smuggle drugs or do anything illegal. I just need you to talk to them."

Val sighed and put her hands on her hips. "Ariadne, I really wish I could help you..."

Ari's shoulders slumped. "I understand. It was worth a shot, anyway."

When she reached the door, Val said, "Those little girls..." Ari looked back at her. Val was looking at the table. "Where did you find them?"

"Melody and Jenna? The guy who took them had them locked up in his study."

"He was going to kill them."

It wasn't a question, so Ari didn't answer it.

"You saved them," Val said.

"Yeah."

Val rolled her head and stared at the ceiling in surrender. "Damn it. Okay, fine. What do you need me to do?"

Dale and Gwen were finally allowed to visit Diana, although they were warned to keep it brief. Dale had to hold back tears as she very, very carefully gave Diana the tightest hug that wouldn't hurt her.

"Thank you," she whispered, kissing the salt-and-pepper hair above Diana's ear.

"I would do it again in a heartbeat. I'm just glad you're okay."

Dale looked guiltily at Lucy, who squeezed her hand. "I married a cop. I know stupid dangerous stuff comes with the territory. I'm fine with it."

"No, you're not," Diana said with a smile.

"No, I'm not," Lucy admitted. "But I'm not going to change the woman I love." She stroked Diana's hair away from her face and smiled down at her. "I'll just keep nagging her about always wearing her vest."

Diana looked down at her chest. "Yeah, I don't think you're going to have to nag very hard after today, sweetheart."

Dale kissed them both on the cheek and made Diana promise to take it easy. "We'll take care of it from here on."

"But if you need anything--"

"You'll be our last resort."

When they got back to Gwen's house, Dale opened her laptop and added everything she knew about Hector Cook to the file she had built. GG&M kept him on their payroll for years just so they could use him for something like this. He was a sacrifice in a game they hadn't even known they would be playing. How many other people like Cook were being paid by the firm? Dale looked up their history and found multiple occasions where lawyers - usually not Cecily Parrish - provided pro bono representation to small-time career thieves. Break-ins, car theft, vandalism... she counted at least four different defendants who were kept out of prison by GG&M.

Milo leaned over the back of her chair and examined the screen. "Are you... is it legal for you to be in these records?"

"Let's say it is."

Milo kissed the top of Dale's head. "I love you, girl."

Dale made a note of each name on the list and did searches for their current whereabouts. A year ago, Scott Riddy had been sentenced to twenty years for kidnapping and murder. Five years before that, a man named Henry Gordon pled guilty to another murder. Dale made notes of the victims in each case. It seemed like GG&M had a bad habit of collecting bodies.

She had lost track of time when the doorbell rang. She snapped out of her investigative tunnel vision to realize Hannah and Mia were cooking dinner. Gwen touched Dale's shoulder as she passed on her way to answer the door. She peered through the window before she undid the lock.

"May I help you?"

"Wow. I was going to ask to speak with Ariadne Willow's mother, but I don't think I have to. Gwen, right?"

"Yes?"

Dale had gotten up and approached the door. The brunette at the door looked nervous, tugging at the sleeves of her red jacket as she introduced herself.

"My name is Valerie Byrne. I'm a doctor at King County Correctional."

Dale was now at Gwen's shoulder. Without looking, Gwen reached out and touched Dale's hand. "Should you be here right now?" Gwen asked.

Valerie laughed without humor. "No, definitely not. But it's special circumstances."

"Is Ari okay?" Dale asked.

Valerie looked at her. "You must be Dale. Ari is okay. But she was... there was an incident this morning."

Dale squeezed Gwen's hand.

"She's relatively fine. But someone tried to hang her in the bathroom."

"*Hang* her?" Gwen said.

"Damn it," Dale said. "I knew it. I fucking knew it."

Valerie linked her fingers together, head hung almost sheepishly.

Gwen said, "Oh, come in. Please."

"Thank you." Valerie came inside and looked toward the kitchen, acknowledging the women there before she drifted into the living room. Gwen closed the door and joined her. Valerie took a seat while Gwen and Dale remained standing. "Ari told me about what she believes is happening. That she's been framed, and the person behind it is trying to tie up the loose ends."

"And you believe her?"

Valerie shrugged. "I saw the bruises on her throat myself. Prisoners don't generally get attacked like that in their first week." She put her hands in her jacket pockets and then seemed to remember something. "Oh, *canidae*. I know about the *canidae*. I'm the one who... I gave Ariadne a drug that can halt her transformations."

Dale walked across the room and hugged Valerie. She didn't think about it, she just felt it was something that needed to be done.

"Thank you."

"Sure. I'm... there are other *canidae* who are in the same situation." She looked into the kitchen again. "Ari told me she didn't have a pack."

Dale stepped back from the hug. "These are friends. They're from England."

Gwen said, "You're not *canidae*?"

"No. It's a long story." She cleared her throat. "Ari wants to coordinate. She needs to know what you know, and vice versa."

Dale said, "Well, I just found out GG&M has a stable of criminals they use to cover up their own crimes. It seems reasonable they have someone who was willing to turn herself in the same day Ari went to prison. Then she just waits for a signal."

Gwen said, "Dale, you were listing the people who were likely to be GG&M's sacrificial lambs. Were any of them women?"

"Not that I'd found yet. But who knows how many there are that I just haven't uncovered?"

Valerie said, "I want to help as much as I can. If someone really is plotting to kill a prisoner, it's worth a little risk to keep everyone informed."

Dale said, "How is she doing?"

Valerie looked at her. "Outside of a bad habit of making people hit her..."

Dale laughed. "Yeah, that's my puppy."

"She's doing well," Valerie said gently. "She misses you like crazy."

Milo came downstairs, slowing when she saw the stranger. "Who's this?"

Gwen said, "Dr. Valerie Byrne, this is Milo Duncan. Milo, Valerie is the doctor at the prison."

"Ariadne?" Milo said.

"Someone tried to kill her this morning." Dale managed to keep her voice even and emotionless.

Milo's posture straightened, her shoulders squaring as her eyes darkened. She took a deep breath and let it out so slowly she seemed to be deflating. She went into the kitchen and placed her hands flat on the counter. She stared at Mia until their eyes met, and then she held her gaze.

"Go home. Tonight."

Mia furrowed her brow. "We're..."

"Go home. Take the rest of the pack with you. Be on a plane in the next few hours."

Hannah said, "Milo..."

"Milo," Gwen said, "what are you doing?"

Milo walked to Gwen and cupped her face with both hands. "I'm doing what should've been done the night Ari was arrested. I'm not blaming you for not doing it, babe. We didn't know how far this would go. But the hag tried to kill Ari, Dale, and Detective Macallan all since this morning. Who knows what the hell she's going to do tomorrow if we don't stop her?"

Gwen gripped Milo's wrist. Dale was startled to see how hard the grip was; Milo seemed to be in sincere pain.

"Don't," Gwen said.

Milo didn't flinch, but she pressed her lips together. "You're hurting me."

"I'll chain you up in the basement if it'll stop you from doing something stupid." Her eyes were watering. "I can't lose you, Millicent."

"Let go of my hand, Gwyneth."

Dale stepped closer. "Mom, let her go."

Gwen closed her eyes in defeat. "Damn it..." She released her grip, but maintained the touch, drawing Milo's hand to her lips. She softly kissed the red skin where she'd been squeezing. "I'm sorry."

Milo kissed Gwen's forehead. "It's been a rough week. You'll make it up to me when it's all over."

"Will I?" Gwen asked. "Will you be around?"

"I swear."

"It might not be up to you if you go running into the fire right now."

"What would Ariadne be doing right now if it was any one of us in her situation?"

A tear rolled down Gwen's cheek. "That's not fair."

"That's exactly right." Milo kissed her, then pulled her into a hug. "I love you."

"I love you. So much."

They stayed like that for a long moment before Milo stepped back. She looked at Mia and Hannah. "Get the others, go to the airport, change your flights. Be in the air as soon as you can. I don't want any of you getting in trouble if this goes sideways. You were already planning to go home, so we just have to move up the timeline a bit to make the alibis work."

"We can't leave you, Milo," Hannah said. "And I won't walk away from my debt to Dale."

"Go," Dale said. Hannah started to argue, but Dale shook her head. "No. Get out of here, stay safe. You think I jumped in front of a bunch of hunters with guns to save your life just so you could throw it away later? Go home. Be with your partner. Do that and I'll consider the debt paid in full."

Hannah looked like she was about to cry. Mia put a hand on her shoulder and nodded to Milo. "We'll start packing now."

Dale had an arm around Gwen's waist for support. "What do you need from me?"

Milo said, "I want Cecily Parrish's home address."

CHAPTER TWENTY-FIVE

CECILY'S SPRAWLING living room was mostly dark, save for a few running lights under the shelves behind the seating area. A large picture window looking out over the driveway was next to the main entrance. The kitchen was on the other side of the stairs, and it also had a few dim lights to prevent full darkness from filling the space.

When Cecily came in, she stepped out of her heels and pushed them to one side before continuing on in her stockings. She went directly to the kitchen and retrieved a bottle of wine without looking at the label. She had just started to pour when Milo, who was sitting in an armchair in the darkest corner of the ground floor, aimed a remote at the stereo and turned it on. She had adjusted the volume before Cecily arrived so, when it came to life, some kind of electronica music shrieked to life loud enough to make Cecily drop the bottle.

She cursed in an ancient language and spun around, preparing for an attack. Milo turned off the stereo and tossed the remote casually onto the couch.

"No version of my first name works with Willow."

Cecily narrowed her eyes.

"I'm not saying marriage is even on the table at this point, you know? Or that either one of us are going to change our names if that did someday happen. But I was sitting here waiting for you, and my mind just wandered some. Milo Willow. Millie Willow. They're just both garbage, aren't they?"

"You're the wolf who came to the office," Cecily said.

Milo nodded. She came forward, hands in her pockets. She was wearing a long black coat that was a little big on her, but she made it work. It was unbuttoned to show the white button-down shirt and black slacks she was wearing underneath.

"I expected you a lot earlier. But I guess you had to unwind, eh?" She sniffed the air. "They smell young. Hope you checked their IDs before you defiled them."

Cecily smiled, the predator in her coming out. "They consented."

Milo kept her face neutral to conceal her disgust. She wanted to appear calm and collected, even though her wolf was raging at the back of her mind.

"Have you come to make another deal for your friend?" Cecily asked. She was fully relaxed now, eyeing the spilled wine with regret. It had fallen on the counter and was now slowly pumping dark merlot into the grout.

"I'm here because today, you came very close to killing three people I hold very dear. Well... two of them, anyway. I don't really know Diana. I'm sure she's a great lady and all, we just haven't spent much time together. But Ari got hurt in prison because of you, and Dale had a fucking gun aimed at her head. *Dale Frye*. She's one of the sweetest, best people I've ever met, and you had someone aim a gun at her. I'm inclined to tear you apart for that alone."

Cecily said, "Then why haven't you? I half expected one of you mutts to show up here in wolf skin to try to take revenge."

"I thought about that. I really did. But there's disadvantages. Like I couldn't have pulled off that stereo trick if I was the wolf. And we wouldn't have been able to have this little conversation."

Cecily retrieved the paper towels to clean up the spill. "I do appreciate the human touch."

Milo grinned. "Oh, and there's the other thing. Wolves don't have fingers."

Cecily looked up as Milo drew the taser from her coat pocket. She fired and the prongs shot out, stabbing Cecily in the shoulder and upper chest. The voltage made her jump back, slamming her hip against the island before she hit the ground. Milo advanced on her so the prongs wouldn't be pulled out by the fall. Cecily jerked and danced on the kitchen tile, eyes wide and staring over the top of her head at the windows over the sink. Milo knelt down next to her and stared impassively at her until the seizures became mild twitches.

Milo snapped her fingers in front of Cecily's open eyes to make sure she was unconscious. "Okay," she said. "We'll talk more in a little while. You just... you should have told the bastard Dale was off-limits. You don't... you shouldn't have threatened to hurt her." She chewed her bottom lip and thought hard for a minute. "Gwen Duncan doesn't work much better, either, you know? Ah, well. We've got plenty of time to work that out."

She patted Cecily's face with her palm, a very mild slap, and stood up to prepare the second half of her plan.

Cecily was startled back to consciousness by the ground sliding out from beneath her feet. She instinctively grabbed hold of the bar in front of her to keep from falling and discovered her wrists were bound to it using zip ties. She almost tripped over her feet trying to keep upright as the fog lifted from her brain and she realized she was on the treadmill in her home gym. Her bare feet slapped against the belt. She was still in her work clothes, and her skirt was less than ideal for running. Fortunately the machine was nowhere near the highest setting.

Milo was standing in front of the treadmill, arms crossed over her chest. She smiled. "I'm not sure how the whole succubus thing works, but I figured if you'd just screwed two people, you might be at full power. So I thought I'd help you burn some of that off while we had a conversation."

"You're going to... regret this."

"Nah," Milo said.

Cecily laughed breathlessly, shaking her head. "Assault and battery, breaking and entering, harassment. All you've done is reserve yourself a cell next to your friend."

"I'm British. Diplomatic immunity."

"What are you even... That's not... *what?*"

Milo reached over the control panel and increased the speed. "Shut up and run."

Cecily stumbled but managed to remain upright. "So what's your plan, wolf?"

"My plan is to keep my people safe. You had a big day today. I'm going to make sure you don't repeat it. Because this, what we've been doing? It's done. No more threats, no more people trying to kill Ariadne in prison. We're going to sort everything out right here, right now."

"Or what? You'll put a bullet in *my* brain?"

"Nothing so crass. You know who you're dealing with, Cecily. I'm a wolf, and wolves don't really like using guns. That's more of a Hunter thing, you know." She rested her arms on top of the control panel. Her eyes were cold, flat. "All I'd do is bite you."

Cecily tried not to react, but her face betrayed her. She tightened her jaw as a trickle of sweat moved down her temple. It felt cold against her skin.

"See, all it takes is one bite." Milo kept her voice completely calm. "It doesn't even have to be a particularly bad bite. But it'll be enough. And then in a week or two, you'll start to feel the itch. You can fight it at first. It's like stopping a sneeze. You can stifle it for a little while. But eventually, you'll have to give in. It might be in the middle of the night. Or in court. But it'll happen. Your muscles will tangle themselves pulling your bones out of shape. If you're lucky, you'll die from it. But nobody dies quickly." She bared her teeth. "So what do you say, Cecily? Feeling lucky?"

"You're not a murderer."

Milo said, "Maybe I'm not. But I have a family now. I thought I knew what that meant, 'cause I always had a pack. But family is something different. It makes you feel superhuman and vulnerable at the same time. It makes you want to tear your own guts out when they're hurting. I hate that and I never want it to go away at the same time. You know what that's like?" She looked around the house and made a derisive noise. "Nah, I guess you wouldn't."

"You can't possibly... expect me to... confide everything to you."

"Ariadne Willow, Dale Frye, Diana Macallan. One of 'em was in the hospital today. Another one had a gun aimed at her head. The third was hung by a sheet in a bathroom stall. So you understand that I'm not feeling particularly reasonable right now. I want what I want, Cecily, and you're the one most likely to give it to me."

Cecily was panting now. "Your threat... carries... no weight. You can only... follow through... on it... once. And once... you do... all your leverage... is gone."

"Oh." Milo blinked. "Oh, you misunderstood the incentive. No, no, you see, I'm not leaving this place with you alive. I'm going to kill you no matter what happens. You can either tell me what I want to know and I do it quickly, or you keep quiet and I bite you.

Let you die in a month. Either way, you're done hurting my friends."

Cecily kept her eyes forward, hands gripping the rail, forcing herself to run.

"Let me tell you what I know. You tried to get Ari to work for you. She said no, because she's a smart cookie. But you wouldn't take no for an answer. You decided that she needed to be punished. So you arranged to have Shannon Hardy killed and framed Ari for it using one of the criminals you have on retainer at the office. How's that work, by the way? You just have all their names in a hat, and when you need one to take the fall for something, you just throw a bunch of money at the family?

"Doesn't matter. You have someone else in jail waiting to make sure Ari never makes it to trial. How much does that cost? Rhetorical question. But I've been a hired gun. The woman I now love once hired me to break up her daughter's relationship. It sounds more sordid than it ended up being, trust me. And she paid me a *buttload* of money. I mean, just a ridiculous amount of cash. I spread most of it around to the rest of my pack and I'm still living off what I had left. So for a murder, that's gotta be an insane receipt."

"Cost doesn't... matter in our business."

"Right. Because you lot have been doing this for ages. Maybe not you specifically, but Louis and Bart and Lillian."

Cecily almost fell, her steps breaking rhythm and forcing her to slump against the rail to keep from being thrown.

Milo grinned. "Ah, didn't think we'd know those names, did ya? And we know how long they've been part of this city. What we don't know is why they're wasting time with these criminals just to throw them under the bus later on. Why does GG&M have so many murders they want covered up? And why do you need werewolves and succubi and whatever the hell else you got running around in there? Hm? Want to fill in those last little blanks for me, Miss Parrish?"

"And... then what? Your plan will be... attacking the senior partners?"

"Sure."

Cecily laughed as hard as she could, which came out as a weak wheeze. "You haven't... the faintest... clue... what you're dealing with."

"Then tell me. C'mon. If you start talking, I'll slow down the treadmill. Give you a chance to catch your breath."

Cecily glared at her, then slowly smiled. She tightened her grip on the rail and moved her feet to either side of the belt. Milo took a step back as Cecily flexed her arms and pulled, letting the zip ties cut into her skin until blood was running down over her knuckles. She cried out victoriously when the plastic finally snapped, and she stepped off the still-running machine. Milo stood her ground as Cecily approached.

"You should run, wolf."

"I made you a promise."

Blood dripped off both of Cecily's hands. "Little Millicent Duncan, so eager to be a hero. You've learned so much but you don't understand any of it. You see the power they hold and how long they have been a part of this city. What makes you think that you and your sad little pack stands a chance of stopping them now? Pathetic little mutts.

"You gave me a choice of deaths, but I won't be so kind. I'm going to allow you to leave here and run back to your doghouse. I'll let you carry on with this plan, because I know Gilles, Girard, and Moreau will have far more fun with you than I will. They will enjoy making you suffer, and I will get immense satisfaction as well. But you invaded my home. You strapped me to this machine in an effort to humiliate me. You threatened my life. I can't let that go unpunished."

Milo reached for the taser but Cecily was too fast. She propelled herself off the balls of her feet, one hand slapping away Milo's dominant arm while the other closed around her throat. She twisted in the air and pulled Milo with her. It was almost like a dance that ended with Milo's back pressed hard against the wall. Milo kneed Cecily in the stomach but it did nothing to loosen the lawyer's grip. She was still sweating and breathless from her time on the treadmill, but her strength was stunning. She kept her hand on Milo's throat and stepped back, reaching for something in the darkness. Milo grabbed Cecily's arm with both hands in an attempt to pull her off, but the arm was rigid as steel.

"That little human you run around with is actually pretty clever," Cecily said. "I heard all about your little plan to prevent Ariadne from transforming in prison. It would have worked, too. I found anecdotal evidence of it through the ages."

Cecily let go of Milo's throat and grabbed her wrist instead. She swept Milo's leg, knocking her to the ground, and clambered on top of her. She slammed Milo's hand down hard against the concrete floor and adjusted her grip on the object she'd reached out to grab: a twenty-five pound cast-iron dumbbell with hexagonal heads. Milo's eyes widened when she saw it.

"No, don't~"

"Say goodbye to your wolf, Millicent."

Milo screamed even before Cecily brought the weight down, and the impact turned the sound into a mournful howl.

CHAPTER TWENTY-SIX

THERE WAS half an hour left on Ari's shift when members of the so-called kennel club began arriving in the library. Kunz arrived first with her entourage, pausing just long enough to share a nod with Ari before she went toward the back. They were followed a few minutes later by Frankie and a woman Ari didn't know. Segura was the last to arrive. Vogel came with her and took a casual sentry position in the hallway. Gladys closed the door and motioned for Ari to follow her to the reading area behind the shelves. Ari looked at Vogel through the glass and decided she might as well go along with it.

Gladys was sitting at the head of the long table, with Kunz to her right. Henning and Frankie were on the opposite side of the table and Segura was leaning against one of the low half-shelves that ran along the wall. The woman Ari didn't know was sitting beside Kunz. She was leaning forward with her elbows on the table, shoulders hunched and head low. She only moved her eyes when Ari appeared, and she tracked her movements without actually turning her head.

Kunz gestured at the newcomer. "Willow, meet the last member of our little group. This is Beatriz Moran."

"You really fuck a human?" Beatriz asked.

Ari blinked. "Uh. My girlfriend is human, yeah."

"That's twisted." There was no judgement in her voice. In fact, she almost sounded impressed.

Kunz said, "Dr. Val told us what happened to you this morning. I know it sounds strange considering the fact I stomped your head into the ground, but are you okay?"

"Yeah, I'm feeling a lot better." Ari took one of the empty seats. "I'm a little bruised, but nothing that won't heal." She looked at Segura. "No offense, I'm glad you're here, but... you're not a wolf."

"No," Kunz said, "but she knows about us and she's your cellmate. So I figured she should be part of this."

Ari said, "Makes sense. Part of what?"

Gladys said, "Someone tried to kill you. You don't think we're going to just ignore something like that, do you? We didn't just give up our wolves when we got locked up. We gave up our packs. So we became our own pack. We look out for each other. You might be new~"

"And already more of a handful than some of us have ever been," Frankie said.

"But," Gladys continued, "an attack on you is an attack on all of us."

Henning said, "Until you find out who is trying to kill you, at least one of us is going to be watching your back at all times. I already got reassigned to the library so I can help Gladys. And Segura is going to take care of you during your free time."

"Vogel, too," Segura said. "You can trust her."

"It's probably not going to be much fun having someone following you around all day, every day," Gladys said, "but definitely better than getting jumped in the shower."

Ari said, "That sounds great, honestly, but I couldn't ask you to-"

"We all know what you did," Beatriz said. "Wolf manoth came back. Wolfsbane. Hunters on every street corner. Some of us were locked up in here when it happened. You don't know what that was like. We're already vulnerable but then... we couldn't even eat without worrying that shit was in our food. Guards thought we were doing a hunger strike so they punished us. You put an end to it. For that, we can spare an hour or so to keep an eye out while you're on the shitter."

Gladys said, "You protected us. It's our turn to repay the favor. As long as it takes."

There was a lump in Ari's throat, and she fought it down before it could become tears. She nodded and finally managed to say, "Thank you."

"We're going to work out shifts," Segura said. "I'll be at your side during free time, and we'll take meals together for as long as you can stand my company. But someone's going to be with you all the time, no matter what."

"That sounds good."

They spent the time left on Ari's shift working out the schedule. Ari tried to make sure none of them were sacrificing too much of their time just to stand guard while she took a shower. When they finished, Ari thanked each woman individually. Beatriz tightened her grip after shaking Ari's hand, keeping her from pulling it back.

"Offense isn't going to work. You need to think defense. Don't give whoever this is an opening to attack you. They've got the benefit of knowing who you are and planning ahead. All you can do is keep your wits about you."

"Understood. Thank you."

Gladys said, "I know you'll have Henning here as support, but don't count me out. I may be old, but I can take any fool who comes through here."

"I know you're including me in that," Ari said, "And I don't doubt it for a second, Gladys." She kissed the older woman on the cheek. "Thank you."

Segura was waiting by the exit with Vogel. She swept her arm toward the door and bowed from the waist. "Shall we, ma'am?"

"Okay, you can cut that shit out right now," Ari said.

"Come on, I just found out werewolves exist, and I'm surrounded by them, and I get to play bodyguard for one. Let me have a little fun with it."

They started down the corridor shoulder-to-shoulder, with Vogel lagging behind as their escort.

"If there's anything I can do to make up for this inconvenience, let me know."

"Well..." Segura glanced over her shoulder at Vogel. "I mean, you're not the only one who might need someone to stand guard outside the showers, if you get my meaning."

Ari laughed. "I think I can handle that. And I'll do my best not to eavesdrop."

"Well," Vogel said, "if you hear something, you hear something."

"She's kind of a freak," Ari said.

"You have no idea." Segura sighed. "So, you want to grab dinner before we head back to the ol' homestead?"

Ari thought about what Beatriz had said about thinking defensively. "Actually there's somewhere else I think I should go first. Is there a barber shop in here?"

"Barber?" Segura said. "Yeah, sure."

They detoured to another corridor to a room which looked like any number of beauty shops Ari had visited in her life. A tall woman with red hair piled on top of her head turned to face her when she came in.

"You're new. Looking for a classic prison buzz?"

"Uh." She looked at the tools on the table. "Is that the only option?"

The redhead grinned. "No, sweetie, we won't make you go the full Sinead. Lots of girls just don't have the skull for it, know what I mean?" She patted the back of her chair. "I got an opening right now. Hop up here." Ari got into the seat and let the woman wrap a cape around her. "So, what *are* you looking for today?"

Ari looked at her reflection. Her hair was past her shoulders, and had been for as long as she could remember. She rarely got more than a trim. And currently it was actually kind of short for her liking. She'd just gotten a haircut two weeks earlier. But now she had to think defensively, and that meant taking less time in the shower and not providing anything a potential attacker could grab and hold onto.

"Don't shave it," she said, "but short. Cut it really, really short."

The redhead gathered Ari's hair in her hands, holding it like a rope. "How's this?"

"Shorter," Ari said.

The hand moved closer to her skull.

Ari fought a grimace. "Shorter."

A little closer.

"There. That should be close enough."

"You sure? You don't look very sure."

Ari let the question hang for a second, considering it. She looked at Segura and Vogel's reflections in the mirror, and then she nodded.

"I'm sure. Cut it all off."

"Okay, sweetie." She patted Ari's shoulder and moved to get her scissors. "Just remember, in the end, it's just hair. Eventually it all grows back."

Ari kept her eyes locked on her reflection as the redhead made the first snip.

Gwen's house was eerily quiet without the wolves filling up every empty space. They had all packed their bags and headed to the airport so they would have an alibi for whatever Milo was doing at Cecily's house. Dale couldn't even hope to sleep, so she was sitting in the living room while Gwen scrubbed kitchen surfaces which looked immaculate to Dale's eye. Neither of them spoke or suggested putting on music. Occasionally Dale would check her phone for messages from Milo or news alerts about cops being sent to a familiar area.

The doorbell rang, startling both of them, and Dale shot to her feet. She took the time to look through the peephole and saw a body slumped on the stoop. Her face was turned away, but the clothes confirmed that it was Milo.

"Oh, god... Gwen!"

She threw open the door to check on her. Cecily stepped out of the blind spot next to the door and shoved Dale back into the house. Dale was only wearing socks and they failed to find traction on the foyer tile. She flailed and hit the ground hard, sliding a few inches as Cecily grabbed Milo by the shirt collar and hauled her into the house. She flung Milo forward like she was a bowling ball, sending her tumbling into the back of the couch. Her right arm took the brunt of the impact and the pain brought her back to consciousness with a cry of pain that turned into a whimper. There was blood on the cuffs of Cecily's silk blouse.

Gwen drew a chef's knife from the wooden block next to the oven but only managed to take one step before Cecily placed her foot on Dale's shoulder and pinned her to the floor.

"How many of your girls are you willing to sacrifice, Gwyneth?"

"You want to hurt me, then fine. Leave them alone."

Cecily said, "I didn't come here to prolong our ridiculous war. I'm simply returning a lost dog to her owner and issuing a warning. You seem to think I'm your villain, but I assure you I'm not. I'm a lieutenant, someone who was hired to do a job. You are coming very close to drawing the ire of my employers and trust me, that is something you *do not want*." She pointed at Milo. "I left her alive. I didn't have to do that. I could have waited for her to change into the wolf and broken a bone, trapping her in that form until it healed. I chose not to. We are done. This is finished."

Gwen said, "We're not finished. As long as my daughter is still in jail for a crime she didn't commit—"

Cecily held up a hand. "That is the ending she chose, Miss Willow. She refused our offer of employment. We discovered that she would never accept our offer, so the decision was made to simply eliminate her. Nobody refuses us, Miss Willow, and Ariadne will serve as a cautionary tale for those who come after her. She will prove to those who came before her that they made the right decision coming to work for us. There's nothing for you to win. No victory. You're simply prolonging your own suffering and making things worse for everybody you love.

"I suggest the next time you visit Ariadne, you take the time to say goodbye. Then move on. The firm is not interested in you, your girlfriend, or the girl who may have once been your daughter-in-law, but if you continue to make nuisances of yourselves, you will be dealt with. To you, this is a war. To my employers, it is nothing more than an inconvenience. Count yourselves fortunate that Ariadne will be the only loss you've suffered."

She took her foot off Dale's shoulder, looked at Milo with disdain, and walked out of the house without looking back.

Gwen dropped the knife and ran to Milo, who was still cradling her broken arm. Her whimpers had grown quiet, but her face was pale and beaded with sweat. Gwen cradled her head against her chest and stroked her hair.

"She took my wolf," Milo whispered.

"I know, sweetheart, I know." Gwen looked at Dale. "Are you okay?"

Dale nodded, but she looked understandably shaken. She was brushing at her shoulder where Cecily's foot had been seemingly without realizing she was doing it.

"What do we do now?" Gwen asked.

Dale looked at Milo, utterly shaken by how defeated she seemed. And Gwen, who had sacrificed so much to fight the hunters and finally had a chance at real, true love. She thought about Diana in the hospital bed, and the bullet holes in her blouse. She thought about Cecily and the partners at GG&M, and what they could do. They had silently dug their claws into Seattle and remained there for over a hundred years with no one even realizing.

"We stop," Dale said.

Gwen furrowed her brow. "What?"

Dale slumped against the back of the couch and shook her

head. "I'm sorry, Mom. But you heard her. We can't fight them, not without losing someone else." She put a hand on Milo's leg. "Ari wouldn't want any more of us to get hurt to save her. If she knew..." Her voice caught in her throat. She had to take a moment to fight the tears before continuing. "If she knew sacrificing herself would keep the rest of us safe, she wouldn't hesitate."

Gwen was openly crying now, holding Milo. "She's my daughter."

"She's my everything," Dale said. "But look at what we've learned about GG&M and where it's gotten us. Where do we go from here? A kamikaze run? What good is saving Ari if she comes out of prison to find us all dead or mourning someone she loves? My job is to protect Ari's interests and... I know this is what she'd choose. She would want us to stop."

Gwen closed her eyes and pressed her lips to the top of Milo's head. Dale brought her knees up and covered her face with both hands. She tried to smother the idea she had just signed Ari's death warrant. She knew in her heart she'd done the right thing, knew it was what Ari would want in her place. But laying down arms just felt so much like surrendering.

I'm sorry, puppy, she thought. *I'm so sorry.*

CHAPTER TWENTY-SEVEN

ARI ONCE read somewhere that it only took about three or four weeks to create a habit. It didn't take her that long to adjust to her new routine, but maybe whoever came up with the number didn't have a whole platoon of guards enforcing the new habit. Mornings were awake at six, bathroom and shower, breakfast, work. Lunch. Then more work, free time, and in bed by ten. Everywhere Ari went, she was trailed by at least one member of the kennel club. The first couple of days, her bladder refused to cooperate while Frankie was leaning against the sink outside the stall, but soon enough it wasn't a problem. She got to know far more about Segura and Vogel's sex life than she ever wanted to know, but it was a small price to pay for safety.

She still wasn't used to her hair. Every morning she reached up to straighten it, only to find that it barely reached past her ears. It was less of a hassle, sure, but she hated it. She absolutely hated the breeze on her neck, and the way it just barely reached her eyes. She couldn't tie it back so it was always just slightly inconveniently in her face. It had grown out a little, but she still had a long way to go before she was back to normal.

Dale, on her first visit after the scalping, had very gently stroked it with her hands before declaring the new look made Ari look "so handsome."

After that, the meeting became bleak. Dale explained what had been happening out in the real world. While Ari was shaken by what happened to Diana, she looked like she might become physically ill when Dale told her about Milo.

"Is she...?"

"She's depressed, of course, and she's angry at herself. Your mom is taking care of her. I think she's traumatized. You had time to process what was going to happen. She had her wolf torn away from her. I worry that it's not really going to hit her until later."

Ari put her hand on top of Dale's. "Baby, you have to stop."

"What?"

"Stop this. Just leave it alone. Walk away, right now, before anyone else gets hurt because of me. I know it's going to be hard..."

Dale started crying and put her head down on the table. Ari put her hands on top of Dale's head.

"I know. I know. But I can't... if Milo or Diana had been hurt in a more permanent way, to try to save me... I can't justify that, Dale. Please tell me you understand."

"I love you so much, puppy."

Ari kissed Dale's hair. A guard across the room said her name with just enough warning to let her know she was pushing the limits of the rules, so she sat up straight and moved her hands back. Dale sat up and wiped at her cheeks.

"I told Gwen and Milo to stop. I put an end to it. I didn't know how I would tell you." She sniffled and laughed. "I told them it was what you'd want. I don't know why I'm surprised I was right."

"You do know me better than anyone ever has."

When their time was up, Ari stood and pulled Dale into a hug. She breathed in her scent and kissed her hair. "I would give up my wolf for a full year if I could just have one night with you."

Dale held her tighter, gripping the back of Ari's prison uniform with both fists.

The male guard standing just behind them said, "Willow..."

"Please, Burke..."

He didn't say anything, but he also didn't force the hug to end.

Dale said, "Every time I leave here, it might... I may never..."

Ari stepped back and cupped Dale's cheek. "Don't think like that."

"Just stay alive. Okay?"

"I've got some good people in here watching out for me."

Dale kissed her. Ari closed her eyes and let her hand slip into

Dale's hair.

"Willow, we've really got to go."

She sighed and pecked the corner of Dale's mouth. "I love you."

"I love you, too."

The rest of the day was almost unbearable, a comedown from the high of holding and touching Dale. It only reinforced the fact she was in prison and cut off from all the most important people in her life. She kept quiet and did her work. She followed Henning to the cafeteria and the gym, ate dinner with Gladys and Segura, and said less than a dozen words throughout the evening.

Every inmate with blue shoes became a suspect. She spent so much time watching feet that Vogel finally commented on it.

"Keeping your head down is one thing," she said, "but if you always have your eyes on the ground, people might start mistaking you for a weakling."

"Right now, it's the only clue I have to her identity."

"Unless she got a new pair of shoes that happen to be white."

Ari groaned when she realized that was a valid point. "So much for that lead."

The days began to bleed together. She didn't read any of the books she got from the library, she didn't pay attention to the rotation of the lunch and dinner menus. The only thing she cared about were Mondays, the morning meetings with Dale where she could feel like herself again. But even those quickly got harder. She could see the worry on Dale's face compounded with each meeting, and she knew Dale could see Ari growing more and more despondent.

Dale was still living with Gwen and Milo. They were officially cohabitating, a true couple, and Ari managed a sincere smile at that. It might not be a happy relationship, given the circumstances, but she was glad her mother had someone there to support her.

"I feel like an adopted daughter," Dale said. "They dote on me. I think it gives Milo something to do other than worry about her arm."

"How is that going?"

Dale shook her head. "She's depressed. Withdrawn. I've walked in on her crying a couple of times, but she always pretends I'm imagining it."

"Mom?"

"She's..." Dale ran a hand over her face. "Sad, but happy about Milo, and guilty about feeling happy, and worried for you. She keeps saying she wants to come visit you, but then when I get ready to go, she says she doesn't want to take away from my time. I think she blames herself for not doing more to get you out, or for being happy while you're in here."

Ari said, "I'd love to see her. And I'm thrilled she's happy. The last thing I want is for all of you to be depressed all the damn time."

"Easier said than done, puppy."

"I know."

That day when they parted, Dale put her lips against Ari's ear and whispered, "Tonight at eleven, I'm going to be thinking about you. Will you think of me at the same time?"

Ari curled her fingers in the small of Dale's back. "Yeah. I promise."

Dale kissed Ari's neck and ended the hug.

Gladys and Segura commemorated her first month in prison with a cupcake in the commissary. "No candles," Segura said, "but you can still make a wish before you chow down."

"Something tells me everyone in here makes the same wish," Ari said.

"That would probably be a safe bet," Gladys said, licking frosting from her finger. "But go ahead and make it anyway."

She met with her lawyer, Graham Cosgrove, and gave him her side of the story. She left out any talk of wolves and succubi, but told the rest of it exactly as it happened. When she was finished, Cosgrove carefully chose his words as he capped his pen.

"This goes along perfectly with what I heard from your mother and partner. But it just sounds so bizarre. No offense, but why would a law firm like GG&M go to these lengths for you? Are you really that singular? Are you *that* good at your job?"

"I am," Ari said, "but that's beside the point. I think it's been a long time since anyone has told Cecily Parrish no, and she got obsessed."

"Well, I'm pretty good at my job, too. You have my word that I'll do everything in my power to sort this all out."

Ari thanked him, hoping she hadn't just put a target on his back as well.

Elise Gilpin caught up with Ari as Vogel escorted her back to the library after the meeting. "Hey, Willow. Got a minute?"

"Not really. I have to get to work."

"I understand. I just..." She glanced at Vogel and lowered her voice. "I just noticed that you seem to have built up quite a posse the past few weeks. I was wondering if you had room for one more. You know, safety in numbers?"

Ari said, "Everything okay?"

"Sure, I mean, I guess. No one's knocked my head into the ground like Kunz did with you. But I haven't quite bonded with my cellmate the way you have. It's kind of lonely in here without a support group. Look, I don't want to be the pathetic girl asking the cool kids if she can sit at their table at lunch. I was just hoping you could maybe throw me a bone."

Ari nodded. "I understand. And I think we can make some room for you."

Elise grinned. "Really? Thank you. Thanks so much."

When she was gone, Ari looked at Vogel. "What do you think about her?"

Vogel shrugged. "She's quiet. Keeps to herself, doesn't cause trouble. Of course, compared to *you*, everyone in here is a model prisoner."

"Yeah, yeah, yeah," Ari muttered.

"Blue shoes, though," Vogel pointed out. "Could be damning."

Ari said, "You're the one who told me the shoes didn't matter."

Vogel said, "Unless they do."

"I hate you."

Vogel grinned and followed Ari into the library.

Gwen switched her focus from tactical to triage. Her first order of business was getting Milo to the hospital to take care of her broken arm. Milo was silent throughout her examination and the application of her cast. Gwen was obviously concerned but also relieved to have something to take up all her focus. She doted on both of the girls as the days turned into weeks, and Dale's decision to give up on helping Ari became more and more real.

She couldn't bring herself to visit Ari, though she pestered Dale for details every Monday when she returned. "Is she healthy? Is she taking care of herself? Have her bruises healed?" Dale patiently answered everything she was asked. She knew that Dale was worried every visit would be the last time she'd see Ari alive, and Gwen had the same fear. She dreaded the phone call that Ari had been killed in prison. With that cloud hanging over her head, along with Milo's depression, and Dale's resignation, the house was in a constant state of melancholy.

Gwen made the decision that as long as her girls couldn't

transform, she would also abstain. She would have to do it at least once a month, but she could make sure she did it where Milo couldn't see. Her attempt at abstinence only lasted a few days. They were getting ready for bed when Milo said, "I know what you're doing."

"Moving the decorative pillows to the chair so I'm not sleeping all propped up by them?"

"You're chaining up your wolf. I don't want that. Ari doesn't want it, either. If our positions were reversed, would you want us to hold ourselves back?"

Gwen said, "It's not that simple."

"Yes, it is." Milo got into bed and smoothed the blankets over her legs. "Change."

"What, now?"

"It's been a couple of days. I'm sure the wolf is aching to get out."

Gwen thought about arguing but, in the end, knew it would be a battle she lost. She stepped away from the bed and stripped off her pajamas. She couldn't help but notice Milo's appreciative examination once the clothes were gone.

"If this was just an excuse to ogle me..."

Milo grinned and raised an eyebrow. "Added bonus."

Gwen got on her knees beside the bed and steepled her fingers on the carpet. She hunched her shoulders, then arched her back into a wide stretch. Her skin rippled and burst forth with thick, dark hair. Milo had leaned forward to watch the transformation and smiled when Gwen leapt up to join her in the bed. Milo wrapped her arms around Gwen's neck and buried her face in the thick fur just above her shoulders.

"Hey there, gorgeous," she said.

Gwen nuzzled Milo and settled heavily across her lap. Ordinarily she would have gone for a long run, but even the animalistic side of her brain knew where she needed to be.

A few nights after that, three weeks after Cecily broke her arm, Milo startled Gwen awake by suddenly leaping out of bed and running to the door. She clawed at the knob before she turned and ran to the window. She was making frantic whimpering noises in the back of her throat as she scraped the fingernails of her uninjured hand over the glass. Finally she dropped to the floor and began clawing at the plaster of her cast.

"Millicent," Gwen said as firmly as she could. "Wake up."

Milo pulled her arm up and bit it just above the cast. Gwen got out of bed and ran to her, stopping her before she could break the skin.

"Milo, stop it. Stop."

"I have to change. I need the wolf."

Gwen said, "You can't. You need to heal, sweetheart."

Milo kicked and tried to pull away, but Gwen held her tight. "I can't do it anymore. I'm going to explode. I need the wolf, Gwen, I need her. She's dying. She's dying."

"She's just asleep, Milo. When you heal, she'll be back, good as new."

"She's not coming back. She'll think I don't want her. She's never going to come back." She began crying. "I can feel her fading. I can't... she's not there, I can't... she's not even asking to come out, Gwen. I can't hear her."

Gwen kissed Milo's cheeks and eyebrows, rocking her on the floor. "She'll be back. I promise you, Millicent. She's just giving you time to heal."

"What if she really is gone?" Milo whispered.

"Then... we'll find a way to deal with that."

She let Milo cry until she fell back to sleep, but Gwen was up for the rest of the night hoping that Milo's panic was unfounded. She'd been spending her days looking up stories about *canidae* who had to stop their transformations for one reason or another. There was a private forum which required her to jump through nearly a dozen verification hoops before it allowed her to view any posts. She found former prisoners, mothers, and athletes who were forced to 'silence the wolf' for their various needs. They all mentioned the drug Ari was using in jail, and Gwen kicked herself for not thinking of the internet before they sent her to get beaten up. She let herself wallow in guilt before she focused on finding help for Milo.

That night at dinner, they gathered at the table as had become their habit. They all pitched in shopping, cooking, and cleaning up, and tonight it was Dale's turn to make the meal. When she put the plates in front of Gwen and Milo, they were surprised to see she'd made lamb chops.

"What's the occasion?" Gwen asked.

"I'm going home."

Gwen's smile fell. "Dale, you're more than welcome to--"

"I know. You're not pushing me out, I'm making the decision on my own. I miss home. I miss Neka. I miss... normal. And I know it's not going to be normal, because Ari isn't there and I'm not going to the office every day, but it will feel more like real life than living here. Living here is starting to feel like the new normal, like my life has changed so much that I'm living in this big house by the lake. I need to go home to make sure Ari has the life she remembered when she gets out. I appreciate everything you've both done for me. The sacrifices you've made. And I really hope we can keep having dinners like this even when I'm staying across town. But it's been over a month. It's time."

"If you're sure." Gwen stood up to hug Dale. "You're welcome back here any time. I mean that."

"Thank you, Mom."

Milo reached out with her good hand to squeeze Dale's fingers. "You're a good wolf, Dale."

"Thanks, Milo."

She packed the next day and was gone after lunch. Gwen fled the suddenly cavernous house and went into the backyard. There was a squat stone wall at the edge of her property where she could sit to watch the boats on Lake Washington. Milo found her there and offered her a cup of coffee. Gwen smiled, took the mug, and sipped it as Milo settled beside her. Milo let her plastered arm rest across her lap like a piece of driftwood she'd picked up on the beach.

"This is perfect," Gwen said, lifting the mug in a toast. "Thank you."

"You spent the last month taking care of me and Dale. Can it be your turn now?"

Gwen said, "I take care of people."

"Alphas are bullshit. The pack takes care of the pack."

"I'm..." Gwen's voice caught on the next word, so she shook her head. "I'm afraid if I... let go just a little, I'll lose my grip and I'll never get it back. The day after I was attacked, I knew I had to fight. When I found out I was pregnant, I found a purpose. Ariadne became my whole life. The idea of losing her, of outliving her... I'm..." She balled her hands into fists and looked away from the water. "I can't risk losing my grip."

"Let me hold on for you," Milo said. "I might only have one good paw at the moment, but it's yours."

Gwen looked at Milo, gratitude in her eyes, and leaned in to kiss her. She put her head down on Milo's shoulder and put her hand on top of Milo's cast.

"Maybe I can let you take care of me. Just for tonight."
"Good enough for now. Baby steps."
Gwen smiled and watched the water as her coffee grew cold.

CHAPTER TWENTY-EIGHT

ARI AND Dale sat across from each other, nine weeks into their forced separation. They were holding hands, silent, letting the white noise of the other prisoners and their visitors fill the air between them. When the guard who was making the rounds moved out of earshot, Dale began speaking again. She kept her voice low so it wouldn't travel to the other tables.

"Greer."

Ari thought before shaking her head.

"Hansen."

"Louise?"

"Jenny."

Ari shook her head. "No one here named Jenny Hansen."

Dale tried not to look despondent. She was running out of names. "Ford."

"There are a couple of Fords," Ari said.

"Lisa."

Ari thought again and finally gave a slow shake of her head. "Doesn't sound familiar."

Dale sighed. "That's all I have this week. I'll keep digging."

Ari nodded. "You're doing great. One of these names is bound to mean something."

"Yeah. But there's bound to be a limit to how many I can find."

She had been spending her days digging as deep into GG&M's records as she could without being discovered. She was looking for any and all clients defended by the firm for relatively minor crimes, anyone who had benefited from their inexplicably generous pro bono work and then ended up in prison for a severe crime. It didn't make sense for GG&M to defend someone on vandalism charges only to remain silent when the same person went to court for murder. She also noticed the person always pled guilty or no contest, essentially walking themselves directly into a prison cell.

Once she had those names, she looked into their families. Sarah Calvert. Multiple possession charges dismissed, sentenced to fifteen years for murder. Three months into her sentence, her cousin received a kidney transplant after three years of being on the wait list. Anthony Short, six counts of armed robbery and domestic violence, currently in prison for a double homicide but, as a man, probably not relevant to their investigation. If GG&M did have a man trying to kill Ari in the prison, he would be a guard and not a prisoner.

Ari glanced to make sure the guard was still out of earshot. "You should keep yourself safe. If Cecily finds out you're still looking into it..."

"She won't. I covered my tracks well. I move on little cat's feet." Ari couldn't resist a smile at that. She bent down to kiss Dale's fingers. "The important thing is that everyone else is safe. We're the only ones in danger."

"You and me against the world, huh?" Ari said with a smile.

"What else is new?"

Ari ran her thumb over Dale's knuckles. "This drug I'm on... I'm kind of getting used to it. Maybe when I get out of here, it wouldn't be the worst thing in the world..."

Dale furrowed her brow. "What? You want to keep taking the drug?"

"It would give you the chance to have a normal girlfriend."

"Pass," Dale said.

"I'm serious."

"So am I. I fell in love with you knowing full well everything about who and what you were. You can have butch short hair or super-long freak hair, you can be sickly thin or get some damn curves, I don't care as long as you're still you. That includes the wolf. Living with Milo and your mom proved that I need a wolf in my life, and you're it, baby."

Ari said, "If you insist."

"I do."

Ari bit her bottom lip and let her mind wander. "You know... the people GG&M send to prison probably aren't actually doing the murders. They're most likely just taking the fall."

"So somebody has to be killing all these people," Dale said.

"Maybe the firm has a hit squad? Maybe that's why they wanted a wolf on their payroll."

Dale squinted. "I don't know about that. Cecily never saw you being particularly bloodthirsty. I mean, *I* know you can go Big Bad Wolf when you want to, but how would she know you're capable of it? No, she wanted you for your brains. But there could be a GG&M hit squad. It might be who was really responsible for Shannon Hardy's death. I could look into it."

Ari said, "Safely."

"Of course safely." She smiled. "I've missed this so much."

Ari winked at her. "We'll get it back."

When their time was up, they kissed goodbye. When they hugged, Dale said, "Eleven tonight?"

Ari smiled. "I'll be thinking of you."

They separated and Dale went back to the real world while Ari slipped back into her routine. The only time she felt like herself, or like a real person, was the hour she spent with Dale every week. She didn't even pay attention to the book covers as she shelved them. The food was an anonymous gruel. Salisbury steak, green beans, mashed potatoes, chicken, broccoli, it didn't matter what the menu said because it all tasted the same. She liked Segura and the *canidae* she'd grown to think of as friends, but part of her kept them all at a distance. Getting too close would mean she was settling in. It would mean surrendering to her fate.

She liked spending time with them. She liked hearing stories from the older *canidae*, and sharing experiences of being wolves in Seattle with Henning and Frankie. They ever put stashes of clothes in public parks, and neither of them had a partner like Dale who would come get them in the middle of the night after a transformation.

"And she's human?" Frankie said, still unable to believe it.

"Yeah," Ari smiled, "a hundred percent human."

"I'm not judging. To each their own. I've dabbled from time to time, but I could never be with someone who was incapable of understanding what I'm going through."

Ari laughed. "I agree with you on that. I'd never be with someone who didn't understand me."

"But..."

"Dale understands. She's never been through a transformation, but she knows as much as any wolf I've ever met."

Frankie looked skeptical but didn't fight her on it.

Elise was the only member of Ari's new circle who didn't know about her status as *canidae*. She enjoyed having one little area of her life that wasn't overwhelmed with the threat of Cecily Parrish. One evening the guards made an announcement that both inmates assigned to laundry duty had fallen ill and they needed volunteers to take over the next day. Elise raised her hand almost immediately and Ari remembered she was assigned to the cafeteria. Any assignment had to be better than waking up at three in the morning.

"Thank you, Gilpin," CO Burke said. "Anyone else?"

No one raised their hands. Ari felt bad for her, like watching a kid being shunned when it was time to choose kickball teams. Elise tried not to look around but it was clear she was feeling pretty unpopular at that moment. Ari decided to save her future humiliation and raised her own hand.

"Willow just saved someone from being forcibly reassigned. Thank you, Inmate Willow. Everyone else, back to your bunks."

Segura said, "I doubt the kennel club can get any of your bodyguards reassigned to the laundry on such short notice."

"Elise will be there. She's like an honorary member of the club."

"You really trust her to watch your back? She looks like a strong sneeze would knock her down."

Ari said, "She's tougher than she looks. She's in here for assault."

Segura laughed and stretched out on her bed. "Yeah, sure. I'd get the whole story there before I used it as proof she can kick some ass."

"Even if she's not imposing, she's security just by being there. Whoever is after me probably won't take a chance of having a witness around."

"That just means she'll have to take Gilpin out, too. You want someone getting seriously hurt just to keep yourself alive?"

Ari couldn't help thinking of Diana and Milo. "No. I really don't."

"Just food for thought," Segura said.

"Right…"

She spent most of the night thinking about it, distracted only when she made good on her promise to think about Dale at the predetermined time. She was surprised by how easily she got used to the idea of masturbating with someone else in the room, but needs must.

In the morning, after breakfast, she and Elise followed a guard into the laundry room. She was hit by the scent of bleach, detergent, and warm linen, but the effect was muted. She'd never realized how acute her sense of smell was, or how much of it was because of the wolf. Now she could smell the way normal people did, and she understood why Dale never complained about that mildew scent in their kitchen. If it was faint to her, then there was no way Dale could smell it.

The guard gestured vaguely at the machines. "I assume you ladies know how to run one of these."

"I think we can figure it out," Elise said. When he was gone, she looked at Ari. "Was that a sexist comment?"

"I'm going to say yes." Ari went to the double-level table in the middle of the room. There were piles of clothes on top and gallon bottles of bleach on the bottom. A huge dumpster-sized cart was placed to one side with even more clothes inside. "I guess we should just get started."

"Is it just the two of us?" Elise said. "None of your bodyguards?"

Ari smiled. "No, I think we can get by a day without them. We'll watch each other's backs."

"Cool." She went to one of the washers and examined its controls. "This is slightly different from the Maytag I have at home. But between us, we can figure it out."

"I like the optimism," Ari said.

They got to work, Elise humming just loudly enough to be heard over the rumble of the machines. Ari watched her and couldn't help smiling.

"I hope you take this as a compliment," Ari said, "because I definitely mean it as one. But I find it kind of hard to believe you're in here on a real charge. What was it, forced entry, assault…?"

"Grand theft auto," Elise said.

"Right. I've gotten to know you sort of well, and I can't see you actually doing any of that. So be honest, am I the only wrongly-accused woman in the room?"

Elise smiled and continued sorting shirts. "Sad to say it's true.

People adapt to their environment, you know? And this is prison. *Prison.* There's killers in here! I might kick someone's ass when I get mad, but I've never killed anyone. And even when I did get nabbed, I never actually had to do any time."

Ari had her back to Elise. Her mind clicked to what she and Dale had been talking about. "Friends in high places?"

"Something like that," Elise said. "When I'd get in trouble, I could always wriggle out of it. But I knew I was just borrowing from a well that would eventually run dry. I guess I could've been preparing better for it." She sighed heavily. "It's different in here. I wasn't expecting that. I'll fight when I feel like I've been shortchanged or insulted. But that's defense. That's just smart. In here you have to be on the offensive all the time so no one fucks with you. I can't do that."

Ari turned slowly to face Elise. "So the people in high places who would get you out of trouble. They didn't help you this time?"

"This time was different. I don't really want to talk about it, though."

Ari said, "This time was different because... why? Someone told you who to go after? And I'm sure getting yourself arrested and sent to prison was part of the deal. What did you get in exchange? I know it's selfish, but I hope it was something more than just money. I'd like to think I'm priceless."

Elise had gone still, staring at a spot on a wall. When Ari stopped talking, Elise slowly turned her head to look at her. The silence hung between them as Elise appraised Ari, then sighed and stood up straighter.

"Son of a bitch. You figured out the whole thing?"

"Dale did."

Elise nodded carefully and rolled her head back to look at the ceiling. Her entire demeanor changed, her shoulders straightening and both hands curling into fists. In an instant she had gone from a victim to a boxer waiting for the bell. She pushed her jaw forward and lowered her head to glare at Ari.

"I guess you'll be happy to know I didn't sell my freedom for anything as small as money. My sister is trying to get into the country. Immigration issues. She has a record. GG&M is greasing the wheels to get her through with my niece. It's a matter of life or death. Your life for theirs."

"And Shannon Hardy," Ari said.

"She was going to die anyway. She was marked a long time

before you even met her. Cecily just elected to wait until her death could serve a greater purpose."

"So the meek little mouse act..."

Elise shrugged. "I needed to get close to you. At first I just thought we could be friends, and then you surrounded yourself with the goon squad, so I had to mix things up a little. I figured you wouldn't suspect me if you pitied me. I didn't plan on getting you alone down here, but sometimes things work out." She slowly moved forward. "The truth is, I like to fight. Usually I like to have a good cause, like my sister and my niece. Nothing personal against you, Willow, but you aren't family." She held her hands out to the sides. "Want to make this easy? Just put an end to the whole thing now, get it over with?"

"You tried to kill me in the damn toilet," Ari said.

"I would have dragged you back to the cell, geez."

"Still."

"Fine. I'm getting paid for the hard way anyway. Might as well earn it."

She threw herself forward. Ari swung her leg out to the side and knocked a bottle of bleach off the table's lower shelf, then kicked it at Elise. She swatted it away but ended up splashing the bleach up into her own face. Ari lunged and grabbed the back of Elise's head with her left hand to pull her forward. Elise was thrown off-balance so Ari twisted at the waist and cracked her elbow across the bridge of Elise's nose. The move made them both stumble in opposite directions. Elise hit the machines while Ari grabbed hold of the table to keep from hitting the floor.

Elise recovered first. Ari's attempt to flee was hindered by the bleach suddenly pouring across the tile under her feet. Elise grabbed Ari's shoulders with both hands and threw her against one of the washing machines. Ari's head bounced off the glass and left her dazed long enough for Elise to get an arm around her neck. She turned it into a choke hold and squeezed hard.

"I actually did like you, Willow," Elise said, out of breath. "You were kind when you didn't have to be. That's a good quality. But it can only get you so far."

Ari could see their reflection in the washing machine's door. Her eyes were half-closed and her face was turning an awfully dark color.

You took me from Dale. You took Bitches and my freedom. You took my wolf. You're not taking another goddamn thing from me.

She bent her knees and leaned forward, forcing Elise to subtly change her position. She grabbed the arm around her neck with both hands and used it as leverage when she threw her body to one side. Elise tripped over Ari's legs and gave up her dominant position. Ari slammed them both into the machine as hard as she could and dug her fingernails into Elise's forearm hard enough to draw blood. Elise let go and brought her fist down on the back of Ari's head. The effect was like ringing a bell, and Ari's limbs spasmed. She went down and Elise climbed on top of her.

"Forget what I said about liking you," Elise said. She had one hand in Ari's hair, which was just long enough to grab a handful, and the other on her shoulder. "You're a fucking bitch."

"That's uncalled for," Ari said, her voice rough from her near strangulation. She thought of Milo's broken arm. She flattened her palms on the tile and arched her back, then rolled them both. It effectively bucked Elise off of her, but she was thrown in the direction of the only exit. Ari was trapped and Elise was stronger than she looked. She doubted she would eventually come out on top in their fight without a little help.

She reached out for the wolf. *I know the drug is holding you down for a little while longer, baby, but I need your voice. Just for a few seconds.*

As Elise got back to her feet, Ari ran to one of the washing machines and threw open the door. She leaned inside and opened her mouth in a wide O. The howl that boiled up out of her was a sound that no human should've been able to make, a spine-chilling keen that slid fluidly around the concave interior of the machine's basin before projecting back out at a hugely amplified volume. Elise winced, but still grabbed Ari by the hair and yanked her back. She threw Ari to the floor and climbed on top of her.

Frankie heard the howl first. She sat up straight, her ear physically twitching at the unmistakable sound of a wolf in danger.

Blood flicked from Elise's knuckles as they came back down for another blow.

Kunz knocked over a table and a chair on her way out of the woodwork shop. Segura, who hadn't heard anything but what she assumed was a strange and distant siren, pursued. CO Burke started to call it in, but Vogel stepped in and stopped him.

Ari closed her hands around Elise's throat, but the next blow caused her grip to release before she had done any damage.

Gladys stood in the library door. Henning ran from the library without waiting to see if anyone was paying attention to her. Guards pursued, and

Gladys threw herself in their path.

"Look at the bright side, Willow," Elise said. "It's finally going to be over."

Kunz didn't slow down when she entered the laundry room. The big woman was moving so fast her shoes didn't even skid on the spilled bleach. She saw Ari on the floor and grabbed the woman on top of her without considering who it was. The effect was like a train snatching up a mail bag hanging from a wooden post. Kunz slammed Elise into the washing machine hard enough to dent the metal. From there, Kunz's attack was methodical: two punches to the head to cotton her brain, a trio to her stomach to disrupt her breathing, another punch to the face to keep her upright, and then back to the abdomen.

Henning and Frankie arrived at the same time. They each took one of Kunz's arms and pulled her back, using all their strength to keep her from pummeling the other inmate to death. Segura saw that Kunz was restrained and ran to Ari, checking to be sure she was breathing. Ari's lips were covered with blood from her nose, and she would have an ugly collection of bruises from the shoulders to her hairline, but she was breathing.

"Willow?" Segura said.

Kunz had her eyes locked on Elise. "She alive?"

It was clear from her tone and posture that if Segura said no, Kunz would make amends with Elise's life. She said, "She's alive. She's conscious, even, but I think she's a little dazed." She lightly patted Ari's cheek. "C'mon, Willow. Look at me."

Ari's eyes moved from the ceiling and focused on Segura. "Hey..."

"Hi. Don't try to move, okay?" Vogel had just arrived and stared at the scene in horror. "Mel. *Melissa.*" Vogel looked at her. "Get Dr. Val."

Vogel ran to comply.

Ari coughed and cradled her abdomen. "She was right."

"Who was right? About what?"

Ari smiled. There was blood on her teeth, but she looked genuinely happy. "I think it's over."

CHAPTER TWENTY-NINE

Someone was holding her hand. At first she thought someone had smuggled Dale in, but the fog quickly cleared enough for her to know that was unlikely. She also had a pounding headache, soreness all throughout her body, and swallowing felt like her saliva was on fire. She grimaced and carefully opened her eyes to see that Dr. Val was the hand-holder. She was sitting beside the bed with her phone in her free hand, typing with her thumb.

"You really go all out for your patients, huh?" she rasped.

Val looked up and smiled, putting her phone down on her lap. She brushed a loose curl away from her face. "To be honest, I don't have that many patients. It will surprise you to learn that the majority of prisoners manage to go weeks, sometimes even months, without making an infirmary visit."

"I think you made that joke last time."

"See? You're here so much I'm running out of material." She moved her phone into her pocket and stood up to examine Ari's wounds. "How do you feel?"

"Like I got my ass kicked."

"Yeah, well, I think technically you won. So you've got that going for you."

Ari grunted. "Seriously, though. Holding my hand? Is that a normal thing you do?"

Val hesitated. "Honestly? No. But I met your partner, and she didn't seem like the type to want you waking up alone after something like this."

"Yeah, she tends to hover when I get hurt. How bad is it this time?"

"Not as bad as last time, actually. You might feel shittier because of your throat. It was still healing from your near-strangulation, so getting choked didn't really help matters. But no matter how scrappy she might be, Gilpin is no match for Kunz."

Ari looked at the other empty beds. "Where did Gilpin end up?"

"There's another ward for violent offenders. She's there with a bunch of guards watching over her. They'll page me when she wakes up, but I should go check on her. Make sure she *will* wake up at some point."

"Kunz really took her down, huh?"

"Yeah, you *canidae* really look out for each other. Try to get a little rest."

Ari said, "Wait. First, can I borrow your phone?"

Val hesitated.

"Come on, I just proved I'm innocent. I'll be out of here soon enough anyway, but it'll be even sooner if I can make this phone call."

"I'm starting to understand why so many people punch you," Val said as she handed over the phone.

"Hey, I'll have you know, just as many people want to kiss me."

"Uh-huh, sure. If you get caught with that—"

"I picked your pocket."

Val left to check on her other patient. Ari had to think for a moment to remember Dale's number. She closed her eyes, carefully lowered her head back onto the pillow, and listened to the buzz on the other end.

"This is Dale Frye."

"Hey, you sound sexy. What are you wearing?"

Dale tried to gasp and laugh at the same time. "Puppy? This... you're... what number is this?"

"It's Dr. Val's phone. I'm kind of in the infirmary again."

This time a sigh. "Damn it, Ariadne..."

"I'm fine. It's not as bad as last time."

"I don't care! Your voice..." She grunted angrily. "Stop getting yourself hurt like this."

"I'm sorry. If it helps, I found out who was trying to kill me. She tried again, but the rest of the *canidae* in here saved my ass."

Dale was quiet for a long time, and Ari let her process it. When she finally spoke again, it was with guarded hope. "So it's... it's almost over?"

"I think so, yeah. Knock on wood. Her name is Elise Gilpin." She spelled it. "She's the one who killed Shannon Hardy. Then she got herself arrested so she could take me out as well. Cecily promised to help bring Gilpin's sister into the country."

Dale said, "So..."

"Unleash hell, babe."

"Fire in the hole. I'm getting you out of there, puppy."

Ari grinned. "Go get her. I love you."

"Oh, I love you."

They hung up and Ari put the phone on the table next to her bed. Her chest hurt but she couldn't help laughing. She didn't want to jinx things so she didn't say anything out loud, but it was hard not to be hopeful with Dale Frye on the warpath.

Dale waited patiently across from the desk sergeant, watching the ebb and flow of police officers moving through the lobby. The sergeant asked several times if she needed help, but Dale only smiled and told him she was fine waiting. He let her wait but kept an eye on her. Finally, after close to two hours, her target appeared and moved quickly toward the elevators. Dale stood and pursued him.

"Detective Rojas?"

"Ma'am," the desk sergeant warned.

Rojas turned, recognized her, and signaled the sergeant to stand down. "Miss Willow."

"It's Frye, actually. Dale Frye. I need to talk to you about the Ariadne Willow case. Or... I guess it's the Shannon Hardy case. She was the victim. She was killed in her apartment..."

"I remember the case," he said, already moving toward the elevator again. "And I know Ariadne Willow has a lawyer. What's-his-name Cosgrove. Any evidence you have needs to go through him."

Dale held up her tablet. "I have evidence that Cecily Parrish conspired to have Shannon Hardy murdered and set Ariadne up to take the fall. Ari told me Cecily called you Detective Roaches in the interrogation room. I assume she has the same relationship with most of the cops in this town. How would you like to be the one who brought her down?"

He looked at the tablet and then at Dale. "Do you think you're the first person to try taking that woman down? People have gone after her before."

"I've spent the past month digging into what her firm has been doing. I have solid evidence that GG&M has been involved in at least eleven murders over the past fifteen years, and every single one was covered up by finding someone to take the fall. Clearing the charges against Ari is just the tip of the iceberg. Take this, and I promise you will never have to deal with Cecily Parrish again."

Rojas looked at the tablet like it was gold-plated. Dale held her breath. Everything hinged on his reaction. If he was too afraid to go after Cecily, there was a chance that all their hard work would be for nothing.

"What's the name? Let's start there. You found Shannon Hardy's real killer?"

"Her name is Elise Gilpin. She's currently incarcerated at King County with Ari."

Rojas sighed and muttered something in Spanish before slipping back to English. "–regret this. Okay, Miss Frye. Come with me and we'll talk."

"Thank you, Detective."

"Don't thank me yet. All I'm agreeing to do is listen."

Dale grinned. "That's all you have to do."

She followed him to the elevators.

A few hours later, Dale knocked on Gwen's front door. She was out of breath, flushed, and trying hard to keep her expression neutral. When the door opened, she immediately gave herself away by smiling wide. Gwen was in a robe that was open just enough to reveal she probably wasn't wearing much, if anything, underneath. Behind her, Milo was wearing a V-neck and buttoning her jeans. Dale pushed past the visuals and the meaning of what she had just interrupted and focused on Gwen.

"Get dressed. We're going to get our girl."

Gwen said, "What do you mean? You said we should stop."

"I know. I said we should stop, but I meant *you* should... I mean... Mom. You've sacrificed enough. Ariadne might be your daughter, but you shouldn't fight her battles anymore. Not when you have something else to protect." She looked past her at Milo.

"But it doesn't matter, because we won."

"What do you mean?"

"I mean," Dale said, "Graham Cosgrove is on his way to the prison right now to break the news that all charges against Ariadne Willow have been dropped."

"Dale..." Gwen grabbed Dale's hand. "She's coming home?"

"It'll take a little while to process the paperwork, I'm sure," Dale said, "but yeah. She's coming home."

Gwen laughed and pulled Dale into a hug. When she let go, she stepped around her and started to the driveway.

"Mom," Dale said, "I think you might be naked."

"Shit," Gwen said, turning to go back into the house. "Sorry. It's a wolf thing."

Dale smiled and nodded. "Ari has the same problem sometimes."

Gwen went back into the house, and Milo came out onto the porch. She had the fingers of her uninjured hand in her pocket with the thumb in a belt loop. Her hair was mussed, a large shock of it hanging from one side of her head as if it had been weighted. She looked casual-cool, like a street racer in a movie from the fifties. All she lacked was the cigarettes rolled in the sleeves of her shirt.

"You lied to us," Milo said.

"I had to." She nodded at the cast. "You... Gwen has sacrificed enough."

Milo tilted her head to the side. "You get more and more wolf every time I see you."

Dale grinned proudly, then jerked her chin toward the house. "Go on. You should probably get dressed, too."

"I'm dressed."

"I mean with a bra. And maybe something that isn't thin enough that I can definitely tell you're not wearing one."

Milo rolled her eyes and went inside. "Maybe you're not a wolf after all. Such a prude."

Dale chuckled and put her hands in her pockets, bouncing on the balls of her feet as she waited for them to get ready.

Ari and Segura sat across from each other in their cell. Ari's bed was made and, since she hadn't bothered to accumulate any belongings, that was the extent of her preparations. She was feeling much less sore, but she didn't know whether to attribute that to healing, the drugs, or the knowledge she was about to walk out the doors of the prison as a free woman. She was wearing her own clothes and her collar had been returned to her, but she refused to put it on herself. She held it with both hands, running her thumbs over the leather and buckle.

Segura said, "Collar, huh?"

"Dale and I... it's a promise. It isn't anything kinky, like most people think when they see me wearing a collar."

"I get it. And she has to be the one to put it on you."

"Right." Ari looked at her. "Shae, I couldn't have made it through this without your help. You have my word, I'm going to find out what happened to your sister."

Segura nodded, accepting the promise. "Thank you, Ariadne."

Vogel appeared at the door. "Ready?"

"Yeah." Ari and Segura both stood. "Are you a hugger?"

"God no." Segura offered her hand. Ari took it, and Segura pulled her into a hug. "Stay safe out there, Willow. I'm worried about you when we're not all watching your back."

Ari said, "I've got Dale. She's enough."

"Seems to be, yeah," Segura said, letting her go. "All right, get the hell out of here. Don't stick around this hellhole any longer than you have to on my account."

"I'll start looking into your sister's case as soon as things settle down," Ari promised. "But no matter what else happens, come find me when you get out. Okay?"

"You got it, wolf girl."

Ari looked at Vogel. "Take care of her."

"It's my job."

"Yeah, I know, I meant~"

"I wasn't talking about being a CO," Vogel said, smiling. "I meant... it's my job."

Ari nodded. "Right. Okay, I'm ready."

Vogel led her to the elevator. Ari looked up and saw the majority of the kennel club lined up along the edge of the second level. Kunz was still in solitary for her "attack" on Elise, but Vogel had promised that the higher-ups were about to declare her actions justified. The *canidae* available to see her off were all there, however - Henning, Frankie, Gladys, and Beatriz - and Ari nodded her thanks to them. Gladys smiled, and Henning offered a quick salute.

Ari returned the salute and followed Vogel into the elevator. This time they were alone for the ride down to the lobby. Vogel looked at her.

"This place is going to seem downright boring without you here. Sure I can't convince you to stick around?"

"That would have to be one hell of an argument, Vogel."

"Fair enough." She chuckled and watched the numbers count down. "I am going to miss having you run interference for me and Shae, though. You were a good lookout."

"I'm sure you'll find someone who can pretend they're not listening."

"You listened?"

"I listened a little bit."

Vogel nodded, smirking a little. "Good."

They arrived at the ground floor and Vogel offered her hand. "You were a good prisoner and a pain in the ass, Willow."

Ari shook her hand. "Thanks, Vogel."

"Melissa."

"Melissa," Ari said.

Vogel said, "Be good."

Ari walked across the lobby and, after pausing at the exit, stepped out into the sunshine.

In the movies, prison was always out in the middle of nowhere with a road stretching off into a mysterious distance. In reality, she was standing on an ordinary city street. It looked so normal that she felt as if she had just been transported to a completely different world. The air smelled strongly of the sea, and it was cold, and the breeze felt magical against her face. She tilted her head back and let it wash over her for a moment: freedom. Finally she opened her eyes and looked down the block, toward the bus stops.

Dale.

She had been walking toward the building's entrance, hands in the pockets of her hoodie, but broke into a jog when she saw Ari.

"Puppy."

Ari grinned and grabbed Dale, lifting her off the ground as they greeted each other with a kiss. This time it was a proper kiss, a kiss that would only end when they decided it was over, a kiss no one would scold them for. Ari finally let Dale's feet touch the ground and, a moment later, moved her lips to Dale's cheek. She stroked her hair and let her hand rest heavily on Dale's shoulder to prove she was real and solid.

"Hey," Dale said.

"Hi. Where are Mom and Milo?"

Dale gestured back the way she'd come. "They're in the car.

Mom said she wanted to give us a second alone first."

Ari said, "Did you just call her 'Mom'?"

"Yeah."

"First person you've called that since your mother passed?"

"Yeah," Dale said softly.

"Are you okay?"

"Oh. Yeah. Yeah, it's good. It feels right."

"Okay." Ari held up the collar. "Would you...?"

Dale took it from her. Ari moved to lift her hair out of the way, but it was still too short to be an issue. The leather was cool against her skin but it started to warm up almost immediately, its familiar weight welcome against the back of her neck. Dale poked her tongue out as she worked the buckle and fastened it carefully where it was bent just enough to show where the buckle usually rested.

"How's that? Too tight?"

"It's perfect."

She kissed Dale again, and Dale grabbed hold of Ari's hips to keep from being walked backward from the force of it.

Dale leaned out of the kiss and moved her hands to Ari's face. She catalogued the bruises, both healing and fresh, and examined the cut above her right eyebrow.

"I wish I was a murderer."

Ari kissed her palm. "No, you don't."

"Yeah. Just this once, in this specific case, I really wish I had it in me."

"I'm glad you don't. I don't want to see you go to prison."

Dale said, "Was it terrible?"

Ari thought of Segura, Vogel, and the club. "It... could've been worse, I guess. But you weren't there. So it was unbearable."

"I'm here now," Dale said. "What do you want to do?"

"Well..." Ari said, looking Dale up and down. "A couple of things."

Dale blushed.

"But first, we should probably go take care of the bitch who tried to take me away from you."

Dale's smile was diabolical, her eyes shining with potential mischief. She kissed Ari's knuckles and pulled her to the car.

"I'll drive."

Chapter Thirty

Dale offered to go home so Ari could change into something nicer, but Ari passed. There was something poetic about the confrontation she was about to have happening in the clothes she'd been wearing when she was arrested. She explained what she needed to Gwen and Milo and dropped them off so they could put their part of the plan into action. Ari called in her backup and drove to the Patkanim Building. She parked at the end of the block where they could wait without being seen.

The street was full of people, everyone going about their day. Ari knew she'd only been in prison for a few weeks, but she really did feel like she appreciated things more. She could open the door, walk to the monorail, ride to the end of the track, and then just walk north until she got tired. No one would stop her or ask what she was doing. But the best and most appealing part of being free was seated right beside her.

She looked and caught Dale staring at her. "What?" she said, smiling.

"Nothing," Dale said. "I can look at you as much as I want."

"I might get creeped out by that."

"Tough luck. Try to stop me."

Ari said, "I'll just watch you all day and if you start staring, I'll just cover your eyes."

"Try it."

Ari put her hand over Dale's face. Dale kissed her palm. Ari sighed. "Random kisses. I missed that." Dale leaned across the car so she could place a random kiss on Ari's lips. "Yeah, that's the stuff."

Dale retreated back to her side of the car, adjusting the seatbelt which had slipped down during her romantic lean.

"You know," she said, "I won't think less of you if you wanted to leave. Put this off for a while. Recuperate before going in for another round."

Ari shook her head. "It has to happen now." She looked at Dale. "Unless *you* want to pause. I would understand if you wanted a time-out."

"No, you're right. And if we wait, Cecily would just go after Mom or Milo."

Ari smiled. "Really digging you calling her that."

Dale covered Ari's hand with her own. "It has to be now. I know. I just thought I'd give you the option to back out without feeling like you were running away."

"Thank you."

An unmarked sedan pulled up behind them and Detective Rojas got out. Ari rolled down the window as he approached, and he bent down to look into the car.

"You look rough, Miss Willow."

"I don't know what they tell you about that place you keep sending people, but it's nothing like the brochures. I didn't see a single yoga class."

"I'll have a word with the management." He looked at the building, then craned his neck to look past Ari at Dale. "That stuff you found was good. It was really good. I've gotten most of the detectives who worked on the individual cases to sign on with me. She might still wriggle out of this, but we've got a better chance of taking her down than I'd ever hoped for. You sure you want to do it this way?"

Ari nodded. "Absolutely."

He straightened and motioned at his car. A uniformed officer got out and climbed into the backseat of Ari's car.

Ari said, "Not that I think you need a bodyguard."

"I'll happily accept him, thanks." She kissed Ari. "Be safe, puppy."

"Promise." She got out of the car and let Rojas lead the way across the street.

Once they were out of earshot of the car, Rojas said, "Puppy, huh?"

"Yep."

"That have—"

"Collar, yep," Ari interrupted.

He said, "That's cool. Your business is your business." He coughed into his fist. "My wife calls me *oso de peluche*. Teddy bear."

"Cute," Ari said.

"Mm-hmm."

One of the receptionists got to her feet when Ari and Rojas entered the building, but remained silent after he showed her his badge. He continued without looking at her. The security guard posted at the elevator was equally cowed, stepping to one side so the detective could hit the call button.

"Having a good day?" Ari asked the guard.

He stared at her. The elevator arrived.

"Good talk," Ari said as she stepped into the car.

The doors closed, and Rojas hit the button for GG&M's floor. "You really do antagonize everyone you meet, don't you?"

"Aw. Did you think you were special?"

"You realize I'm *helping* you, right?"

Ari said, "You're right, I apologize. But you were the one who sent me to jail, so I feel like I have to give you a little shit."

"Fair enough."

The elevator doors opened to reveal GG&M's receptionists all standing behind their desks. The one in the center, obviously nervous, said, "I'm sorry, Detective, but—"

"Obstruction charges," Rojas interrupted. "This is on top of the potential conspiracy charges every employee of the firm risks being slapped with."

She opened her mouth but no sound came out. Rojas continued into the main office and Ari followed. Lawyers had come out of their offices and lingered in doorways to watch as they advanced, as if everyone already knew exactly where he was headed. The door to Cecily's office opened just before they were close enough to knock and she emerged with an expression of bemused irritation.

"Hello, Roaches. Ariadne. You look well, considering where you spent the past few weeks. I hope your time behind bars was long enough for you to become rehabilitated. I hear the recidivism rate is something like thirty percent. You might want to be careful."

Ari said, "Oh, my time was very enlightening."

Rojas said, "Cecily Parrish, I'm here to ask you to come with me, voluntarily, so I can ask you a few questions regarding several murders that have occurred over the last ten years."

Cecily arched an eyebrow. "If you're asking me to divulge privileged information related to my clients, I can assure you~"

"No, Miss Parrish, I want to ask about *your* involvement in the murders and subsequent cover-ups. I thought we could do this the nice way, given our relationship over the years, but if you'd prefer to make an issue about it, then I could call in the uniformed officers parked around the block and we can turn this entire firm into a scavenger hunt."

Cecily's body language changed. She lowered her chin and squared her shoulders. Her smile shifted ever-so-slightly, and she narrowed her eyes. Ari could almost smell the pheromones wafting from her as she sashayed forward.

"Detective Rojas... hm. *Alonzo*. Why don't we step into my office and~"

Ari took a small spray bottle from the pocket of her coat and spritzed it in Cecily's face. She spluttered and wiped the water away with one hand, glaring at Ari.

"What the hell are you doing, Willow?"

"Nothing," Ari said. "Carry on."

Cecily exhaled slowly and focused on Rojas again. "As I was saying, Alonzo..."

Ari sprayed her again, twice this time, and Cecily shouted in frustration.

"Sorry, Cecily, you just seemed to need a little cool-down. Please, continue."

Cecily's face was red. She started to speak, but now she was anticipating another spritz from Ari's bottle. Rojas held up a hand before either woman could do anything else.

"Let me save us some time. We're not going into your office, Miss Parrish. You're either coming to the station with me for a friendly conversation, or things around here will become very unfriendly very quickly."

Cecily looked at Ari. Ari pretended to examine the spray bottle's trigger mechanism.

"I am a powerful woman, Detective Rojas. If your intention is to slander my name, I assure you that~"

"Actually, you're not." Cecily's teeth snapped together. Ari didn't smile, but she was finding it enormously entertaining to interrupt Cecily. "You said as much to Dale. Your bosses have the real power and you're just a go-between. A go-between who, I'm afraid to say, has just become a huge liability to the firm. How long do you think it will take the partners to come to the same conclusion and decide you're expendable?"

Cecily opened her mouth and closed it again. Her eyes darted toward the floor, then swung back up to focus on Rojas. He smiled genially.

"We really should get going if we want to beat traffic."

"Fine," Cecily said through clenched teeth.

"I should mention," Rojas said, "that Elise Gilpin has agreed to discuss the murder of Shannon Hardy in detail. That's the main reason for my visit today. She had a lot of interesting things to say."

Cecily looked as if she was going to stand her ground. Ari could see her considering the options. Beads of water from the spray bottle were still glistening on her forehead. It looked like flop sweat, and Ari wished she could take a picture. Finally she focused on Rojas again and forced a casual smile.

"Fine. Lead the way, Detective."

Rojas dipped his head in a sarcastic bow, then turned to walk back to the elevators. Cecily followed but slowed after a few steps and looked back at Ari.

"Are you coming, Miss Willow?"

"Nah. I'll stick around for a little while. I bet your bosses will be pretty pissed off when they find out what happened here today."

Cecily said, "They will most likely be pissed off at *you*, Miss Willow."

Ari said, "I'm counting on it. I think it's about time I met the partners. Have a good time with the interrogation, Detective Rojas." She turned and walked down the hall. She tapped a random lawyer on the shoulder as she passed. "If someone whose name is on the front wall shows up, tell them I'm waiting in the conference room. And be sure to tell them I am *really* looking forward to having a chat with them."

Ari chose a seat in the middle of the table. She was framed by large picture windows looking out over Elliott Bay. She had her feet up on the polished wood, idly poking at her phone. She had been texting with Dale, Milo, and her mother since Rojas left with Cecily.

There was a chance Cecily would use her juju on Rojas now that Ari and her spray bottle weren't standing watch, but Ari doubted it. There were records now, and Cecily would be hard-pressed to explain how she'd gotten Rojas to let her go without divulging she was a succubus.

The conference room door slid open and three people entered in single file. Ari purposefully didn't look up, pretending to be rapt by what was on her screen.

"Just a second, guys. You would not believe how many games of Words with Friends I racked up while I was in the joint. People never think about that, you know, the little inconveniences. They sneak up on you." She poked the screen one final time with an elaborate flourish, then slipped the phone back into her pocket. "Okay, that should do it. Now..." She put her feet down and folded her hands on the table as she finally looked at the partners. "Introductions?"

The two men were exact opposites: tall and short, cadaverous and rotund, cruel-featured and plump. The woman had a regal bearing, with ash blonde hair pulled back in a severe bun. Their outfits were indistinguishable from any other businesspeople she might have seen on the street, but something about them seemed off. Both men had facial hair - full beard for the smaller man, tiny mustache for Lurch - and the woman seemed like a Victorian headmistress.

The plump man started to speak.

"Wait!" Ari held up one finger. "No one said you could go first. My name is Ariadne Willow. I'm sure you knew that. But it's about politeness."

They stared at her. After a moment, the same one opened his mouth, but Ari interrupted again by pointing at the woman.

"You're Lillian Girard. I mean, you're the only woman and I'm a detective. I can put two and two together." She swung her finger to the plump man. "And you're Louis Gilles."

His smile was condescending. "Very good. But you had an equal chance of being wrong."

"No, I had an eighty percent chance of being right. Maybe higher. You tried to be the first person to speak. Twice. Now, would someone like that allow himself to be named last on the letterhead? Nah. You're the type who has to have top-billing. Gilles Girard and Moreau. Although kudos to you, Bart, for letting the woman be second. Not a lot of guys in the nineteenth century would have been cool about that."

Gilles and Moreau exchanged looks.

"Oh, come on," Ari said. "I knew your names. You're surprised I know you've also been around for over a hundred years?"

Moreau spoke for the first time. His voice was like stone sliding on stone. "As entertaining as this might be, Miss Willow, this is still *our* domain."

"Oh, no, no, no. After everything you've done to get me here, all the shit you've thrown into my life just to make me sign up, you're going to listen to me. Now, where was I? Hundred years old. Right." She rapped her knuckles on the table. "I couldn't stop thinking about the people you were sending to prison on murder charges. Dale found a lot of them, but I can't imagine it was a comprehensive list. You guys have probably gotten really good at covering your tracks. But those are a *lot* of tracks to cover, even just going by what Dale was able to find. A lot of bodies, even for a law firm.

"So we had to ask ourselves why would a law firm need to cover up so many deaths? It took us a while, because we could only talk for an hour every week. And even then we had to be careful. We didn't know if any of the guards might be on your payroll. Dale's the one who figured it out. It's pretty obvious, really. You're siphoning their lives. We're not sure how you're doing it. Whether it's because of what you are, or maybe some spell you're casting, but whatever it is, you're stealing life from these people and taking it for yourselves. And you've been doing it since the Great Fire."

Gilles gave a weary sigh, lowering his head. "Oh, this is unfortunate."

Moreau stared at Ari without blinking. "We hoped to utilize your skills as an employee of this firm. The arrangement can be mutually beneficial, as it is with Cecily."

"Ah, yes. You wanted a wolf. You were *desperate* for a wolf."

"Not just any wolf," Girard said. She kept her chin up as she spoke, as if chiding Ari. "You are singular among your species."

Ari said, "Aw, you big flirt. I bet you say that to all the girls. *Canidae* have a longer lifespan than ordinary people. I imagine I'd be like the jackpot for you. Get a couple of free decades for the price of a single death."

Moreau said, "You would have been well-compensated for your sacrifice. As our employee, you could have named your salary. You could have ensured Miss Frye would never have to work while living a life of luxury. You chose to dig your heels in the dirt."

"I chose to live my life freely. I chose not to barter my life away for money."

"Pride." Girard smiled. "So many people have cut off their own hands in the name of pride."

Gilles said, "Pride is probably why you came here now. You decided to take a stand. I would call this foolish, but even a fool wouldn't walk into a situation like this."

Ari smiled.

Moreau narrowed his eyes. "She is certainly no fool. What ace do you have up your sleeve, Miss Willow?"

She held up a finger to silence them and listened. "Not yet. Okay. I walked in here because I know you're going to leave before I do. You've got some packing to do."

"This is our town, Miss Willow," Girard said. "We're not leaving because you came in and glowered at us, little girl."

"It was your town. For a very long time. You sunk your claws in and held on tight, and that's commendable. But it's over. See, a couple of years ago, I walked into a room on behalf of every wolf in Seattle and talked a bunch of bullheaded humans to lay down their weapons and stop hunting us. I put an end to a war and saved countless *canidae* lives. I did it selfishly, really, to protect myself and my friends, but every wolf in Seattle... every wolf in the world, really... benefited from it. I don't have an ace up my sleeve, Mr. Moreau. I finally cashed it in."

The sound of a siren was building outside. Ari grinned and held her finger up again.

"There it is."

At that moment it became clear that the sound wasn't a siren; it was a howl. But even that was inaccurate, because it was a fluid and shifting tone which could only have come from multiple throats. The windows were closed but the howl was loud enough to be heard clearly through the glass. It echoed off the buildings, reverberating through downtown Seattle as pedestrians stopped and drivers turned down their radios to try pinpointing the origin of the sound. People on the ferries heard it as well. For anyone in or near Seattle that afternoon, it was impossible not to hear the unmistakable sound of dozens, if not hundreds, of howling wolves.

"You wanted a wolf," Ari told the partners. "You're getting every fucking wolf in town. Or as close as we could get on short notice. Milo and my mother had to move fast to spread the word.

One thing I learned in prison is that I'm pretty popular among *canidae*. They felt they owed me a debt. I'm not comfortable with that kind of thing, so I was more than happy to get rid of it for a good cause."

Gilles actually looked wary. "Are... do you plan to have us torn limb from limb?"

"No. I'm really not a killer, Lou. Not when there are other options. You're going to leave. All of you. Don't bother packing up, just take whatever you have on you and go."

"Where, exactly, would you have us go?"

"I don't care. This is my town, and I don't want you in it anymore. I don't want you deciding who goes to jail for what, or who has to die so you can live. Shannon Lisa Hardy. She was taking business classes. She was working here to pay her tuition, and you turned her into a pawn. You treated everyone who worked here like your personal chess pieces. It's done. Go somewhere else. Good luck starting over from scratch without your firm to hide behind."

Girard bared her teeth. "You said you're not a killer."

"When there are other options. I'm choosing not to kill you, but to put you in a situation where you'll probably shrivel up and die a normal death. Just like anyone else in the world. You could try to find new victims, but I don't think you'll have much luck with your accounts frozen."

Shock passed across Moreau's face. "Pardon?"

"Oh. Yeah, apparently when you go to the police with evidence that a law firm has engaged in the systemic coverup of multiple homicides over the years, the police tend to freeze any money the partners of that firm might use to flee. Hope you hit the ATM this morning."

Moreau rounded the table, one hand extended for Ari's throat. She turned to face him, arms still at her sides.

"I walked into this building with a homicide detective, you stupid motherfucker. You three are boned even without me turning up dead in your conference room."

He glared at her, face red, nostrils flaring, but he dropped his hand without touching her.

Girard kept her voice level and measured. "If we are to have a chance of avoid arrest, we should most likely make haste."

"Sure, cops," Ari said. "Personally, I'd be more worried about how many wolves it had to take for that chorus you just heard. They're down there in the street and they didn't sound too friendly.

Look, you don't have to run. I personally think it would be the most entertaining trial in the world. Who do you think would flip on you? Cecily? Elise Gilpin, of course, is already prepared to talk now that it looks like you guys won't be around to honor the deal you made with her sister. So please. Stay. Fight."

Gilles was backing toward the door. All amusement had drained from his face. "We spent a century building this firm."

"And you threw it all away by going after the wrong bitch."

Gilles fled first. Ari watched him go, the roll of his hips becoming more pronounced as his trot turned into a run. Moreau paused at the conference room door to sneer at Ari before he followed at a gallop, his long limbs making him look like a giraffe. Lillian Girard stepped closer to the table and regarded Ari for a long, silent moment.

"We could have changed the world together, Ariadne."

"Sure. Run."

Girard smiled, turned, and strolled from the room. Ari waited until she and the other two had a chance to board the elevators and descend to begin their retreat. She went to the window and looked down to see if she could spot any of the *canidae* who had provided the howl, but she couldn't see anything amiss. She took her phone from her pocket and sent the "all-clear" to Dale. A few seconds later, she got the reply.

"Mom+Milo okay 2. Come down."

Ari left the conference room and walked through the offices of GG&M. Most employees were on the phone or engaged in a panicked conversation. The rest were in glass-fronted offices shredding whatever papers they could fit into the machine. The floor was filled with the sound of machinery slicing papers into unreadable ribbons, the chirp of phones going unanswered, and worried demands for answers. Ari didn't slow down as she walked through the chaos.

She had to get downstairs to get her girl.

CHAPTER THIRTY-ONE

BY THE time Ari got downstairs, Milo and Gwen had arrived and were waiting by the car with Dale. Gwen tried to keep her expression neutral but, by the time Ari reached them, she had started crying. Ari smiled and hugged her.

"Careful, Mom. You have to look cool in front of your girlfriend."

Gwen laughed and kissed Ari's cheek. "Are you okay?" She lightly touched one of the wounds on Ari's cheek. "Do you need anything?"

"I'm good." She took Gwen's hands in her own to keep her from pawing at her. "I talked to the partners. I think I convinced them this was the end. They looked pretty spooked when they ran out. But I think we should probably keep our eyes open for a little while, just in case. Mom, maybe you could spend some time in England with Milo?"

Milo said, "You could help me pack."

"Pack... for...?" Ari looked at Milo and raised an eyebrow. "Pack as in... pack up your home?"

"And come back to live here."

Ari looked at Gwen. "Live here?"

"With me."

"With you," Ari repeated. She looked between them again. "It's about time."

Gwen smiled, relieved. "Are you really okay with it?"

Ari said, "You're both adults. And I recently got a very hard lesson in what it's like to be separated from the person you're dying to be with. I'm not going to be the thing standing in the way of your happiness. Not after everything you gave up for me. If you feel like you need my blessing, you have it. But she doesn't get to go in my room." She turned on Milo. "And whatever happens, I am never going to call you 'Mom.'"

Milo said, "I guess that's fair enough."

"Then okay. I'm happy for you. Both of you." She rubbed her mother's arm. "And I know you probably have some big dinner or something planned, but can we maybe postpone it? I'm exhausted and all I want to do is curl up and sleep for a few dozen hours."

"Actually," Gwen said, "we do have a little party planned, but Dale already convinced us to put it off until the weekend. She had something she wanted to do first." She kissed Ari's forehead. "Good job, Ariadne. You made me proud today."

"Thanks, Mom."

Gwen hugged Dale. "Take care of my girl."

"I will. I love you."

"Love you too, Dale." She looked at Ari and then scanned the street. "You should have seen this place about five minutes ago. There were about forty wolves scattered all up and down through here. People were filming with their cameras."

Milo grinned and affected an American accent. "Hey, man, where were you when all them wolves started howling downtown? Man, that was, like, totally insane!"

Gwen and Ari exchanged a look. Gwen whispered, "I'll talk to her about the accent."

"My accent is great."

"Okay, honey." Gwen looped an arm around Milo's shoulders and guided her to their car. She blew a kiss to Ari. "Just remind me again which state you were aiming for..."

Ari and Dale were left alone on the street. "Hey," Dale said.

"Hi there. I seem to remember you saying something about kissing me whenever you wanted. Does that also go for whenever *I* want you to kiss me?"

"Maybe." Dale stepped forward and kissed her. "You ready to get out of here?"

Ari nodded. She walked around the back of the car and got into the passenger seat.

Dale said, "If you wanted to nap, we have a bit of a drive ahead of us."

"We're not going home? When Mom said you had something planned tonight, my mind went to a dirty place."

"We can go home if you want. But I did have something else in mind."

Ari said, "Okay. Do your thing, Red."

Dale rubbed Ari's leg and started the car. She drove north and, as she crossed the floating bridge to Eastside, Ari took her up on the offer to get some sleep. She wouldn't say the car seat was more comfortable than the prison bed, but it was familiar and it meant she was free, so she wouldn't have traded it for anything. She never fell into a full sleep but remained aware of Dale's presence beside her. About half an hour into the trip, Dale turned on the radio and sang along quietly with the music.

When Ari woke and looked at her phone, she saw they'd been on the road for an hour. She looked around and only saw thickly-wooded forests. The road was flanked on either side by steel guardrails, but otherwise she couldn't see any signs of civilization.

"Where are we going?"

"We're almost there."

Ari accepted the non-answer. Eventually Dale pulled into the spacious parking lot of a small brewery and pulled up next to the dumpster in a spot labeled for employees.

"Did you get me a job?"

"Hush, puppy." Dale unfastened her seatbelt and got out of the car. "I talked to the owners and they're going to let us park here for a couple of days."

"A... wait, a couple of *days?*" Ari followed her to the back of the car, where she was unloading a tent, sleeping bags, and two backpacks stuffed to capacity. "What are you doing?"

Dale hesitated with her hand on the trunk. "I wanted it to be a surprise. But now I'm thinking you might just want to spend a night in your own home, in your own bed... shit. I may have fucked up."

"Just tell me the plan," Ari said.

"I thought after prison, anything with four walls would feel like a jail to you. Even if it was your home, even though you can't wolf out yet. I don't know. I thought the idea of closing a door and locking yourself up inside... I thought you probably had enough of that the past few weeks. So I found a spot where we can camp. It's going to be kind of cold, but that means we'll have the spot all to ourselves. But if you want to go home--"

Ari kissed her. Dale leaned into the kiss, letting one of the backpacks fall so she could put both hands on Ari's hips.

"You're my mate," Ari whispered.

"And you're my pack," Dale said.

They kissed again. When they stepped back, Ari picked up the bag Dale had let fall. She slipped her arm into the strap and let it hang off her shoulder.

"Okay," she said. "Lead the way."

They split the supplies between them, including a cooler full of food, and headed into the forest. The fresh air tasted delicious, and her muscles loosened up almost as soon as they started walking. It wasn't the same as a run, but the knowledge she could keep walking forward for as long as she wanted was enormously intoxicating. The trees closed behind them and blocked the brewery from view, which meant there were only trees, rocks, and brush in every direction. She was in the wilds with only Dale for company, and it was euphoric.

Ari braced herself for a long journey but Dale started to slow down after less than half a mile. She headed off the trail until she found a wide outcropping of rock. It was large enough for a tent and a campfire, flanked on two sides by winter-bare trees and on the other by a rocky shore of a lazy stream. On the other side of the water was a small hill covered with evergreens, hemlocks, and maples covered with red-orange leaves with moss on their trunks.

Dale put down her bags and faced Ari. "What do you think?"

"It's a bit of a commute," she said, "but I'd be willing to move here if you are."

Dale smiled, and it lit up her whole face. She was absolutely gorgeous, Ari realized. She'd fallen in love with Dale and started taking her for granted, had stopped seeing her a stranger might, but now she could see it. Their time apart had shifted her perspective just enough that she could see just how jaw-dropping she was. Her breath caught in her throat and she found her eyes burning with tears. Dale's smile wavered.

"You okay?"

"Okay?" Ari scoffed and looked at the trees. "Okay. Okay. No, Dale, I'm not 'okay.' I'm feeling humble and unworthy and... and touched. This is finding me a home that feels like a wolf's den all over again. You found this place and you brought me here, and I'm going to remember that for the rest of our lives. Thank you."

Dale ducked her head. "Imagine how I feel. A woman who can summon every wolf in Seattle to help her out at a moment's notice? That's a lot to be worthy of."

Ari closed the distance between them and took Dale's hands. "You're worthy. You're... everything I've ever wanted or will ever need. Trust me, I've literally had everything taken away from me. Our house, my job, my wolf. The only thing that truly broke my heart was being away from you. You always come first. And you always will."

"Same."

Ari hugged her, eyes closed so she could focus on Dale's scent and the sounds of the wilderness. It was exactly what she needed after the cold brick and steel of the prison. Even though the drug was still in her system and her ability to transform was still paralyzed for a long, long time, she finally felt like she was completely and utterly at peace.

Dinner was sandwiches and chips, which was actually a step down from what Ari had gotten in prison, but it tasted gourmet. When the sun started going down, Dale went to the backpack and pulled out a small camp lantern. Ari watched, a little dumbstruck, as she chose the best position for it and turned on the small blue light.

"We didn't already own all this stuff, right?" Ari asked. "I don't remember owning any camping supplies."

"No, I bought them for this trip."

"When?"

"Uh. About a week after you were arrested, I guess? I don't remember the exact day. I just knew you'd get out soon and you'd need to camp out for a while."

Ari got onto her knees and leaned forward as Dale turned back toward her. Their lips met and Dale smiled, one hand coming up to rest on Ari's collar as she tilted her head into the kiss. Ari moved closer but stayed on her knees. Dale pulled back but kept her first two fingers hooked under Ari's collar.

"Want to get in the tent?"

"Yes," Ari said, trying not to sound too eager but also rising to her feet and almost flinging herself into the tent. Dale had already put down a foam pad and Ari scooted to the center of it as Dale joined her. She straddled Ari and settled onto her lap as she resumed their kiss. Ari was desperate but also eager to make what was about to happen last as long as possible. She wanted to appreciate Dale like it was their first time, wanted to remember every amazing thing about being with her.

But at the same time, it had been over a month.

Dale's shirt was tossed, slapping against the wall of the tent and sliding down. Ari nuzzled Dale's breasts and reached behind to undo her bra, and Dale ran her fingers through Ari's still-shockingly short hair. She kissed the top of Ari's head, gasping when Ari's tongue found a nipple and began teasing it mercilessly. Dale managed to get Ari's shirt off as well, and Ari dropped one hand to blindly work at her belt and the button of her jeans. Dale did the same.

"You planned everything else so perfectly," Ari whispered, "you couldn't have worn a damn skirt?"

Dale chuckled breathlessly. "I didn't know... I thought I'd have more time to prepare. I was going to seduce you."

"I'm easy prey."

Ari lifted up, pressing her lap between Dale's legs, and together they muscled her pants down. She kicked them away and dropped back onto the pad. Dale had to reposition to get her pants off, but Ari felt it was worth losing the weight of her for a second when she dropped back down. Ari sighed as Dale's naked thighs slid across hers, eyes closed and smiling as she dug her fingers into the warm skin and pulled Dale closer.

"Eager puppy," Dale whispered.

"You're damn right."

"Fingers," Dale requested, and Ari brought her hand up. Dale took it and closed her lips around two fingers. Ari groaned quietly as Dale sucked them, then guided Ari's hand back down between her legs. They looked at each other in the dark, the light from the camp lantern glowing eerily against the wall of the tent to make them both look bluish-green, and Dale's breath caught in her throat. Ari bit her bottom lip as she moved her fingers and extended her thumb. Dale shivered in her arms.

"Ariadne."

Ari smiled. That was what she'd missed, almost more than freedom and fresh air and good food. Dale had one hand on the back of Ari's neck and the other on her breast, her body rising and falling as she slowly moved against Ari's fingers and thumb. The time apart had done nothing to diminish Ari's skill; her hand moved with the same sure strokes as always. Ari bowed her head to kiss the freckles between Dale's breasts.

"Tell me when you're about to come," Ari said against Dale's breastbone.

"I want to come."

Ari said, "I want to make it last…"

"It's okay," Dale whispered, bending down to kiss the top of Ari's head. "We've waited long enough, puppy. Let it happen. We've got all the time in the world." She pushed Ari's hair back and arched forward, pressing her hips down. "Make me come."

It was hard to argue with a request like that. Ari moved her free hand to Dale's ass, squeezed, and thrust with her other hand. Dale sat up straighter and whispered, "Yes, yes," and gave a pronounced finishing shudder that ended with a choked cry. Her hands slid across Ari's body until they rested on her shoulders, then moved up into her hair. She brought Ari's face to hers and kissed her hard, passionately, before forcing her backward until she was lying down.

Ari smiled when she felt moisture on her cheeks. "I can't believe I'm crying," she said. "I don't think I cried after our first time."

"This is better than our first time," Dale said quietly. She kissed Ari's tears. "This is reunion sex. You don't get reunion sex that often."

"Knock on wood," Ari said.

Dale smiled. "Given our luck, that's pretty smart." She repositioned herself and began kissing her way down Ari's body. She closed her lips around Ari's nipples, used her tongue to draw shapes on her stomach, and then eased her legs apart so that her feet were resting on the slick-smooth bottom of the tent. Ari put one hand behind her head and teased Dale's hair with the other hand.

"What are you doing down there?"

"Taking my time." Dale wet her lips and lowered her head.

Ari's eyes rolled back and her face slumped into a drunken smile.

They had all the time in the world.

Epilogue

DALE WOKE up when it was still dark outside. She was alone in the sleeping bag, but the fact she was in a tent in the woods was enough reassurance that she hadn't dreamt the day before. She was still naked so she took the time to put on her underwear and a T-shirt before she left the tent. Ari was sitting on a folded shirt near the edge of the rock platform, legs crossed in front of her, leaning forward with her elbows on her knees. Even in the pre-dawn light, Dale could see she was naked.

"I said there aren't many other people around. There still might be a few." She sat down next to Ari. "You want everyone to see your tits?"

"They've all seen tits before. And if they haven't, I'm doing them a favor." She gestured at the wilderness. "You're welcome, phantom forest virgins!"

Dale put her head down on Ari's shoulder. "I like your short hair. But it's not permanent, right?"

"God, no."

"Good. I mean, it's your body..."

Ari said, "You can be the short-hair one in the relationship."

"Good."

Dale looked out across the stream. In the few seconds since she'd come outside, the sun had already risen high enough to color the clouds at the far horizon. She could see the shapes of the forest and hear various animals moving through the underbrush on the other shore. Hopefully the campsite would keep them from crossing over.

"What are you thinking about?"

Ari sighed. "Lots of things. How hard it's going back to normal will be. I can't imagine going in to the office on Monday and just investigating a case."

"So take a week. Or two weeks."

"Mom has already done so much for us. I don't want to take advantage of her charity."

Dale said, "It's not charity. She's your mother. She's happy to do it."

"I know. But the point stands."

"Fair enough. I'm thinking about Cecily Parrish and GG&M. I hope they're really gone and they stay gone, but I'm scared. What if they decide now they have nothing to lose and come after us again? What if this time they don't pull their punches?"

Ari said, "Then we'll be ready for them."

"We *barely* survived this time, Ariadne."

"I know." She kissed the top of Dale's head. "But I don't want to live in fear. So I'm going to keep an eye out, and be as ready as I can be, and live my life."

Dale said, "I think I can do that."

"Mm." She put her arm around Dale. "I was also thinking that the last time I went out camping in the wilderness was with Mom, after you helped cure me of the pain. I came back to Seattle to testify in court, and that was when we crossed paths with Cecily Parrish in the first place. Being out here again after getting her out of our lives feels like closing the door on her. Bookends."

"I hope so," Dale said.

Ari took a deep breath. "You call my mother 'Mom'."

"I do. Is that okay? If it's weird..."

"No. No, I like it. I like it a lot."

There was even more light now.

"You don't have to do anything, puppy," Dale said. "We can close up Bitches and get normal jobs. We can move to Portland. The agency is just a thing we do, it's not us. Seattle isn't us. The wolf isn't us. No matter what happens or what gets taken away from us, or what we have to sacrifice to protect each other, as long as this-" She wiggled her finger to indicate the two of them. "-remains intact, then that's all that matters. And you don't have to decide right now. Spend the weekend not thinking, not worrying, and just being here with me. And when we get back to the real world, whatever you decide, I'll be right there with you. No matter what."

"I want this. You. The life we've built together. Everything Cecily tried to take away from us. That's what I want."

"Then that's what I want, too. After this weekend."

"After this weekend," Ari confirmed. She hooked her finger under Dale's chin and bent down to kiss her. "My partner."

Dale smiled. "My mate. My pack. Welcome home, puppy."

Ari looked out over the forest. Dale put her head down on Ari's shoulder again. Birds were chirping, and she could hear the wind pushing through the higher branches of the trees. It would have been ideal if Ari stood up, stretched her arms over her head, and effortlessly became the wolf so she could go for a run through the trees. Dale's heart broke a little to think it wasn't possible. But in a few months, the drug would be out of her system. The wolf would be back. And now that they knew about this place, they could easily plan another weekend away. Maybe in the summer, when it would be warmer. There was no need to figure it out immediately.

For now, Dale was determined to simply enjoy the moment and appreciate having the woman she loved by her side. They had plenty of time later to think about later.

About the Author

Geonn Cannon lives in Oklahoma. He is the author of several novels, including the Riley Parra series which is currently being produced as a webseries for Tello Films, and an official Stargate SG-1 tie-in novel. Information about his other novels and an archive of free stories can be found online at geonncannon.com.

MORE FROM GEONN CANNON

"Riley Parra is a strong, badass heroine for those that like their coffee and their cop fiction bitter." - P Industry

No Man's Land isn't the kind of place you go after dark, even if you have a badge. But Detective Riley Parra was born there, and she refuses to surrender it to the drug dealers, killers and criminals who have made it there home. The case of a body stuffed into a drainage pipe leads her to discover that there is far more at stake than she ever imagined.

~ **Riley Parra, Season One.**

"A good novel to while away a few hours in front of the fire." - *Kitty Kat Reviews*

Three years ago, Sofia Kennedy reported the tragic death of her girlfriend live-on air. Still in the closet even with her closest friends, she was forced to suffer her loss in silence. In the years since she's become isolated and sticks strictly to a routine that prevents her from encountering painful memories of the woman she lost.

Marion Vogt runs a small but well-respected catering service that feeds the elite of Seattle. When Sofia's consumer reporting segment does a story on Marion's company, the two women immediately butt heads. An unintended insult results in a scathing report that nearly shuts down the business. Marion's attempt to defend herself results in a deepening of their conflict until both women are ready to destroy one another.

They quickly find out Seattle can be a very small town when trying to avoid someone. As much as they want to avoid each other, fate keeps forcing Sofia and Marion to cross paths. Before long they realize they'll have to decide if they're going to hold on to bad feelings or risk forgiveness to discover just what they have to offer each other.

~ **Breaking Anchor**

www.ingramcontent.com/pod-product-compliance
Lightning Source LLC
Chambersburg PA
CBHW070923190726
48292CB00004B/1088